# MURIALE

## BOOK THREE OF THE DAUGHTERS OF MOIRRA DUNDOTTER SERIES

### SUZAN TISDALE

Copyright 2022 by Suzan Tisdale

Cover art by Wicked Smart Designs

# ALSO BY SUZAN TISDALE

### The Clan MacDougall Series

*Laiden's Daughter*

*Findley's Lass*

*Wee William's Woman*

*McKenna's Honor*

*The Clan MacDougall Boxed Set*

### The Clan Graham Series

*Rowan's Lady*

*Frederick's Queen*

### The Mackintoshes and McLarens Series

*Ian's Rose*

*The Bowie Bride*

*Rodrick the Bold*

*Brogan's Promise*

### The MacCulloughs

Black Richard's Heart

Lachlan's Heart

### The Clan McDunnah Series

*A Murmur of Providence*

*A Whisper of Fate*

*A Breath of Promise*

*The Clan McDunnah Boxed Set*

<u>Moirra's Heart Series</u>

*Stealing Moirra's Heart*

*Saving Moirra's Heart*

<u>Stand Alone Novels</u>

*<u>Isle of the Blessed</u>*

*<u>Forever Her Champion</u>*

*<u>The Edge of Forever</u>*

*<u>In the Echo of a Kiss</u>*

The MacAllens and Randalls Series:

*Secrets of the Heart*

The Daughters of Moirra Dundotter Series:

*Mariote*

*Esa*

*Muriale*

*Orabilis*

<u>The Brides of the Clan MacDougall</u>

(A Sweet Series)

*Aishlinn*

*Maggy*

*Nora*

*For Kate Robbins and Melanie Martin.*
*You know why.*

# PROLOGUE

Muriale McCullum was in mourning. The love of her life, Patrick MacConnell, had been killed ten months and nine days ago, leaving an ache in her heart so profound and intense that she firmly believed she would never be the same again.

She was still wearing black and would continue to do so all the rest of her days, though she frequently prayed her remaining days would not be many. If her heart didn't stop beating soon, she'd just curl up on his grave and wait for the sweet release of death.

Mourning was agony.

Had Patrick not been killed in the senseless attack by the Buchanans, they would have been married in August, and God willing, she'd be with child by now.

When the Buchanan's stole Patrick's life, they'd also stolen Muriale's future—and her heart. So, not only would she mourn Patrick's death until the last beat of her heart, she would hate and despise the Buchanans throughout eternity.

'Twas a dreary spring afternoon, nearing the end of May. The gray skies, the blustery wind, and the heavy mist kept most people indoors. But not Muriale.

As she had done every day since Patrick's death, she was at his gravesite. Muriale didn't care about the puddle that soaked her blue woolen gown or the water seeping into her boots. Neither did she care about the gusts of winds swirling around her, pulling long strands of hair from her braid and turning her skin to goose-flesh.

"Patrick, I miss ye," she whispered to his grave. "I dinnae believe I can live much longer without ye."

Her heart, she firmly believed, had been cleaved in twain the day Patrick died. Each morn, she was surprised by the fact that she was still among the living. How could a crushed heart still beat?

Oh, how she wished he were here to make everything all right. Fervently, she wished she could turn back time and keep him from going on the hunt that day. "I am so sorry, Patrick. Had I kent that ye were goin' to be attacked, I would have kept ye home."

With her attention entirely focused on her broken heart, she hadn't heard the footsteps that approached from behind. "Muriale?"

'Twas Braigh McAllister, her sister Esa's husband. He was a former priest, a man of good character, with a giving heart.

She didn't even bother to turn around.

---

"Lass, yer mother has asked that I fetch ye," he said as he stepped closer. His voice, soft and warm, was filled with concern—concern she didn't believe she deserved.

"I shall be along soon," she all but whispered her reply.

The despondent tone of her voice nearly brought tears to Braigh's eyes. He crouched beside her. "Muriale, we are all worried about ye," he said.

"Why are ye worried about me?" she asked, without looking up at him. "'Tis poor Patrick that is stuck in the cold, dark ground."

'Twas true that her mother, Moirra, had asked him to fetch her.

But she'd also asked that he talk to her. Until last summer, he'd been a priest. But he had left the church for a myriad of reasons, and now he was happily married to Esa, and they had a beautiful wee bairn.

Moirra hoped that Braigh might be able to get through to her third-born daughter. Everyone else had tried, unsuccessfully, to coax the poor young woman out of her grief-stricken state. Mayhap Braigh would have more luck.

"Muriale, let us walk together back to the keep," he said, extending his hand to her.

"Nay," she said with a shake of her head. "I like talking to Patrick."

"Lass, if ye dinnae get in out of this weather, ye shall be layin' in the ground beside him."

'Twas then that she finally tore her gaze from Patrick's grave and looked at Braigh. "Ye make it sound like that would be a bad thing."

'Twas worse than he or her family had thought. Muriale's anguish was far greater than any of them had realized.

The poor girl was a shadow of her former self. No longer did she smile or whistle a happy tune while she sewed. No longer did she play with her younger siblings or even visit her elder sisters and their families. If she wasn't here at Patrick's graveside, then she was tucked away in her room, all alone.

Braigh looked into her eyes and realized they were damned near vacant—empty and devoid of life. Her cheeks were sunken from eating less than a bird does for nearly a year. Pale skin made the dark circles under her once bright eyes look even darker. For all intents and purposes, she was a walking corpse.

And, if someone didn't intervene soon, she *would* be lying in the cold earth beside Patrick.

# CHAPTER
# ONE

"Muriale needs to get away from Patrick's memory as much as she needs to get away from his grave."

Moirra agreed with her husband's observation. She was more than just worried about her daughter; she was terrified for her. The poor girl's grief was consuming her.

'Twas after the midnight hour, and most of the inhabitants of the keep were fast asleep, save for Moirra and Alysander. Snuggled together in their bed, Moirra had one arm draped over her husband's chest. The only light in the room emanated from the soft, low burning fire in the hearth.

"I fear I dinnae ken how to help her over her grief. 'Tis consumin' her like a plague," she whispered.

Alysander gently patted his wife's hand. For days now, he'd been mulling over an idea that he thought might help Muriale begin to move forward. The trouble was that he was quite certain his wife wouldn't agree to it.

"My mother has family in Edinburgh," he began with some reticence.

"You are *nae* sendin' my daughter away."

"Of course nae," he replied quietly. "But I would like to *take* her away. She and I could go to Edinburgh together. 'Twould only be for a few weeks."

Moirra was quiet for a long while. Alysander took it as a good thing, for at least she wasn't hitting him over the head with a candlestick or cursing him to the devil for even thinking of such a thing. Her silence meant she was giving some consideration to his idea.

"That might nae be a bad idea," Moirra said as she stifled a yawn. "Mayhap you should take Orabillis with ye?"

"Are ye tryin' to kill me, woman?" he asked playfully. "Orabillis, in Edinburgh?"

Of all their children, Orabillis was the daughter who caused them the most anxiety and aches of the head. At six and ten, she was still of the belief that men were idiots. Romance was a concept she simply could not understand, and she believed it a complete waste of time.

"She would hate it, aye?"

"Yes, Orabillis would hate Edinburgh. So, why are ye tryin' to punish *me*? What did I do wrong?"

Moirra giggled softly as she began to caress his chest with her fingertips. "Nothin', as far as I ken. But think about it, Alysander. We could get Muriale away from all her memories of Patrick. You would take Orabillis to keep Muriale occupied. We both ken that Orabillis can be a handful."

"Lass, that is the biggest understatement in the history of the world."

Moirra giggled again. "Muriale will be so busy tryin' to keep Orabillis out of trouble that she will be too busy to think of Patrick."

While that hadn't been his original plan, Alysander didn't think it was such a bad idea. But then, the path to hell was paved with good intentions and seemingly good ideas. "Verra well," he said with a yawn. "But ye shall give me your word that no matter what trouble Orabillis gets into, ye will nae hold me responsible."

"I would nae dream of it," she replied sleepily.

Of course, he knew she didn't really mean it. If anything happened to either daughter while under his watch and care, Moirra would most definitely hold him responsible. He fell asleep moments later, wondering what on earth he had gotten himself into.

———

The following morn, Alysander and Moirra put their plan to their daughters. They'd just finished breaking their fasts when he garnered the courage to inform them of his plan. "I have business in Edinburgh," he told them. 'Twas a lie, of course, but they didn't need to know that. "And I have family there, from my mother's side. I want Muriale and Orabillis to go with me."

Orabillis's eyes grew wide in horror.

Muriale's eyes filled with tears.

"Edinburgh?" Orabillis exclaimed incredulously. "I'd rather be gutted and my-"

Moirra wouldn't allow her to finish speaking. "Aye, Orabillis, we all ken what ye'd rather do. But your father and I think a trip would do ye both a world of good."

Neither young woman was convinced. While Muriale remained mute, Orabillis felt it important to let her parents know just what she thought of the idea. "I am nae goin'. Take Hugh and Andrew with ye." Hugh and Andrew were her twin brothers, aged ten now. "I'm certain they would enjoy the trip."

Her suggestion did exactly what she'd hoped it would. Hugh and Andrew's faces lit up like the midday sun. "I want to go!" they said, gleefully and in unison.

Their excitement at the possibility of going so far from home was contagious. Their little brother, Jamie, and youngest sister, Alysandria, began to chime in. "I want to go!"

With her parents sufficiently occupied with the chaos that was her younger siblings, Orabillis felt rather victorious. If her siblings protested enough, then mayhap her parents would give up the idea.

Excitement gave way to disappointment when the little children heard their father *and* mother say, "Nay, ye cannae go." That led to cries of "Why nae?" and pleas of "It is nae fair."

As the chaos ensued, Orabillis looked across the table at Muriale. She was looking more and more like the walking dead each day. Her grief was consuming her like the wasting disease. She was staring blankly at her trencher, which was still very nearly full. The poor thing hadn't been eating enough to keep a field mouse alive, let alone herself. Orabillis supposed that God's divine intervention was the only thing that kept Muriale's heart beating.

Orabillis couldn't quite understand *why* Muriale felt the way she did. But, then, matters of the heart often escaped her comprehension. Still, her heart hurt for her older sister.

She gave a quick glance at her father. He was busy trying to keep his tone even as he explained again why the younger children couldn't go.

Her mother, however, was focused on Muriale. Moirra's pretty eyes were filled with worry and concern. 'Twas then that Orabillis understood. This wasn't a trip meant to punish her but rather a way to try to bring Muriale back to the land of the living.

The ache in her heart intensified. Some might have called what she said next a self sacrifice. Orabillis, however, felt 'twas simply a way to help keep the sister she loved so dearly from turning to dust and blowing away in the wind.

"Wheest!" Orabillis shouted at her younger siblings. "Ye cannae go this time." All eyes turned to look at her. The younger children sat with mouths agape and eyes wide. "Mayhap," she said after taking a deep breath, "ye can go next time. For now, Muriale and I are goin' to Edinburgh."

Her parents looked profoundly dumbfounded, but that immediately turned to skepticism. No one was used to Orabillis giving up anything without a fight. Turning her attention back to her parents, she gave a nod towards Muriale and a look to her mother that said, "I understand."

Relief washed over Moirra; her shoulders relaxed as she closed her eyes. She mouthed, "Thank ye," and gave Orabillis a warm smile.

Muriale looked up from her trencher, surprised as well as confused. To no one in particular she asked, "But what about Patrick?"

———

Muriale firmly believed that no one could possibly understand her grief and heartache. Going to Edinburgh was simply out of the question. "Who will take care of Patrick?"

Didn't they understand that she couldn't leave him? She had to visit him every day so that he didn't feel alone. He was, after all, in the cold, dark ground.

"Muriale," Moirra began using the softest tone she could muster. "Patrick will be fine, lass."

Her brows furrowed, and she felt a tinge of anger bubbling up from her stomach. "Fine?" she asked incredulously. "Nay, Mum. He will never be fine again. He is dead. He is in the cold ground all alone."

The room was deathly still. For months now, everyone had tiptoed around her, letting her alone with her grief. They had tried everything they could to console and help her out of her despair. But she wasn't quite ready yet to leave this dark place she was in. And she wasn't sure if she ever would be.

Nay, this was her penance, and she knew it. Penance for the sin she had committed all those many years ago. Penance for killing her stepfather, Delmar Wiggart.

God was now punishing her for that mortal sin by taking away the only man she would ever love. While Delmar had been a nasty, perverse man, he was still one of God's children. And she had purposefully taken his life.

Although she hadn't killed him just for the sake of killing him—

he'd been trying to rape her sister Mariote at the time—she still felt guilty.

Patrick's death was God's way of saying, "Ye took a man's life, so I shall take the life of the man ye love most."

"We will take care of Patrick," Hugh said. Andrew nodded his agreement.

"I will help as well," Jamie offered, looking most solemn and serious.

Muriale looked at her younger siblings. They meant well. She knew they did. But, still, she couldn't agree. Patrick was *her* responsibility and no one else's.

"Muriale, I *need* ye to go with me," Orabillis said. "Please, dinnae make me go to Edinburgh with Da all by myself."

"Excuse me?" Alysander asked, clearly insulted.

Moirra quieted him with a shake of her head.

"I love ye, Da, I truly do. But I fear we would drive each other mad after a few hours. Can ye imagine what a few weeks together would be like?" Orabillis explained.

"But I cannae leave Patrick," Muriale told them. "He needs me."

Moirra placed a comforting hand on Muriale's shoulder. "Sweeting, I ken ye love Patrick verra much. But do ye truly believe he would want ye to spend all the rest of yer days mournin' him?"

Her anger continued to build. "Nay," she said, choking back tears. "I think he would have preferred to still be among the livin' if he'd been given a choice."

Moirra was doing her best to maintain her calm composure. But her daughter certainly wasn't making it easy. She took in a deep breath and shook her head. "Muriale, yer grief is yer grief. There are nae rules on how long someone can mourn a loss. But there comes a time when ye have to make a decision. Will ye choose to keep livin' and enjoy all the *happy* memories ye had with Patrick? Or will ye choose to shrivel up and die?"

Muriale knew her mother meant well. Truly, she did. But it didn't make her feel any better. It also did nothing to assuage her anger. "If I were given the choice, I would choose to die right this verra moment and be buried right beside Patrick!"

She shoved away from the table and raced up the stairs, into her room. All the while, her parents were calling out her name.

Ignoring them, she slammed the door shut and fell onto her bed. Consumed with grief, the tears fell down her face and onto her pillow. *They will never understand.*

When the door to her room opened moments later, she didn't bother to look to see who it was. Quite simply, she didn't care. She was fully prepared to ignore the intruder, no matter what.

"Muriale McCullum, I have had enough."

'Twas her mother speaking, and she sounded furious. Startled by her tone, Muriale sat up in her bed and clutched her pillow to her chest. Aye, her mother was angry, all right. But there was more to it than that.

Moirra stood at the end of the bed, her lips pursed and her hands on her hips. It had been a long, long while since Moirra had given her *that* look. The look only mothers get. The look that warns, "Ye better listen and listen well."

"Muriale, I love ye. We all love ye. And we all ken how much ye loved Patrick."

"Love! I *still* love him, Mum!" Muriale was exasperated.

Moirra wasn't about to be deterred. "I ken that ye do. But, as yer mum, I refuse to allow ye, at the age of nine and ten, to spend the rest of yer days dyin' a slow, agonizin' death over Patrick MacConnell. Or any man, for that matter. I refuse to watch ye die that way."

The retort on Muriale's tongue was quashed by another motherly look that said, "Dinnae ye dare talk back right now."

"Ye are goin' to Edinburgh with yer da and Orabillis. Ye leave tomorrow, and I'll nae argue the matter with ye."

Edinburgh? Had her mother lost all sense of kindness?

Quietly, she shed more tears. *Nay, they will never understand.*

Seeing her daughter's grief, Moirra blew out a frustrated breath. She sat on the bed and pulled Muriale into her arms. "Daughter of mine, I love ye. I truly do. Ye have a good and giving heart."

Muriale couldn't hold on to her guilt any longer. Her resolve to keep the secret was gone. She didn't have the energy to hold onto it any longer. "'Tis my fault Patrick is dead."

Stunned, Moirra gently pushed her away so that she might look into her eyes. "Yer fault?" She shook her head in disagreement.

"But it is," she replied. "God is punishin' me for killin' Delmar."

Moirra felt relieved knowing where at least some of her daughter's grief was truly coming from. Drawing her in for another warm embrace, she couldn't help but smile. "Muriale, I am quite certain God is nae punishin' ye. Why, if he punished everyone who ever took a life for any reason, there would nae be a soul left. We would have died out long ago."

"But what other explanation is there?" Muriale asked. "Why else would God have taken him from me?"

Moirra gave her another gentle squeeze. "Lass, God dinnae take him from ye. The Buchanans did."

---

Just hearing the name Buchanan made the hair on her neck stand up and her skin prickle. "Please, dinnae say that name," she said as she shivered. "I hate them."

If she lived to be a thousand years old, she would never forgive them for what they had done. Not just to Patrick but to her Uncle Connor and the other fine men they had murdered that day. It had been a senseless, unprovoked attack. An ambush, her father had called it. Unprovoked ambush or not, the results were the same:

Many fine men died that awful day. And Muriale's world would never be the same.

"Aye," Moirra said with a nod. "I am nae fond of them either. But yer da and the others, they did avenge Connor's death, as well as Patrick's and the others. They did a tremendous amount of damage to their keep as well as to their warriors. I dinnae think we will have to worry about them again for a good long while."

The imagery of the Buchanan keep burning and dead Buchanan warriors littering the earth did nothing to satisfy her need for more vengeance. It fed the hatred coursing through her veins. She loathed the Buchanans as much as she loved Patrick, if such a thing were even possible.

"But they dinnae kill *all* of them," Muriale pointed out.

"Of course not. Yer father and uncle dinnae kill innocents. They dinnae kill mothers and children or the auld. Ye ken that."

A twinge of guilt stung at her heart. Truly, she didn't want to see any innocent people killed. She wasn't that full of hatred. "Do ye think they will rebuild?"

Moirra shrugged her shoulders. "Most likely, aye. But ye will be a grandmother before they regain the strength and power they once had."

Muriale sat up and dried her cheeks on the sleeves of her dress. "I fear I will never be a mother, let alone a grandmother. Those dreams are buried with Patrick."

"The nice thing about dreams, Muriale, is that ye can always create new ones."

She wasn't quite as convinced as her mother in that regard. Still, she did feel slightly better.

"Instead of languishing in a sea of bitterness and guilt, try to cherish all those happy moments ye had with Patrick."

That was something she had refused to do since his death. She had been intensely focused on her grief and guilt and the future that was stolen away from her. On those rare occasions when a happy memory slipped into her mind, 'twas too much to bear. She wasn't certain she had the strength to do that, to relive those cherished moments spent with Patrick. It somehow made losing him all the more painful.

"I dinnae ken how I can go on without him, Mum."

Moirra kissed her forehead and gave her arms a gentle squeeze. "The only way any of us do, lass: one heartbeat at a time."

The rest of Muriale's day had been busy preparing for the journey south to Edinburgh. Her mother insisted she pack a few elegant and colorful dresses because, as she said, "One just never kens."

She, however, was perfectly content to wear black all the rest of her days. Besides, arguing with her mother was futile at best.

And Orabillis's constant grumbling was enough to make anyone go mad. "If ye dinnae wish to go, then why did ye insist that *I* go?" Muriale asked as she looked at the contents of her trunk one more time.

Orabillis was tossing gowns out of her own trunk. "If Mum thinks for a moment that I will be prancin' around Edinburgh in fancy dresses, she has gone mad."

Forgoing the trunk, Orabillis carefully packed her satchel with tunics, trews, woolens, and weaponry. She didn't feel the need for much else.

"Again, I ask why," Muriale said as she counted the number of chemises for the third time. "Why did ye insist I go?"

"Och!" Orabillis groused. "Because I kent that they were goin' to make me go, and I dinnae want to go by myself."

What Orabillis sometimes lacked in logic, she more than made up for in sheer willpower and determination. "Mayhap it will do ye some good to see another part of the world," Muriale told her. "Mayhap ye will learn that nae all men are eejits."

Orabillis stopped what she was doing and looked aghast. "If ye think for one minute that I am comin' home with a husband, ye are more demented than our mother."

Muriale rolled her eyes incredulously. "I dinnae mean it like that," she said. "I mean that ye need to see that nae all people are the same."

"Then, why did ye nae say it that way?"

Muriale was growing more and more frustrated with her sister. Truly, she didn't wish to argue with her, but Orabillis didn't always make it easy.

"Just forget what I said," she told her. She grabbed the dresses Orabillis had tossed away and went back to her own trunk.

"What are ye doin'?" Orabillis asked. "I am nae wearin' those."

"Of course nae," she replied. "But ye ken mum will check. And if she sees that ye dinnae take any of the dresses, she will come after us."

"I suppose ye are right," Orabillis said. "As long as we both agree that I will nae be wearin' them."

Muriale smiled and folded the gowns carefully. "Aye, I ken." What she said and what she thought were two entirely different things.

By the time she laid her head down to sleep later that night, she was exhausted. There was a time in her life when she didn't feel so bone tired, but that time was before Patrick's death.

She had no desire to go to Edinburgh with her father and sister. In truth, she had no desire to go anywhere. She'd have much rather preferred to stay at home, where she could visit Patrick every day.

Had she truly possessed the energy to argue, she would have

adamantly refused to go. However, she was old enough and smart enough to know that once her mother made up her mind about something, it would take God himself coming down from Heaven to make her change it.

Mayhap her mother was right. Mayhap, just mayhap, Patrick's death wasn't her penance. His death, she knew, lay entirely at the feet of the Buchanans, how she wished she had snuck off like Orabillis did last summer. Snuck off and fought their enemy. Mayhap it would have made her feel slightly better to have run a sword through a few of the Buchanan warriors.

She fell asleep to the images of doing just that. Battling against the men responsible for taking her Patrick. Just envisioning doing such a thing made her feel better.

Who knew? Someday she might even get the chance to exact her own revenge against those Buchanans who remained. Not the women or children or the auld, but killing a few of their warriors might be the one thing she needed to move on with her life.

They would leave at first light and head south. Their path would take them right through Buchanan lands. For the first time in more than ten months, Muriale McCullum fell asleep with a smile on her face.

———

"Orabillis, might I borrow your sword?"

They were standing in the courtyard this sunny morning, waiting for their father to finish speaking with their uncle Archibald. Thus far, Archibald was doing a remarkable job as the new chief of their clan.

"My sword?" Orabillis asked with more than a bit of astonishment. "Ye have never held a sword in yer life. And ye dinnae *borrow* a sword, Muriale. I swear, for someone so smart—"

"I only want it until after we pass through Buchanan lands," Muriale said, interrupting her sister's growing tirade.

Orabillis stopped mid sentence as understanding set in. 'Twas a simple request, as far as Muriale was concerned. However, she knew how much her sister valued her sword.

"I will give it to ye when we reach their border, aye?" Orabillis replied.

Muriale thought about it for only the briefest of moments. It was probably the best offer she would ever receive from her sister, considering weaponry was involved in this particular negotiation.

"Thank ye," Muriale replied.

Alysander came racing down the steps of the keep. With a nod of his head, the order was given to the dozen men who would be traveling with them to Edinburgh. Everyone was soon mounted and ready to leave.

Their goodbyes to their family had been said earlier, but Moirra and the younger children poured out of the keep for one last farewell.

"Remember to write when ye get there," Moirra instructed Muriale. "And remember, we are but a few days away if ye need us."

Muriale knew the only 'us' in that statement was her mother.

"I shall keep a close watch over her, Mum," Orabillis said.

Moirra offered her a warm smile. "Thank ye, Orabillis. And please, dinnae drive yer father to madness."

Truly, Orabillis didn't understand why everyone believed she annoyed her father. As far as she was concerned, they were as close as two blades of Highland grass. She was given no time to argue the matter, though, for the gates opened with a creak and a groan, and the time to leave had arrived.

With Alysander and his second in command, Red John, leading the way, their small group was trotting through the gates and heading for Edinburgh.

---

The last time Muriale had travelled such a lengthy distance had been more than a decade ago. Not more than a little girl then, she'd been filled with excitement and hope.

At the time, she'd been leaving the only home she had ever known: a small cottage on a tiny farm near Glenkirby.

After the events that led to her mother being accused of murder and spending weeks in the gaol, Muriale had felt a tremendous sense of relief at leaving.

Lord only knew where they'd all be if her mother hadn't met Alysander. A shiver of dread tickled her spine at the mere thought.

They had made a new life with Alysander and his brothers. A life she treasured and appreciated beyond measure.

Now, as they travelled through a beautiful valley, she didn't feel the same relief or excitement as she had all those many years ago. Nay, today she was filled with sorrow and regret.

Leaving Patrick behind was difficult. Aye, she understood he was gone and that there was naught to be done about it. She hadn't lost her mind completely, no matter what her family might think.

However, it still felt like a betrayal of sorts to leave him.

She rode next to her sister, who, thankfully, was too busy looking out for thieves or marauders to give Muriale any notice. That left her alone with her own thoughts, which, at times, mayhap wasn't such a good thing.

For nearly a year, her thoughts had been consumed by Patrick's memory and his loss, as well as her guilt. 'Twas a heavy burden to carry for such a long time.

But carry it, she did. Enveloping herself in a cloak of sorrow and despair, it had grown comfortable, like an old friend. Reliable to a fault, the guilt never left her side.

*Mayhap Mum is right that it is time to leave the sorrow behind.* That thought was a shock to her heart. Didn't leaving her sorrow behind mean she was leaving Patrick behind?

Danial Gray Beard's voice broke through her meandering

thoughts. "Look, lass," he whispered. He was pointing to the top of a rocky hill in the distance.

A herd of red deer were grazing on tall grass. Does with their young, casually munching away as if they didn't have a care in the world. The does looked up, ears raised but their tails down, indicating they weren't the least bit concerned by the people passing by.

"'Tis a beautiful sight, aye?" Danial Gray Beard asked with a smile. 'Twas, of course, a rhetorical question. Danial was the same age as her father, but his beard had turned white ages ago.

"Aye, it is," she replied. She couldn't help but smile and look in awe at her surroundings. The grassy hill was dotted with wildflowers in shades of purple and yellow, against a backdrop of tall, deep-green Highland grass. Together, they danced in the soft summer breeze.

"We might run into rain," Danial Gray Beard said as his attention turned to the eastern sky in the distance. "I can smell it."

Muriale smiled at him. "Uncle Archibald says his knee hurts every time it is about to rain."

Danial's lips curved into a mischievous smile. "'Tis because he is an auld man. But if ye tell him I said that, I will deny it." He gave her a wink before turning his attention back to the eastern sky.

"Will ye be quiet," Orabillis groused.

"Why? Do ye smell marauders?" Muriale quipped sarcastically.

Orabillis's brows furrowed into a fine line of consternation. "If we were to come across marauders, ye will be glad that at least one of us was payin' attention."

Muriale knew that her sister was right. Still, it irked her to know that *that* was all her sister was concerned with. "Do ye nae see the beauty that surrounds us?"

"Of course I see it," Orabillis replied sternly. "But a good warrior is nae distracted by such things."

Danial grunted in response. "That is true, lass. But a true Highlander also appreciates the land God has blessed us with."

Their argument was cut short when Alysander called for them to halt. All eyes turned his way. "We shall make camp there." He was pointing to the forest that sat a good distance off their current path. "The rain will be here soon enough."

It seemed every bone and muscle in Muriale's body ached. Unaccustomed to riding across the countryside, her limbs felt as heavy as iron.

But she refused to complain. Complaining would get her nothing more than a displeased roll of the eyes from her sister. And if her father knew, he would likely slow their pace, delaying their arrival to Edinburgh.

'Twasn't that she was looking forward to visiting the great city. On the contrary, she was loathing the idea. However, she knew the sooner they arrived, the sooner they could leave, and the sooner she could get back home.

"I will take the first watch," Orabillis volunteered as she helped young Ardin McCullum set up a tent.

Ardin was a tall, lanky young man, with dark hair and bright-blue eyes. While he might be a scrawny-looking fellow, he was as strong as an ox. According to Orabillis, he was one of the few men who actually challenged her during training.

"I am famished," Red John declared as he set about starting a fire. "I am so hungry I could gnaw off Ardin's arm and eat it."

Ardin ignored the comment.

"But ye'd still be hungry, for there is nae much meat on his bones," Orabillis quipped.

The group laughed at her jest. Ardin was used to having people comment on his slender build, but it didn't mean he liked it. He glowered at Orabillis, who responded with a cheeky grin and a wink.

"Ye are daft," he whispered to her.

"I have been told that before."

Soon, the tents were up and the fire crackling in the evening breeze. Everyone gathered around the fire, save for Ardin and Orabillis. They would be on watch for the first few hours, patrolling the perimeter on foot.

"Ye look done in, lass," Alysander said with a nod toward Muriale.

Mayhap she hadn't been quite as successful as she thought in hiding her weariness. "A bit, mayhap."

Danial Gray Beard and Robert had caught a few rabbits, which were now roasting over the fire. Muriale ate a bit of bread and cheese whilst the rabbits cooked. With her stomach full and her body warmed from the fire, she soon found it difficult to keep her eyes open.

"Why dinnae ye turn in?" Alysander suggested.

She supposed there was no sense in pretending she was anything but exhausted. "I think I might," she replied, trying her best to stifle another yawn.

After bidding good night to her father and the men, she slipped inside the tent she would share with Orabillis. Within moments of crawling into her pallet, she was asleep.

'Twas the first time in an age where sleep came easily. A legion of Roman soldiers could have descended upon their camp, and she would have slept through it.

And, for the first time since Patrick's death, she slept without the interference of nightmares.

———

Muriale and Orabillis were both mighty disappointed as they passed through Buchanan lands the following day. They met one young man—a boy, really—who was patrolling their border on foot. As soon as he saw the group of McCullum warriors heading his way, he hightailed it for home.

"Apparently, we did more damage than I realized," Orabillis said, rather proudly.

The poor boy looked so pitiful running away that Muriale was half tempted to give him her horse. Suddenly, her hatred for the Buchanans didn't burn quite so passionately.

When she found herself feeling sorry for those who remained in the aftermath of their retribution, she immediately pushed the thoughts aside. *'Twas no more than they deserved,* she told herself. *They chose the wrong clan to attack.*

Bitterness began to replace the guilt she'd been feeling all these many months. Her mother had helped her to see that Patrick's death was neither her fault nor her penance. The realization might have helped to lighten the burden of grief, but it somehow made her angrier.

She refused to feel any amount of remorse for despising the Buchanans. In truth, it felt rather freeing to feel something other than grief, anguish, and guilt, for that was all she had been feeling for months now.

The sun was just beginning to disappear over the horizon when they crossed into Clan Graham lands. Three Graham warriors were patrolling the area. Alysander ordered Red John to join him at the front of the line. Red John was a massive man, broad shouldered and narrow at the hip, with a mass of red, wavy hair that fell well beyond his shoulders. He was, by far, one of the most intimidating of all the McCullum warriors.

Muriale and her sister were ordered to stay behind with the rest of the men. Orabillis didn't take insult on the matter. The Grahams, after all, were their allies. But her father still needed to ask permission to cross their lands. Protocol was important.

Muriale paid no attention to the Graham warrior who kept smiling at her. But Orabillis noticed. She supposed her other sisters would have found the man attractive, what with his long, brown hair; his almost perfect, straight, white teeth; and his chiseled physique. The fact that he kept smiling at Muriale annoyed Orabillis to no end. *Why is that all people think about? Love, lovin', rromanc... Och! There is so much more to life than that.*

With a quiet growl of frustration, she moved her horse closer to Muriale as a sign of protection. When she caught the young warrior's attention, she glowered at him. Instead of intimidating him as was her intention, the fool threw his head back and laughed.

"What on earth are ye doin'? Muriale asked. "And why are ye leering at that warrior?"

"I am nae leerin'," Orabillis told her. "'Tis a glower." She was truly insulted that her sister couldn't see the difference.

Muriale rolled her eyes. "But *why* are ye glowerin'?"

Orabillis gave her sister a look that said she questioned her intelligence and soundness of mind. "Because *he* is the one leerin' at *ye*."

"Don't be ridiculous," Muriale argued as she glanced at the warrior in question. Aye, he was smiling at them. And there was something in that smile that she recognized. 'Twas the same smile Patrick would give when he was being mischievous. An overwhelming sense of longing filled her heart. Oh, how she missed him. Not wanting to incite her sister to violence, she said, "He is simply bein'...nice."

"Bah!" Orabillis exclaimed in a harsh whisper. "I think if he had his way, he'd toss ye onto the back of his horse and ride off with ye."

Muriale did something she hadn't done in a very long while: She giggled. While she recognized the look the man was giving her, she thought her sister's assumption was absurd.

"Why are ye laughin'?" Orabillis asked.

"Because he dinnae ken he'd have to get through ye first."

---

They stopped in a small glen near the Grahams' southern border to make camp. Twilight was beautiful, with a lavender sky and the stars just beginning to twinkle.

Muriale wasn't used to riding for such a lengthy time or over such rough terrain.

Her backside and legs ached, and her feet stung like they were being pricked with a thousand needles the moment they touched the soft earth.

Orabillis didn't look the least bit affected. "How on earth are ye able to walk upright?" Muriale asked her. "I feel as auld as dirt right now."

"Because I dinnae spend my days sittin' by a fire. I train with the men. I hunt with them as well."

Muriale quirked one pretty brow. "Ye make it sound as if I spend my days loungin' around like a princess."

Orabillis gave a slight shrug of her shoulders. "All I am sayin' is that I am far more active than ye. My muscles are used to it."

Muriale didn't think a proper lady should have muscles per se, at least not like a man's. But she kept that thought to herself as she pulled her bags from her saddle.

Red John was soon at her side. "I will take care of yer horse, Muriale."

"Thank ye, Red John," she said with a warm smile. "I do appreciate it."

He gave her a nod, grabbed the reins, and slowly walked away. Her brow furrowed with confusion. "Why did he nae take yer horse?"

Orabillis chortled and shook her head. "Because I can take care of my own horse."

*Of course ye can,* Muriale mused. From the moment they left the keep, she had felt wholly unprepared for the journey. She didn't know the first thing about sleeping under the stars, hunting, fishing, or tending to a horse.

Seeing her distress, Orabillis smiled and gave her a nudge. "Dinnae fash yerself overmuch, sister."

"I am nae fashin' over anythin'," Muriale lied.

Orabillis ignored the lie. "I cannae do more than a simple stitch, and usually that is to mend someone's cut. And I cannae cook to save my soul from the devil."

"And yer point bein'?"

"God blessed each of us with a special gift, ye ken. We are—all of us—different."

Muriale felt a slight tug at her heart. *Patrick used to say that.* Oh, how she missed him. If she thought she could find her way back home, she would have retrieved her horse and done just that.

Guilt assaulted her heart and mind. *I have deserted him. I left Patrick behind.*

Tears began to well in her eyes for a host of reasons. Not wishing her sister to see her distressed further, she turned away. "I need to tend to nature's call," she murmured as she headed for a copse of trees.

Thankfully, Orabillis didn't follow.

---

Alone and hidden in the trees, she let the tears fall. Finding a good solid tree, she leaned against it, swiping away her tears.

Oh, she knew most people would think her ridiculous for feeling this way, but she simply couldn't help it. Patrick had been everything to her. He was a good, kind, decent man.

Aye, sometimes he drank a bit more than he should. And occasionally she had wondered if she needed to worry about his roaming eyes. But no one was perfect, least of all herself.

*He loved me, and I him. That was all that mattered.*

She slid down to her rump and leaned against the tree. Twilight was upon them, and soon the sky would be black as pitch. Looking up at the lavender sky, she began to speak to Patrick.

"I am so sorry I left ye behind," she said, swiping away tears with her fingertips. "But Mum and Da insisted I take this trip." She took in a slow, deep breath in hopes of quelling the tears. It didn't work.

"I love ye so much, Patrick. I promise I will never love another as I have loved ye. No one will ever take yer place. Nae in my heart or in my life."

"That's a pretty large promise ye are makin', daughter."

Startled by the sound of her father's voice, she gasped and nearly jumped out of her own skin. So lost in her own thoughts, she hadn't heard him approach.

"Da!" she exclaimed. "Ye scared me half to death!"

Alysander smiled warmly as he sat beside her. "My apologies, lass."

She didn't think he looked the least bit sorry but kept that opinion to herself. They sat in quiet contemplation for a time, before Alysander broke the silence.

"Muriale, I need ye to ken that I love ye. Of all my daughters, I think ye are my favorite."

She openly scoffed at his comment before giggling slightly. "Ye lie, Da. We all ken Orabillis is yer favorite."

"I love all my daughters," he said. "But ye? Ye hold a verra special place in my heart."

Rolling her eyes, she brushed off his compliments as nothing more than a father wishing to make his broken-hearted daughter feel better.

"'Tis true," he said. "Of all my daughters, ye are the one with the biggest heart. I never knew anyone who loved as deeply. And no one is as devoted to family as ye." He smiled as he patted her hand. "Ye want nothin' more than to keep yer family safe at any cost."

A pang of guilt stabbed at her heart. *Delmar.*

Alysander had learned the truth about her long ago. While she appreciated the fact that he loved her in spite of the fact she had killed a man, she despised speaking openly about it. Having all those feelings of fear and anger and, aye, even remorse brought up made her feel sick to her stomach.

"Da, please," she whispered, turning away. At the moment, she couldn't bear to look at him.

"Muriale, mayhap ye would feel better if ye talked about it."

"I hate talkin' about it," she replied solemnly. "I hate *thinkin'* about it."

"Do ye truly still feel guilty after all these years?" His tone suggested a large amount of disbelief.

She chose not to reply.

"Muriale, ye did what ye had to do to protect Mariote. There is nae shame in that. What else could ye have done?"

"I could have run to get Mum," she whispered harshly.

"And by the time ye got back, the deed would have been done," he pointed out. "And yer mum would have been the one to kill him."

Truly, she hadn't thought of that before. Quickly, she turned to face her father, appalled with the idea of her mother killing Delmar.

"They would have hanged her!"

Alysander smiled proudly, glad that he had finally been able to get his point across. "Aye, they would have."

The thought of her mother being hanged all those years ago made her want to retch. Truly, she couldn't have born it. If she was having this much difficulty mourning Patrick, just imagine how her mother's death would have affected her.

"So, ye see, lass, ye saved a few lives that day. Ye saved Mariote from bein' raped, and ye saved yer mum from bein' hanged for it later. And I dinnae ken how ye and yer sisters would have survived in this world without her."

He spoke nothing but the truth. A truth she hadn't been able to see through her own guilt.

*Mayhap 'tis time I put that guilt to rest,* she thought to herself.

"I never want ye to feel guilty again for killin' Delmar Wiggart," Alysander said. "Do I have yer word?"

Sitting a bit taller, she made the promise. "I have wasted many a year filled with guilt for what I did. I will nae give any more of my time to a dead man."

Alysander tilted his head slightly and smiled. "'Tis good to hear." Once again, he patted her hand gently.

"Now, let us talk about another man's death ye cannae seem to get over."

M uriale wasn't quite ready to have *that* conversation with her father. 'Twas highly unlikely that he would be able to understand her plight.

"I ken that ye love Patrick with all yer heart," Alysander said. His voice was low and filled with fatherly warmth and concern.

"I also ken that ye will never love anyone the way ye love Patrick."

More than a bit surprised, she tilted her head as she scrutinized him closely.

"God help me, lass, but if anythin' ever happened to yer mum, I ken that I would never be able to love another as I have loved her."

*So, he does understand.*

"But yer mum and I have had a few conversations about this over the years. I ken ye dinnae remember yer real father, Kenneth McPherson."

'Twas true. He died before she was born. When she was little, her mother used to tell her stories about him, about how kind and generous he was.

"Yer mum loved him with every bit of her heart, lass. Every bit."

More confusion set in. "She told ye that?"

He smiled wide. "Aye, she did."

Muriale couldn't make sense of it. Why on earth would her mother tell Alysander about her first husband?

"I, too, loved someone long ago. When I was young."

That was a startling bit of information. "Nay," she whispered.

"Aye, I did. Elsbeth MacReary was her name. Och! She was such a bonny thing. I was goin' to marry her."

Stunned, she asked what happened.

"She died before we could marry."

From the silence that followed and the look of sadness in his eyes, Muriale knew there was much more to the story than he was telling her.

"I am so verra sorry, Da."

He let out a quick breath. "So, ye see?"

Perplexed, she hadn't any earthly idea as to what he was referring. "See what?"

"Both yer mum and I loved others before we met each other. Each of us loved them with every fiber of our bein'."

"Aye, I see that. But what is yer point?" Mayhap 'twas exhaustion from the hard traveling that muddled her mind.

He sighed with a bit of frustration. "If ye can love once, ye can love again."

---

*Love again?*

Nay, that wasn't possible. Oh, it might work for some people...but not Muriale. She refused, even for the briefest moment, to believe that such a thing were possible.

Why, if she were to allow herself to love another, that would be akin to leaving Patrick behind. And she already felt guilty enough for leaving him now, just to travel to Edinburgh.

"I ken it might not seem possible now, Muriale. But please, lass, dinnae close yer heart off to the chance of finding happiness again."

"I don't think I can do that, Da." Truly, she wasn't being insolent or stubborn. She simply couldn't imagine the possibility. Her love for Patrick had been so profound.

"Ye're young, lass," Alysander said. "Yer heart will mend if ye let it."

# THREE

'Twas impossible to miss the great castle on the rock. Carved from dark-gray stone, it was a marvel to behold. "It looks as though it could touch the clouds!" Muriale exclaimed in a whisper. "Have ye ever seen anythin' so grand?"

Orabillis had to agree. Even she was impressed with it.

Danial Gray Beard let out a low whistle. "'Tis amazin', aye? I never thought I would see the like."

"I have ne'er travelled this far south before," Richard McCullum replied. His dark-brown eyes twinkled with awe. "'Tis a sight to behold, all right."

The massive structure sat atop a hill overlooking the city below. The McCullum group was entering the city from the northwest.

Alysander chuckled as he called for the group to stop and dismount. "Aye, 'tis a beauty, to be certain. Mayhap we shall dine there?"

Knowing her father was jesting, Muriale could not resist smiling at him. While the idea of dining with the king could make a lass giggle aloud, she knew 'twas about as possible as her climbing to the moon on a ladder—even if her father and Robert II were distant cousins. Besides, she had not true fondness for their current king. He was notoriously weak, and few liked him.

Orabillis found no humor in the conversation taking place betwixt her father and sister. Whilst Muriale was relieved that their journey had been uneventful, Orabillis was a bit more disappointed. They hadn't met so much one lone thief or band of marauders on their travels south.

"Really, Orabillis," Muriale said as they walked their horses down a narrow street. "Why do ye love fightin' so much? I swear, I will never understand yer love of it." Truly, she would never understand anyone's desire for fighting or warring. It inevitably led to someone's death.

Orabillis had often tried to explain it to her, but she always fell short. She chose not to have that discussion again. For now, she was busy looking out for ne'r-do-wells and thieves. They were, after all, in a huge city. No one truly knows what might be lurking in the shadows.

As soon as they walked past the grand castle, the streets began to narrow and grow more crowded. People going about their daily business, merchants calling out the wares they were selling, chickens squawking in cages... The sounds were almost oppressive. But not nearly as oppressive as the odors wafting in the air.

Muriale was doing her best not to wretch. The obnoxious smells of urine and feces—human and animal alike—were horrid. And the narrower the streets became, the worse the stench. Finally, she took the bit of linen she kept tucked into the belt at her waist and tied it around her face to cover her mouth and nose. It didn't help nearly as much as she had hoped.

Alysander's aunt lived east of the castle. Muriale silently prayed it was as far away from the smells as possible. Mayhap many *miles* east of the castle, for she sincerely doubted she would ever grow accustomed to any of it.

They found a livery, where Alysander paid for a week's worth of care for their many horses. When Alysander added an extra groat to the older, burly man's hands, it elicited a broad smile. "We shall take extra good care of them, m'laird."

Muriale watched the exchange in exhausted silence. It had taken them six days to travel from their keep. Covered in mud and muck, she couldn't wait to get to the aunt's home.

Alysander thanked him kindly. Soon, their rather large group was traversing the streets of Edinburgh, with Alysander leading the way.

They found an inn a block from his aunt's home, where Alysander acquired quarters for his men. The innkeeper was happy that Alysander paid a week in advance for four rooms. Richard McCullum and his brother George wouldn't be staying. They had relatives who lived a few miles northeast of the city and would be visiting them for the duration.

Alysander left his men at the inn, with an order to stay out of trouble. He left Red John in charge of keeping the men in line. "The last thing I need is for any of ye to end up in the gaol." Alysander had first-hand experience with gaols and did his best to stay as far away from them as he could.

"I will keep them in line," Red John said with a wink and a grin.

Alysander snorted dubiously. "Why do I nae take any comfort in that?"

***

Thankfully, Aunt Forvelith lived on a less busy and less odiferous street. "This is it," Alysander said when they reached the middle of the street.

"This is a dressmaker's shop," Muriale pointed out.

"I ken that," Alysander said with a smile. "She lives above stairs."

Squeezed in between his aunt's dressmaker's shop and the wooler's next door was a big wooden door. They stepped into a small, dimly lit alcove. A few steps ahead was a set of wooden stairs that led to the second floor. Behind the staircase, on either side of the corridor, were two doors. Forgoing the stairs, Alysander went directly to the door on the left and knocked.

Muriale could hear the sound of shuffling feet coming from within. Moments later, the door was flung open, and there stood one of the most beautiful women she'd ever seen, aside from her own mother. Shockingly white hair was braided and coiled elegantly around her head. Bright-blue eyes twinkled with delight when she saw Alysander. It wasn't until she smiled that Muriale could see even the hint of a wrinkle, and those were around her eyes. She didn't look a day over forty, but Alysander had shared the woman's true age with his daughters on the journey here. Now, Muriale was left wondering if her father had told her the truth.

"My boy! Ye are here!" Forvelith exclaimed as she grabbed him in for a big hug. "It has been far too long!"

"Come in, come in!" she said happily as she ushered them all inside.

Alysander was delighted to see his aunt after so many years. His bright smile said so much. This was a woman he admired and adored. "Ye have nae changed a bit, Auntie. Ye are just as beautiful as the last time I saw ye."

"Of course I am, ye wee beastie!" She smiled and patted his cheek. Muriale fell instantly in love with the woman. She exuded confidence and warmth and honesty.

"Now, who are these lovely young ladies?"

"This is my daughter, Muriale," Alysander said.

Forvelith immediately wrapped her in a warm embrace and kissed her cheek. "Ye are just as beautiful as yer father said in his letters to me."

Muriale couldn't resist returning the woman's smile.

"And ye must be Orabillis," she said as she turned her attention to her. She smiled warmly at her. "Och! Ye are a bonny young woman. I hear ye are quite talented with the sword?" She hugged Orabillis and kissed her cheek.

"I am so happy that ye are all here," she said, before giving each of them another round of hugs.

Once the warm welcome was completed, Forvelith said, "Ye all look as though ye could use a bath, a hot meal, and a warm bed."

The thought of a hot bath was enough to make Muriale want to dance with glee. She hadn't had that luxury in nearly a sennight. "That would be glorious," she replied.

"I will have cook heat water while I show ye to yer rooms," Forvelith said. "We shall feast together this night, and ye can tell me all about yerselves."

---

T he home above the dressmaker's shop was large, spacious, and bright. The living quarters were at the front, with two sleeping chambers at the rear.

Muriale and Orabillis were given the larger of the two chambers. A big, comfortable-looking bed sat to the right of the door, anchored on both sides by dark, heavy tables. In front of the window that looked down to the alley was a table with two chairs. Overall, it was a nicely appointed space.

"If ye need anythin', my bedchamber is right next to yers," Forvelith explained. "Yer da will sleep below stairs."

"Red John and David will be along shortly with yer things," Alysander said.

"And what will yer men be doin' while they are here? Where will they be stayin'?" Forvelith asked, concern etched in her brow.

Alysander chuckled and gave her a warm smile. "Ye have nae changed a bit," Alysander said.

"And what do ye mean by that?" she asked.

"Always wantin' to take care of everyone." He chuckled again. "I brought twelve men with me, Auntie. Some will be visiting family nearby. The others will be stayin' at an inn. I can assure ye none will go hungry or have to sleep in a barn."

Alysander adored his aunt for many reasons but mostly for her giving heart. She couldn't abide knowing a person might be going without.

"Do ye still give coin to the homeless ye encounter on the streets?"

Forvelith tilted her head slightly as she put her hands on her hips. "Nae that 'tis any of your business, but aye, I do."

Alysander hugged her again and placed a kiss on her forehead. "I have missed ye, Auntie. Now, let us go so my daughters can clean up and rest. We have much to catch up on."

———————

The hot bath did wonders for Muriale's spirits and achy bones.

After donning her pretty, blue wool gown, she braided her still-damp hair, affixed a silver belt at her waist, and did her best to ignore her sister.

"I dinnae ken why Da will nae let me go with him on the morrow," Orabillis complained.

"Because he has important business to attend to. He cannae keep ye out of trouble while he is doin' it." That was the same explanation their father had given her twice already.

"I will nae get into trouble," Orabillis said through gritted teeth. "And I sincerely wish everyone would stop saying that."

Checking her appearance in the small looking glass, Muriale quipped, "Then, stop gettin' into trouble."

Frustrated, Orabillis threw her boot at Muriale, hitting her in her backside. Had she truly intended to injure her, she would have put a little more heat into it. Muriale barely noticed.

Being accustomed to her younger sister's occasional outbursts and immaturity, Muriale's only response was to say, "And ye wonder why Da dinnae want to take ye.

Now, shall we go sup with Auntie Forvelith?"

Their supper was nothing short of a feast, with roast duck, beef, and ham served with various vegetables and savory dishes. Three different sweets for dessert. Wines, ales, and whisky were also offered. Muriale was surprised the table didn't crumble under the weight of it all.

Forvelith's cook, Mrs. MacCurdy, was a stout, older woman with ginger hair, dark-blue eyes, and a most serious disposition. However, when Muriale, her father, and sister complemented her fine cooking, she smiled proudly. "Och!" she exclaimed with a smile. "'Tis just a simple meal."

If this was the woman's idea of a simple meal, Muriale would love to see what her idea of a feast might be.

Forvelith and Alysander did most of the talking that night. Muriale didn't mind one bit. She found she rather enjoyed hearing stories about her father as a bairn, a little boy, and later as a young man.

"Ye were the prettiest little boy I ever lay eyes on," Forvelith said as she sipped on her wine. "All four of ye were beautiful bairns. But ye? Aye, ye stole my heart from the verra first time I ever saw ye."

Alysander smiled and gave a wink to his daughters. "But Hugh was your favorite."

"Much like yer mum, I had no favorites," she said indignantly. "I dinnae ken why ye would think otherwise."

"Because ye let Hugh get away with things ye would have skelped my hide for."

"That wasn't favoritism, Alysander. Hugh would have preferred a beatin' over bein' chastised or bein' told we were disappointed in him."

Alysander smiled at distant memories for a long moment. "Aye, I suspect ye are right."

"Why did ye leave the clan?" Orabillis asked as she ate another sweet cake.

Forvelith tilted her head slightly and looked rather perturbed by the question. "I never left my clan."

Those five little words said much. Forvelith still held a deep connection to her people, even after all these years.

"I meant no insult, Auntie," Orabillis replied quickly. "I meant to ask why did ye leave the keep? How did ye come to live in Edinburgh?"

"Oh," Forvelith replied, her smile returning. "Why else would a woman leave her clan but for love?"

Orabillis looked disappointed by the answer. Muriale could almost read her sister's mind. *Love? Och. I'd rather be gutted and my entrails fed to wolves than to sacrifice myself to love.*

"Love," Orabillis replied with distaste.

Forvelith took it as a challenge. "Aye, love. Why are ye so against love?"

Orabillis rolled her eyes and pushed her plate away. "I would rather be gutted and my entrails fed to wolves than to sacrifice myself to the love of a man."

Muriale smiled inwardly. *I was close.*

"But why?" Forvelith asked.

Alysander began to look as though he had an upset stomach. He'd had this conversation with his daughter far too many times over the years. The answer was always the same. *Because men are eejits.*

"Because men are naught more than ill-bred eejits."

He sent a silent prayer heavenward whilst Muriale smiled. Her aunt didn't know what she'd gotten herself into.

"Well, of course they are," Forvelith replied.

Alysander and Muriale turned their attention to her. They were perplexed. That wasn't the reply either of them had expected. Even Orabillis looked surprised.

Forvelith kept her focus on Orabillis. "They are also stubborn to a fault, ridiculously ignorant on what a woman truly wants, and they can be mind-bogglingly jealous at times."

"Exactly!" Orabillis exclaimed her agreement.

Forvelith smiled affectionately at her. "Some men are naught more than wastes of human flesh, if ye ask me."

Orabillis smiled victoriously. Finally, she had someone who agreed with her.

"I fear I have kent a few women in my time who were like that as well," Forvelith said.

Orabillis's brow furrowed. "I have only kent good, strong women. Kind women."

"Then, ye are indeed quite blessed, child. Quite blessed, indeed." She took a sip of her wine before asking her next question. "And how many awful, disgusting men have ye kent?"

Orabillis sat back in her chair and began to list those men by name. "My mum's third husband, Delmar Wiggart. Never a more nasty, perverse man ever walked the earth." She shook her head in disgust. "Then ye have his brother, Almar, and the sheriff of Glenkirby and his deputies. Then our old neighbor, Thomas McGregor. Now *there* was a piece of shite for ye. He tried to kill me when I was but six years of age."

"Oh my!" Forvelith replied with genuine surprise. "I dinnae ken that."

"Were it nae for Alysander and my uncles Connor and Archibald, I would nae be sittin' at yer table this night."

"Well, I can certainly understand why ye dinnae trust men," Forvelith said.

"Damned right I dinnae trust them," Orabillis said with a nod.

"Language, please," Alysander said firmly.

Forvelith's warm smile returned. "But ye lived, aye?"

"Aye," Orabillis replied with a furrowed brow. If there was a point her aunt was trying to make, she couldn't see it.

"Ye saved yerself?"

"Nay," Orabillis said, silently wondering if her aunt wasn't having an apoplexy at the moment. "I told ye, Alysander and my uncles saved me."

Forvelith nodded her head slightly. "So, *men* saved ye?"

Understanding dawned in Orabillis's eyes. "Aye, men saved me."

"So, nae all men are wastes of human flesh and God's time." 'Twas more a statement than a question.

Orabillis wasn't given any time to reply. Her aunt began to push away from the table. "The hour grows quite late," she said as she got to her feet. "While I would love naught more than to stay up till dawn with ye, I am rather tired. If ye will all excuse me, I shall bid ye all a good night and wish ye all pleasant dreams."

Alysander stood and placed a kiss on her cheek. "The girls and I will clean up. We shall see you in the morn."

Forvelith gave each of them a smile and a nod before disappearing into her bedchamber.

Orabillis looked as dumbfounded as she was dejected. She'd been preparing herself for a good, long argument about men. Mayhap the woman wasn't as of sound mind as she previously believed. 'Twas also quite possible that she simply didn't have an argument that could change Orabillis's mind about the opposite sex.

"Stop yer wool gatherin', Orabillis, and help us clear the table," Muriale said, with platters in each of her hands.

Mrs. MacCurdy returned and began to argue that she could very well clear the table. "Ye are guests, after all!"

"Aye, we are," Muriale argued. "But we will nae take advantage of your kindness or our aunt's. Now, please let us help."

Mrs. MacCurdy finally acquiesced but insisted she could do all the washing up. Muriale, however, insisted that she and her sister would be helping.

"Ye are a stubborn thing, aye?" Mrs. MacCurdy said with a fierce glower that even Muriale could see through.

"Aye, I am. I come from a long line of stubborn women," she replied with a smile. "Now, would ye like to wash or dry?"

Mrs. MacCurdy's glower turned into a smile. Before she could reply, Orabillis stepped forward and grabbed a towel. "Ye wash, I will dry, and Mrs. MacCurdy can tell us where everything goes."

"Well, if ye are certain," she said reluctantly, then she sat down on a three-legged stool next to a heavy table.

"Aye, we are," Muriale replied.

Alysander was standing in the doorway, with a tray filled with dishes. "Just sit that here, laddie," Mrs. MacCurdy said with a wave of her hands, indicating the top of the table. "Then off to bed with ye. We three can take care of the rest."

"I fear I am too tired to even pretend to argue with ye," Alysander said with a wide grin.

He bid them all good night before quitting the apartment and heading to his bed below stairs.

"He is a right nice man," Mrs. MacCurdy said.

"Aye, he is," Muriale agreed.

Orabillis carried the kettle to the basin and poured the hot water into it. Steam rolled and billowed upward, leaving her face damp. "Tell me," she said as she put the kettle back onto the fire. "How long have ye worked for our aunt?"

The older woman glanced at the ceiling as she tried to remember. "Nigh on ten years, I believe. Saved my life, she did."

Curious, the sisters asked what she meant by that.

"Och! Ye would nae ken it now, but I was quite a looker in my day." She smiled and winked. "But I dinnae have a lick of common sense, and I made the biggest mistake of my life."

Muriale was more than just a bit curious. As she washed a big, heavy pot she asked, "How so?"

"I married the first bloke who asked me."

Orabillis pursed her lips as if 'twas a story as auld as time and as true as the sun coming up each morn. As if she had all the worldly experience one could ever attain and knew exactly Mrs. MacCurdy's full meaning.

"He was a bastard then, aye?"

Mrs. MacCurdy cackled heartily. "Nay! He was the finest man I ever met. And, Lord above, was he beautiful to look upon."

"Then, how exactly was it a mistake?"

A wan smile formed on her face. "He was a good, kind man, as I said. But he was like me; he dinnae have a lick of common sense. He simply could nae make a livin' for us. So, he convinced me to move here to Edinburgh. I was all of six and ten."

Muriale supposed she would eventually get to the part about the mistake and how Forvelith had saved her life. But she was tired and hot from the small confines of the kitchen and the scrubbing up.

"I grew up a lot those first few years. Far more than Darvid did." She suddenly looked quite sad, her gaze transfixed on the floor, undoubtedly reliving memories of those times.

"Eleven years ago, the fool up and died on me."

"Oh, I am so verra sorry to hear that," Muriale replied.

"Och! 'Twas his own fault. The fool partook of far too much whisky one night and fell off a pier. The drunken lout drowned."

"Ye sound angry with him," Muriale said. She herself had been quite upset with Patrick dying on her, for not fighting hard enough to survive his attack. It took months to realize it simply wasn't his fault.

"That, I am, lassie. That, I am."

"But ye still love him," Muriale pointed out.

"Aye, I do. But life is for the livin', as they say," she said with a smile.

Orabillis wasn't quite as interested in the romantic part of the woman's storytelling. "But how did Forvelith save ye?"

She smiled wide, her eyes twinkling in the candle light. "I dinnae have a bit of coin to my name. I had nae eaten in days. Forvelith caught me trying to steal a hunk of bread off a cart over on Hay

Market. I cried and cried and cried, and she wiped my tears and gave me a job."

Mayhap the story wasn't quite as exciting as Orabillis would have preferred, but Muriale found it quite sweet. "The more I learn about my aunt, the more I love her."

Mrs. MacCurdy cackled again, slapping her hand on her knee. "Lass, I have kent the woman for more than a decade, and I still dinnae ken her well."

Muriale thought that a rather odd comment but decided not to speak that opinion aloud. Forvelith's secrets were her own, as most secrets should be.

CHAPTER

# FOUR

They slept like rocks their first night in Edinburgh. The king's legion of soldiers could have walked through their bedchamber, and neither Muriale nor Orabillis would have noticed.

Muriale woke to the smell of bread and ham wafting into their room. Her stomach growled, and her mouth watered. How long had it been since she'd last looked forward to eating? While the food last night was as delicious as it was abundant, she hadn't truly partaken of much of it. Thankfully, no one had encouraged her to eat more.

For a long moment, she felt the familiar pangs of guilt. Poor Patrick was dead and buried in the cold, dark ground, and here she was, in Edinburgh, with her mouth watering to the sweet scent of ham.

She closed her eyes against the tears and thought about the conversation she'd had with her mother a sennight ago. Being as young as she and Patrick were, they didn't think much beyond the future of their wedding day. Death was something old people thought about, not the young and healthy.

*Would Patrick have wanted ye to spend all the rest of yer days mournin' for him?*

There was no real way of knowing the answer to that question, for they'd never discussed the what-ifs of life. Instead, they only planned for all the things they would do together, such as having as many bairns as the good Lord would allow, building their own little cottage, and raising chickens and sheep.

*Oh, Patrick. I wish I could ask ye what I should do.*

In her heart of hearts, she knew the answer. Patrick had been a kind and thoughtful man. He wanted nothing more than to make Muriale happy. He hated seeing her cry or in any kind of upset.

Her quiet musings were interrupted by Orabillis yawning loudly and stretching out beside her. "Och!" she said as she wiped the sleep from her eyes. "I cannae remember the last time I slept that soundly."

Muriale's answers to the many questions floating around in her head would have to wait. Forvelith was calling their names.

---

M uriale and Orabillis broke their fast over ham, bread, eggs, and sausages. This morn, Muriale actually ate more than a few bites; she ate until she felt near to bursting.

She noticed, however, that Orabillis ate very little.

Their aunt had left them alone to tend to business below stairs. Their father had been up at dawn to tend to that all-important business he'd talked about. But just what that business was was anyone's guess.

"Ye are awfully quiet this morn," Muriale remarked to her sister. 'Twas unlike Orabillis to be quiet unless she was plotting something.

"I have much on my mind," she replied rather absentmindedly.

"I can see that," Muriale said as she got up from the table. "Let us clear away the dishes and go below stairs."

"I swear, if all I have to look forward to whilst we are here is clearing dishes and cleanin', I shall go mad." Begrudgingly, she pushed away from the table to help her sister.

Muriale washed as Orabillis dried, the task done in complete silence. Muriale felt uneasy about her sister's silence. *I'd rather have her grousin' and complainin' over somethin' than to be this quiet,* she mused. *At least then I ken she is nae plannin' to overthrow the king or some other mad scheme.*

She found herself giggling at the thought of Orabillis overthrowing the current king of Scotland. Very few people liked Robert II. Most considered him a weak sovereign and an even weaker man.

Orabillis was too lost in her own thoughts to pay any notice of her sister. Before Muriale could ask her to share her worries with her, the door opened, and Aunt Forvelith stepped inside.

"Och! Lasses, ye dinnae have to do that," she said as she stepped toward them. "The scullery maid will tend to that."

"Then, why were we up half the night doin' dishes?" Orabillis bit out.

Oh, she was in a sour mood all right.

"Because Tuesday evenings and Friday mornings are their days off," Forvelith said. Apparently, she was unbothered by Orabillis's foul mood.

"I fear I cannae take you about the town today," Forvelith said. "I have far too much work to do. Lady MacElroy is comin' in this morn, and I must be there to help her."

Muriale had no idea who Lady MacElroy was but assumed she must be rather important. "That is all right, Auntie. I am certain Orabillis and I can entertain ourselves."

From the look Orabillis gave her, she wasn't nearly as certain.

"I have no doubt that ye can," Forvelith replied. "I would ask a favor of ye, however, if ye would nae mind."

"Of course nae," Muriale replied happily. "What can we do?"

"The butcher is a few blocks away," she began. "He has a goose waitin' for me. I thought mayhap ye'd like to get out for a bit and explore the city on yer own. And, while ye are out, ye could pick up the goose?"

Orabillis grunted her displeasure. Muriale gave her a gentle nudge with her elbow. "We would be delighted to. Just tell us where we can find this butcher."

Forvelith gave them the directions. "Are ye sure ye dinnae want me to write it down for ye?" She had asked that question twice, and both times, Muriale assured her it wasn't necessary.

"We are in search of Clarence MacKinnon's butcher shop," Muriale said with a smile. "We leave here, turn left, go down three blocks, turn right, and then turn left a block later."

Apparently satisfied that she had memorized the instructions, Forvelith handed Muriale enough coins to purchase the goose. "Verra well, lasses. Just mind ye nae to talk to any strangers—man *or* woman. There are many people in this town who would take advantage of yer innocence and kind hearts."

With that warning, she quit the room, leaving the two young women alone.

"Come now, Orabillis," Muriale said encouragingly. "We shall think of it as an adventure."

Orabillis rolled her eyes. "If ye think findin' a goose is an adventure, then ye are indeed a verra sad woman."

CHAPTER

# FIVE

Rory MacLeod didn't enjoy large cities. He much preferred the countryside amd the small villages and hamlets that dotted Scotland. His friends, Gavin MacKendrick and Alyn Buchanan, however, were enjoying Edinburgh with a little too much enthusiasm, as far as Rory was concerned.

Summoned here by their king and sovereign, Robert II himself, a fortnight ago, Gavin and Alyn were taking advantage of everything the city had to offer.

Rory took his duty and oath to his king quite seriously and refused to partake in their incessant need for drink and women.

The three of them, Rory, Gavin, and Alyn, had been knighted by Robert II some five years ago. They'd been traveling not only across Scotland but to the other four corners of the world ever since: France, Italy, Germania, and Ireland.

And now they were home. Or at least back on Scottish soil. Rory had missed his homeland far more than he thought he would.

He missed the thousand shades of green that could be seen across his country. The clear blue lochs and the fat trout swimming in the rivers and streams. He'd missed the bleating of the sheep on the hillside and walking through the tall, highland grass in bare feet.

But he was stuck in Edinburgh for the foreseeable future and not the beautiful countryside he called home.

Gavin and Alyn were just now waking up, and it was nearly noon. Rory had been up for hours and had already broken his fast and trained in the courtyard with the king's soldiers.

"Ye layabouts," he groused.

"Stop spinnin' the room," Alyn mumbled, his voice dry and cracking.

"For the love of God, stop shouting," Gavin said as he pressed his palms into his eyes.

"No one is shoutin'," Rory told him. "'Tis all the wine ye drank last night."

"Stop. Shoutin'." Gavin's words were clipped and sharp, filled with much annoyance.

Alyn moaned and held on to the edges of his bed. "Why is the room spinnin'?"

Rory was more than a bit disgusted with his friends. Aye, they *were* his friends, even if he didn't always agree with their behavior. "'Tis noon, ye layabouts. I have been up for hours whilst the two of ye slept like the drunkards ye are."

Gavin was doing his best not to shout, but he truly needed Rory to lower his voice. "Friar, I swear I will kill ye if ye dinnae stop yer shoutin'."

*Friar.* He'd been given the nickname years ago by the two drunkards still abed, due to the fact that he was such a stickler for rules and order. Rory couldn't stand chaos, and he didn't suffer fools lightly.

"Get up," he said as he slapped Alyn's foot. "Robert wants to see us."

One of the few things that could roust a knight from his sleep or a hangover was a summons from their king.

"I dinnae ken how the two of ye became knights," Rory grumbled as he watched his friends slowly crawl out of their beds.

"The same way ye did, Friar," Gavin said. "We saved one of his illegitimate daughters from a fate worse than death."

Robert II was not a most favored king. Many Scots thought him feeble and spineless —too spineless to rule Scotland, let alone to defend it.

Nothing about his looks or his character stood out. Robert had brown hair, dark eyes, and a long, slender nose. He was neither extraordinarily tall nor short. Neither was he fat or skinny. He was as average as the day was long, a most unassuming man in all regards.

However, he was still king, and that alone made him deserving of respect.

Rory, Alyn, and Gavin were summoned to the king's private quarters, a first for all three men. Rory had to assume that, since they were meeting here, it could only mean one thing: Whatever the king wanted to speak to them about was a matter of utmost importance. It would also require a good deal of secrecy.

They were led into his chamber by one of his personal guards. Robert sat in a grand, opulently carved chair near the hearth. It was the only seat in the room. Last night, their sovereign had been in fine spirits. Quite jovial, actually. But this morn, he looked as angry as a bear who had been stung on its arse by a horde of bees.

The three knights knelt before him, each with one hand over their heart. They'd no sooner knelt than he ordered them to their feet.

"I leave in a sennight" Robert said, wasting no time on niceties or formalities. "I will be returning to Stirling Castle. However, Edinburgh has a most serious problem at the moment, and I want the three of ye to take care of it."

None of the three knights had an inkling to what their king was speaking about. They'd not have to wait long for an explanation.

He snapped his fingers and held out his hand. His man, one Derrik Montegue, stepped forward and politely placed the scroll into the king's palm. He then stepped back into the shadows, doing his best to blend into the scenery. Rory would have hated the man's job.

"It seems there is a fiend on the loose," Robert said as he tapped the scroll against his knee. "And, apparently, catching the man out is too difficult a task for my sheriff and his men."

The word *fiend* sparked a memory in Rory's mind. He'd heard mention of it more than once since they'd arrived in Edinburgh a week ago.

"A fiend, my liege?" Gavin was the one to ask that question.

Robert gave him a glare that warned not to interrupt him again. "This fiend has been raping young women for the past year. At first, the sheriff believed it was multiple men, but now he is of the belief 'tis only one man."

He finally opened the scroll and gave it a cursory glance. "Last night, either by intent or by accident, this fiend killed a young girl of only ten and one."

Robert paused a moment to let that information sink into his knight's heads.

Rory felt his stomach tighten with anger and disgust. Ten and one? She was an innocent bairn.

"She was stolen from her bedchamber," Robert explained, "in the middle of the night. 'Tis believed he gained entry through an open window." The level of disgust he felt was plainly evidenced in his eyes and in the way his lips drew in as if he'd just tasted something sour.

"He stole her from a bed the poor lass shared with her younger sister. No one knew she was gone until her body was discovered just before dawn. She had been sorely abused, and her neck was snapped."

A hundred questions exploded in Rory's head as anger and grief filled his heart. Who on earth could do such a thing to someone so young? And why is the sheriff convinced it was the same man?

"The good people of Edinburgh no longer feel safe," Robert said. "They are crying out for vengeance for this monster's many victims. They are now blaming me. They dinnae believe I can keep them safe."

Rory had to wonder if the king truly cared about the victims and the people of Edinburgh or if he was more concerned with his reputation. That reputation was already precarious at best. Did he hope that, by finding the fiend, he could help bolster his esteem and standing with the good people of Scotland?

He decided that it didn't truly matter either way. There was a fiend on the loose who was raping and now killing innocent young women. And Rory was fully intent on finding the man responsible and bringing him to justice.

The king's reputation be damned.

---

"We should be battling against the English," Gavin groused as they made their way out of the castle. "Instead of lookin' for a madman."

"And what do we ken of such things?" Alyn added. "I dinnae have any idea on how we go about catchin' a fiend such as this."

Rory was in no mood to listen to their grumbling. Abruptly, he stopped to look at his friends. "We do it the same way we would hunt down one of our enemies. We take to the streets, and we talk to people."

Gavin rolled his eyes heavenward. "The sheriff should be doin' that, not us. We are knights, for the sake of Christ."

"Knights who have been given an order by their sovereign," Rory pointed out. "'Tis our duty to fulfill this quest."

"Quest?" Alyn asked in wide-eyed amazement. "This is nae a

quest. This is a futile attempt by Robert to gain the trust of his people—which is severely lackin' at this moment."

"Aye," Gavin agreed, lowering his voice. "He thinks if we catch this fiend, it will make his people admire him."

"He dinnae care about these women," Alyn added in a whisper.

Rory had reached the ends of his patience. "It dinnae matter if he cares or not. What matters is if we do."

Gavin and Alyn glanced at one another, looks of shame etched on their faces.

"So, I ask ye," Rory said, placing one hand on the hilt of his sword. "Do ye care?"

Duly chastised, the men stood a bit taller. They supposed Rory was right. Innocent women, young and old alike, were being attacked by a maniac. "When do we start?" Alyn asked.

"Now," Rory replied drolly. "And we will nae stop until we find him."

CHAPTER

# SIX

Their mission was a simple one: Go to the butchers and pick up a goose.

It might have seemed an easy task for anyone familiar with the streets of Edinburgh, but for Muriale and Orabillis, 'twas like finding the proverbial needle in a haystack.

"We should have gone straight," Muriale said for the second time in as many minutes.

Orabillis was nonplussed. "Aunt Forvelith said it was two blocks down, then a left, then another left."

"Nay, she said three blocks down, then a right and another left," Muriale argued.

Orabillis decided to ignore her sister and continue on the path she believed was the correct one.

"Why dinnae she send Father to do this?" Muriale was growing more frustrated by the moment.

"Because he had work to do," Orabillis said. "Really, Muriale, 'tis just a goose we are in search of, nae the holy grail. We will find the butchers. Ye will see."

Any confidence she had previously held went to the wayside

53

when she realized they were, in fact, quite lost. Orabillis, however, seemed to enjoy that fact immensely.

Where the act of picking up a goose in a strange city seemed like a grand adventure to Muriale, Orabillis thought 'twas altogether a boring idea. That was, until she realized they were lost.

Orabillis needed a mission, a purpose. Finding their way through strange and crowded city streets seemed to invigorate her spirits.

Muriale quickly realized that she didn't like this city. It was far too big, too crowded and loud, and it stunk. She wanted to go home. To the peaceful, quiet, clean countryside where one could breathe fresh, clean air.

She was looking down at the ground, making certain to avoid stepping in garbage or worse, when she bumped into someone. She came close to falling over, but two large hands caught her by her arm. When she looked up to thank him, she was quite startled to see such a handsome man smiling down at her.

Dark, curly locks of hair framed a rather handsome face. Dark-blue eyes, a straight nose, and a dimple in his chin. "I am verra sorry," she finally managed to mutter.

"'Tis all right, my lady," he replied, still smiling. "I can assure ye 'twas my pleasure."

The moment of silence seemed to stretch on as the two people stared at one another. Orabillis, being Orabillis, wasn't having any of it. "If ye will please allow us to pass?" She took hold of Muriale's arm.

The man stepped aside and bowed at the waist. "As ye wish, my lady," he said with a wide sweep of his hand.

Orabillis had to tug twice on Muriale's arm to get her moving. Once they were far enough away, she said, "Truly, Muriale. Is that any way for a lady to behave?"

Muriale scoffed openly at her sister. "And just what do ye ken about bein' a lady?"

"I ken enough nae to stand on a street corner and stare all doe eyed at a complete stranger."

"I wasn't starin' doe eyed at anyone," Muriale said, dismissing the idea entirely.

"Call it whatever ye wish, Muriale. 'Twas still obscene."

"Obscene?" Muriale was taken aback by her sister's choice of words. "I was merely apologizing for bumping into him. Really, Orabillis, ye have the ability to over react at the most ridiculous of things."

Orabillis shrugged her shoulders with indifference. Wanting to change the subject, she said, "We have to find the butcher's."

---

Truly, Muriale didn't think she had acted inappropriately. All she had done was apologize for bumping into a stranger. And now Orabillis was blowing the entire exchange out of proportion.

While it might be true the stranger was a handsome devil of a man, it meant absolutely nothing. Besides, she was still deeply mourning the loss of Patrick. He hadn't been gone a full year yet. 'Twas far too soon for her to even contemplate the idea of having another man in her life. And no matter what her family said, she would mourn Patrick for all the rest of her days if she felt like it.

She pushed all thoughts of the handsome stranger aside. "Yes, let us find the butcher."

---

They ended up going around the block three times, and still, there was no sight of a butcher shop. Not Clarence MacKinnon or any other, for that matter.

Both young women were growing more and more frustrated by the moment. *It truly should nae be this hard,* she complained silently.

"Mayhap we should go back and tell Aunt Forvelith that we could nae find it," Muriale suggested.

"I would rather die than admit defeat in any task," Orabillis said, sounding firm and resolute.

Muriale knew her sister wouldn't give up, no matter how lost, tired, or even scared either of them might become. *And she says* men *are stubborn eejits.*

Muriale finally called a halt to their search. "I will nae go around the same block again," she said resolutely. "Let us step into one of these little shops and ask for directions."

Before Orabillis could offer a retort to that idea, the man she had bumped into walked out of the herbalists shop and almost bumped into her again.

He smiled a rather mischievous smile. "Lass, we truly must stop meeting like this," he said cheekily as he bowed at the waist.

If Orabillis had rolled her eyes any harder, they would have fallen out of their sockets and rolled down the hill.

Muriale felt her cheeks blush—something else that hadn't happened in nearly eleven months. "I fear, kind sir, that we are lost."

He stood a bit taller, that smile growing from mischievous to something undefinable almost in the blink of an eye. "I shall be happy to help ye in any way that I can, my ladies. Moris Desmond at yer service, fair maidens."

Orabillis was not in the least impressed with the man. "No, thank ye," she said as she tried to pull her sister away. "We can find our own way."

Muriale refused to move. Ignoring her sister's good-yet-annoying intentions, she looked up at the man. "We are tryin' to find Clarence MacKinnon's butcher shop."

"Ah," he replied with a knowing nod. "I ken it well," he said reassuringly. "It is but two blocks down that way," he said, nodding over his shoulder. "Two blocks that way and then turn right. The sign hangs over the sidewalk."

"Thank ye kindly," Muriale said. For the briefest of moments she had wished he would simply escort them there. But Orabillis would have complained profusely against it.

He politely bid them good day and walked away in the opposite direction.

"See?" Muriale said as she tugged her shawl around her shoulders a bit more tightly. "Nae all men are stupid eejits. He seemed rather kind."

"Aye, if the directions he gave us actually take us to the butcher's, then I shall admit that."

Exasperated with her sister's flare for the dramatic, she said, "Where else on earth could he be sendin' us?"

"To our deaths," Orabillis replied dryly.

"Really, Orabillis, yer imagination kens no bounds, does it?"

"A good warrior is always prepared for any situation," she said, standing just a bit taller. She put her hand on the hilt of her sword as they headed down the street.

"I will wager ye a whole groat that he has given us the correct and proper directions," Muriale challenged her.

"We shall see," Orabillis replied. "We shall see."

---

Much to Orabillis's chagrin and to Muriale's delight, Clarence MacKinnon's butcher shop was exactly where Moris Desmond said it would be.

Clarence himself tended to their purchase. He tried to hand Muriale the goose, but she politely declined. With a bit of disgust at her sister's weak stomach, Orabillis took the goose and gingerly tossed it over her shoulder.

They thanked the butcher and stepped back out into the crowded streets of Edinburgh.

"Ye owe me a groat," Muriale claimed rather victoriously.

"Nae, I never agreed to the wager," Orabillis argued. "I simply said, 'We shall see.'"

Nonplussed, Muriale shrugged her shoulders. "Either way, I was still correct. Moris Desmond gave us the right directions. He dinnae lead us to our deaths."

"We are nae back to Forvelith's dress shop yet. There is still time for an attack."

Muriale would have laughed had she not known her sister truly believed what she said. In some small way, she was actually quite glad that her sister took things, such as traversing through the strange streets of a city as large as Edinburgh, so seriously. It was comforting knowing that, were they set upon by anyone, Orabillis could defend them in more than adequate fashion.

But she wouldn't admit that to her, at least not at the moment. Later, mayhap years from now, she might make mention of it.

"Do ye think we can find our way home?" Muriale asked as she stepped around a large puddle. Lord only knew what had made it.

"Of course we can," Orabillis told her. She sounded rather distracted at the moment.

Muriale watched as Orabillis's eyes darted from one side of the street to the other. She also took note of the fact that her breathing had changed ever so slightly. As if she were concentrating on some kind of important task. And her hand was also on the hilt of her sword.

"What is it?" Muriale whispered the question. She knew enough not to draw attention to either of them. Something tugged in the pit of her stomach: the familiar lurch of a warning.

Speaking quietly, Orabillis said, "Ahead, on the corner. A ginger-haired fellow in a blue tunic and brown trews." She gave a barely perceptible nod of her head in the man's direction. "And across the street, a dark-haired man dressed all in black."

Muriale gave a quick glance across the street until she caught a glimpse of him. He was doing his best to look as nonchalant as possible, but he was failing miserably.

"They have been following us for some time," Orabillis said when they reached the corner of the street. "Right after our first encounter with your mister Desmond."

Why it felt important to say what she next said, Muriale didn't rightly know. "He isn't *my* mister Desmond."

They had to wait for an ox-led wagon laden with various goods to pass before they could cross the street. The ginger-haired fellow was leaning against the side of a building. If Orabillis's memory served her correctly, one of the many closes Edinburgh was famous for was just a few feet to his right.

Realizing he might intend to pull them into that dark close, Orabillis said, "Let us see what this baker offers."

Quickly, they slipped inside, pretending to be in need of bread. While Muriale busied herself with the baker, Orabillis casually glanced out of the window. She couldn't see the ginger, but the man in black came into her line of vision. He was definitely watching them, trying to peer into the window from across the way.

An older, stout woman with a limp entered the baker's shop. She carried an empty basket in the crook of her arm. "Good day to ye, Missus MacRay," she said to the woman behind the counter.

Muriale paid for a loaf of dark bread before joining her sister in the corner of the shop. "Are they still there?"

"Aye," Orabillis said with a curt nod.

The answer to the unspoken question of *what are we goin' to do* was answered a scant moment before Orabillis could share her plan with Muriale. Their father, blessedly, was walking down the opposite side of the street, with Red John right beside him.

Even Orabillis had to admit to a sense of relief at seeing them.

CHAPTER

# SEVEN

The relief the two sisters felt at seeing their father and Red John was quickly replaced with confusion. He walked right up to the man in black and shook his hand—the kind of handshake that takes place betwixt men who have not seen each other in a very long while.

"What on earth?" Muriale whispered.

"Let us see what happens when we leave," Orabillis suggested. "Let us see if the ginger-haired man—" Her sentence was cut short when the ginger crossed the street and gave Alysander a big bear hug and a slap on his back. Stranger still, he did the same to Red John.

"I still want to see what happens when we leave," Orabillis said. Even if her father did know these men, there had to be a reason why they were following them.

"It has been far too many years," Alysander said as he slapped the back of Rory MacLeod.

"At least a dozen, by my estimation," Gavin MacKendrick offered.

Red John, who rarely smiled, was smiling today. "I believe ye are right. What are ye doin' in Edinburgh?"

Alysander answered the question on their behalf. "Have ye nae heard, Red John? These two fools have managed to get themselves knighted by Robert."

Red John's eyes opened widely with sheer and unadulterated surprise. "Ye jest."

As a way of proving their friend wasn't jesting, each of the younger men pulled aside the collars of their tunics to display the proof. Affixed to gold chains was a round bit of silver with the seal of the thistle engraved upon it. Only knights were given these necklaces.

Still uncertain they spoke the truth, Red John asked, "Who did ye steal those from?"

Rory and Gavin laughed heartily. "No one, I can assure ye," Rory said. "We were bestowed this honor five years ago when we rescued one of Robert's illegitimate daughters from a rather precarious situation."

"Aye," Gavin said with a nod of his head. "A fate worse than death."

Alysander continued to smile. He'd known these two young men for many years, since before either of them could grow a beard. And, now, they stood before him as men. Knighted men, nonetheless.

"Let us find a tavern, and ye can tell us all about how ye came to be knighted," Alysander suggested.

The two men glanced at one another before looking over their shoulders. Seeing Alyn was still closely watching out for the two young women, they decided it wouldn't hurt to have a mug of ale with old friends. Besides, Alyn was perfectly capable of taking care of himself.

***

Muriale was just as surprised as Orabillis to see her father and Red John walking away with the two strangers. "Mayhap 'twas only a coincidence," she offered as an explanation. "Mayhap they have been waitin' for Da and Red John?"

Orabillis wasn't convinced. "I dinnae believe in coincidences," she replied. She possessed far too much skepticism to believe in such things.

"Should we follow them?" Muriale asked rather sarcastically.

"Aye," Orabillis said as she opened the door. "I think we shall."

The two young women were so focused on the group of men they were following that they didn't see there were actually two men watching them closely. They walked right past one of those men. One meant them no harm. He stood in the light of day, pretending to be disinterested in the world around him.

The other hid in the dark shadows. And he had naught but evil intentions in his heart and mind.

***

Orabillis was once again feeling rather let down. They had followed behind the group of men and watched as they entered one of the many taverns along the street.

Muriale was slightly less disappointed. "I think we should get the goose back to Aunt Forvelith's before it goes bad," she suggested.

Orabillis couldn't argue against the idea, no matter how badly she wanted to confront the two strangers. At any rate, Muriale wasn't going to leave without her.

She adjusted her grip on the goose and agreed. "Later, we will tell Father what we noticed."

An idea suddenly struck Muriale's mind. "Why did I nae think of it sooner?"

"Think of what sooner?"

"Mayhap our overly worried father had these friends of his keep an eye on us."

"If that were the case, why, then, did they head to the nearest tavern? Would Da nae have seen us safely returned to Aunt Forvelith's first?"

"Oh," Muriale replied. "I dinnae think of that."

Deciding they'd get no answers in the immediate future, they headed back to their aunt's home. 'Twas an uneventful trip, but Orabillis couldn't shake the feeling that someone was still watching them. What bothered her most was she didn't know if they were friend or foe.

CHAPTER

# EIGHT

M uriale had more questions than answers. Questions that would have to wait until the morrow, for their father sent word via Phillip, one of his trusted men, that he would not return in time to sup with them.

"Where is he?" Orabillis asked.

"The Black Boar Inn," Phillip replied.

"And is he, by chance, alone?"

Phillip shook his head. "Nay, my lady. Red John and the rest of the men are with him."

"And anyone else?" She continued to grill the young man for information.

"Old friends of yer da's and Red John's. Rory and Gavin are their names."

From the way he was glancing at the door and shifting his weight from one foot to the other, Muriale could see the man wanted to leave, undoubtedly to return to the tavern and partake of the merriment with the other men. "Thank ye, Phillip. Please tell Da to be safe and that we shall see him on the morrow."

He bid her good day and quickly quit the room.

"Mayhap we should join Da?" Orabillis suggested after Phillip closed the door.

Muriale openly scoffed at the idea. "Dinnae be ridiculous," she replied. "Da would have an apoplexy."

Aunt Forvelith's appearance at the door stopped any further arguments. This day, she was dressed in navy-blue silk, with her hair braided around the crown of her head. Her smile, it seemed to Muriale, lit up the room. By the hour, she was growing more and more fond of her aunt.

"I hear yer da will nae be here to sup with us this night," Forvelith said. "I, for one, am glad. It will give the three of us time to talk alone, without guardin' our words simply because a man is about."

Orabillis grinned from ear to ear at the prospect, although why was a mystery to Muriale. Her sister never found it difficult to voice her opinion, and neither did she guard her words, no matter who might be about.

"Come, help me set the table," Forvelith said as she slipped into the kitchen. Mrs. MacCurdy was just taking the stew out of the fire. Her face lit up with a smile when she saw the two girls. "How are ye this fine day?" she asked.

"We are well," Muriale replied on behalf of the three of them.

Forvelith stepped aside whilst Mrs. MacCurdy placed the pot of stew on the table. "We will be dinin' informally this night," Forvelith told her. "Come, Florie, join us. The four of us shall eat, drink, and talk ill of men."

Mrs. MacCurdy made no attempt to argue. Instead, she laughed as she grabbed trenchers for the stew.

"I will ne'er turn down an opportunity to eat, drink, and talk ill o' men."

Muriale slept fitfully that night. Visions of Patrick invaded her dreams. He was alive again, hale and hearty. But he was angry. Oh, so bloody angry. But not at Muriale. Nay, he was furious with someone. Someone Muriale couldn't see.

Patrick was warning her. At least, that is the sense she felt rather than heard. He was speaking to her, but she couldn't make out a word of what he said.

Yet, somehow, the impression of a warning was ever present. But what was he warning her about?

There was someone behind him, someone who's face she could not see. Someone lurking in the shadows, waiting like a wolf ready to pounce on its prey.

A flash of something silver and bright. The glint of a dirk, the motion of a hand coming down in the shadows. The dirk sliced through the blackness.

She all but bolted upright in her bed. Her heart was pounding ferociously in her breast. Her breaths were ragged as she fought to breathe. She felt as though she'd just run from one end of Scotland to the other.

"Are ye well?" Orabillis was asking. She was sitting up in the bed, fumbling to light a candle.

"Aye," Muriale replied. "'Twas naught but a bad dream."

Orabillis lit the candle anyway. "Would ye like to tell me about it?"

Muriale swallowed back her fear and trepidation. "Nay, I will be fine," she said. "I am all right now."

Orabillis yawned before asking, "Should I put out the candle?"

"Nay," she replied, her fingers still trembling with fright. "I think nae."

Understanding all about bad dreams, Orabillis didn't argue. She bid her sister good night once again before rolling over and going back to sleep.

It was sometime later before Muriale was able to succumb to

sleep. The dream, she was certain, meant something. But what, exactly, she didn't have the slightest idea. All she knew with any amount of certainty was that Patrick was worried, angry, and warning her about something.

*Oh, Patrick,* she thought to herself. *I wish ye were here.*

———

Orabillis and Muriale were on another mission from their aunt. This time, she sent them to a very specific baker. When they asked why they couldn't simply go to the baker across the street, their aunt's explanation was quite simple: "Because I prefer the bread from Andrew McMillan's bakery."

Neither sister was brave enough to ask for further explanation. If Aunt Forvelith preferred the bread from a baker blocks away, then that is what they would do.

'Twas a warm summer morn, with the sun shining brightly overhead. The sky was a beautiful, brilliant blue, dotted with large, fluffy clouds. When Muriale realized she was growing accustomed to the pungent aromas and the hustle and bustle of the city, she wanted to weep. *We have been here less than a fortnight, and already I am forgetting what home is like.*

An overwhelming sense of melancholy washed over her. She was missing her mother, her brothers and sisters, and the rest of her family. When she realized she'd left Patrick out of her quiet musings, tears filled her eyes. An overwhelming sense of betrayal came over her. *Ye promised him ye would never forget him, and now look at ye. Happily livin' —*

"Watch out!" Orabillis warned, breaking her quiet reverie.

Muriale came to an abrupt halt. She was only inches away from not only running into but falling over some poor creature huddled on the ground in the middle of their path. She felt a jolt of surprise clear to her toes.

"Och!" she exclaimed, covering her now-pounding heart with one hand. "I am so verra sorry!"

Rather rapidly, the huddled mass began to move and take the form of a man. "No worries, lass," he replied after standing to his full height.

He was tall, but not overly so, with light brown hair and dark brown eyes. Or at least, *one* dark brown eye. The other was covered with a black eye patch. Overall, a decent looking fellow, with straight white teeth.

With great flourish, he stood aside, bent at the waist, and waved both women to pass by.

"Good day to ye, lassies," he said with a wide smile.

Muriale was frozen in place for the longest of moments. Orabillis had to grab her by the arm to pull her away.

"Have ye lost yer mind?" Orabillis asked as soon as they were out of earshot of the stranger.

"What do ye mean?"

"Ye were starin' at the man as if he had three heads," she explained rather ashamedly.

"Dinnae be ridiculous," Muriale said, scoffing at the notion. She hadn't stared; she'd simply been startled.

"I hope ye dinnae stare at every poor sot we might come across this day," Orabillis said with a good deal of frustration.

"Ye are in a foul mood this morn," Muriale said, hoping to change the subject.

"I am nae in a foul mood. I dinnae understand why Aunt Forvelith could nae have sent a maid to get the bread."

"Mayhap she thought we might like to get out for a bit," Muriale offered with a feigned smile. Truly, it was exhausting listening to her sister's constant complaints. "Ye yourself have said ye dinnae wish to stay cooped up inside all the day long."

Orabillis chose to ignore the logic in her sister's statement. "Aye, I dinnae want to be cooped up all day. But I still dinnae wish to go traipsin' all over Edinburgh in search of bread."

"What would ye rather be doin'?" Muriale regretted the question as soon as she asked it.

"I'd rather be home, trainin' with Da and the men. I would rather be anywhere else but here."

*At least she dinnae say she would rather be gutted,* Muriale mused with a smile. "Be that as it may," she began with a shrug of indifference, "we are still in need of the bread. Complainin' solves nothin'."

"And what if complainin' makes me feel better?" Orabillis asked sarcastically.

Muriale let out a heavy sigh. "Fine, complain all ye'd like. But dinnae expect me to listen."

Orabillis grunted her disapproval.

"Now, can we get on with findin' the bread?" Orabillis asked.

Hearing no objections, she lifted the hem of her skirt and led them down the street in search of Andrew McMillan's bakery.

---

As he had promised the night before, their father was waiting for them at the table. He had already broken his fast and was waiting for his daughters to join him.

Neither girl was given the opportunity to put their questions or concerns to him. "There ye are," he said with a warm smile. "I have been waitin' an age for ye to finally wake."

To Muriale's eye, he looked positively gleeful.

"Let them sit down and break their fast first, Alysander," Forvelith said. With a nod, she directed the young women to sit down to eat.

"I am far too excited," Alysander said. His smile was bright and filled with excitement. "What are yer plans for this eve?" he asked his daughters as they sat down.

"Plans?" Muriale asked as if he were daft. "We are only here because ye insisted we come along."

"Well, that does an old woman's heart good," Forvelith quipped.

"Dinnae get me wrong, Auntie," Muriale said as an attempt to sooth any injured feelings the woman might have. "I simply meant to say we have no plans."

"Da, ye look like a wolf who just successfully raided the chicken coop," Orabillis said.

Alysander gave her a wink. "I need ye dressed in yer finest dresses this night."

"Why?" Muriale and Orabillis exclaimed in unison.

"Because, tonight, we are dining with Robert."

Muriale and Orabillis exchanged confused glances. "Robert who?" Muriale asked.

"Robert II, the King of Scotland."

---

"I would rather be gutted and my entrails fed to scavengers." Unbelievably, 'twas Muriale who gave that remark.

Forvelith and Orabillis looked astonished, with wide eyes and mouths agape. Her father, however, looked horrified.

Muriale had no fondness for their current sovereign, neither did she have any desire to experience court life. Oh, what she would not give to leave for home now.

"I would have thought ye to be a bit more excited," Alysander replied with equal measure of horror and surprise.

"We all ken him to be a weak man," Muriale said. "Why would I wish to spend an evening with a man such as he?"

"Well, he *is* our king," Orabillis said.

The fact that Orabillis agreed with her father was a miracle in and of itself. While the idea of dressing in a frock wasn't one that appealed to her, getting a chance to meet their king would be worth such a self sacrifice. "I, for one, would enjoy meeting our king," she said.

"Ye?" Muriale was sincerely taken aback. "Ye think him just as weak as I do."

"Aye, that is true," Orabillis replied. "Yet, he is our king. Mayhap we should give the man a chance to change our minds?"

Alysander interjected his own thoughts on the matter. "Might I remind the two of ye that Robert is my cousin?"

All arguing betwixt the two sisters stopped abruptly. "Might I also remind ye that, were it nae for Robert, yer mum and I would most likely be dead?"

Muriale felt ashamed of herself. Her father was right. Were it not for Robert intervening to ensure Alysander received a fair trial, he would have been hanged. The same could also be said for their mother.

"I am sorry, Da," Muriale murmured. "I sometimes forget."

Looking pleased that they had remembered and were sufficiently contrite, he said, "Please try nae to forget that again." He studied them closely for a short moment. "I ken that Robert is deemed weak by many people, and I realize that I am but a distant cousin. But, on those rare occasions where I was able to spend time with him, he was nae weak. He is simply..." He searched for the right word. "He is simply different." In truth, Alysander wasn't quite sure how to describe his cousin and king.

"Now, ye will be on yer best behavior this night, aye? Remember, ye are representin' the McCullum clan as well as yer family."

For a change of what was ordinarily a daily occurrence, neither Gavin nor Alyn were suffering the ills of a night of drunken debauchery and antics. They were as sober as a monk on a Sunday morning.

To make the matter even more unusual, they were up at the crack of dawn, dressed, and ready to continue the hunt for the fiend.

Rory believed he owed these changes in attitudes to Alysander McCullum's good advice the night before. When they explained to Alysander (in confidence, of course) their thoughts and feelings on the matter of their liege's order that they find the man responsible for hurting these women, Alysander had simply smiled and asked, "And if 'twas yer sister, daughter, wife, or mum? How would you feel then? Would ye not want justice for them?"

Rory had known these men for more than a decade. He, Gavin, and Alyn had all fostered with the Keith clan. While they were each completely different in almost all aspects of their character, they had in common a thirst for justice and a strong sense of right versus wrong. They were three honorable men, even if two of them were more than just fond of strong drink and women of loose moral character.

"I pray we catch this monster today," Gavin said as he tightened his sword belt.

Alyn agreed. "I should like to do it before Robert returns to Stirling, if only to send him away happy."

Rory was glad their attitudes had changed. Hopefully, they would be able to maintain their enthusiasm, no matter how long it might take to catch the madman.

"I should like to do it before he hurts another innocent," Rory replied. His fellow knights agreed.

"I should like to speak to the sheriff this morn," Rory said.

Both men readily agreed.

"Do ye think the sheriff will be agreeable to our helpin' him?" Gavin asked.

"Of course he will," Rory replied. "We all want the same thing: We want this fiend caught as quickly as possible. The sheriff will be grateful for extra hands to help in his search."

He couldn't have been more wrong.

———

Magnus MacElroy, the sheriff of Edinburgh, was not a happy man. He and his men had been searching for the maniac responsible for raping more than a dozen young women and murdering one.

As sheriff, he was overseer of twenty-one mostly good men. A few were as inept as the day was long, but there was no way he could fire them. They were distant relations to the king, therefore their employment was as secure as the gates to Edinburgh Castle.

Magnus knew these clumsy men were naught but spies for the king, but since he couldn't release them from their duties, he decided it was best to simply ignore them and do the important work.

There were of the twenty-one undersheriffs, five of whom were of keen intellect. They were honorable men he could trust to help keep the streets of Edinburgh safe. Magnus also believed that, together, he and these five men could catch the madman roaming their streets.

Repeatedly, he had assured his king that they would in fact catch the madman. And, repeatedly, Robert had told him he had complete faith in Magnus's abilities.

Apparently, his sovereign had lied, for this morn, three of the king's knights appeared, by order of their king. Now they were in his office, standing in front of his desk, asking to be given whatever information Magnus and his men had been able to collect.

The scroll the tall, dark-haired knight handed to him was affixed with the king's seal. In it, he introduced the three knights and ordered Magnus to give them whatever they needed to help find the killer.

"I have told our king on multiple occasions that we *will* be successful in bringing this madman to justice," Magnus said. He was sitting at his desk, his back as straight as a lance. And he was doing his very best not to let his temper flare.

Rory, ever the diplomat, smiled and agreed. "We three also have every faith in yer abilities, Sheriff MacElroy. We are only here to offer our services. Certainly, the more men ye have lookin' for this maniac, the better, aye?"

Magnus raised an eyebrow. He was forty and one years of age, a man with much experience in life and, therefore, not easily fooled. Neither could his ego be stroked with a few kind-yet-false words. "Have ye heard the old adage about too many cooks spoilin' the stew?"

"Aye, I have," Rory replied. "And have ye heard the old adage about many hands makin' light work?"

Magnus wasn't sure yet just what he thought of this particular knight. He was quite certain the young man was as stubborn as he was. Which could either be a blessing or a detriment.

There would be no way he could turn the men away. The king

had sent them to help catch the killer. He could no more deny them than he could the blundering fools who were also here under the king's orders.

Mayhap, however, these three men—these three knights—could be useful. 'Twas better, he decided, to accept their help than to fight against it.

"Verra well," he said as he got to his feet. Several sturdy shelves lined the wall to the left of his desk, and a large, heavy table sat against the wall. Multiple scrolls, documents, and maps filled the top of the table. From one of the piles of parchment, he pulled his most recent notes regarding the matter at hand.

"The rapes started over a year ago," he began as he read from the parchment. "At first, he was assaulting the younger prostitutes. Four in all." Three of the victims hadn't come to him directly. He had only learned of the assaults from one Pheobe MacAllister, a young prostitute who herself had been a victim.

He glanced up at the men, who did appear keenly interested. He tossed the parchment onto the table. There was no need for him to refer to the notes. These crimes were ingrained into his very soul. He could recite them from memory.

"Then he turned to sneakin' into homes at night. Usually homes of widows or where the menfolk were nae at home."

Burned into his memory were the names of every victim, their ages, where they lived, and most importantly, how the attacks affected each of them. As long as he lived, he would never forget.

"How many victims thus far?" Gavin asked, his brow furrowed with concern.

"And what about the body ye found yesterday?" Alyn asked.

Magnus took a quick, deep breath before answering. "Five and ten," he said as he looked at Gavin. "And 'twas nae a body that was found yesterday morn. Her name was Lisabeth Montgomery. She was all of twelve years old. As innocent as they come. I have kent the lass since the day she was born. She was nae just a body."

Alyn apologized for his choice of words.

*They cannae possibly understand,* Magnus thought. *Unless this madman attacks someone they ken, they will never understand.*

"On the last four attacks, the madman was able to gain entry into the home either by a window or a door that was mistakenly left unlocked."

"How can ye be certain 'tis the same man who is attackin' all these women?" Rory asked.

"Because the thought of three or four madmen on our streets is more terrifyin' than just one," he said.

The three knights glanced at one another, and Magnus could see the uncertainty in their expressions. "I am nae that big a fool," Magnus said as if he could read their minds.

"Those women who were willin' to talk to me described their attacks."

Rory was studying him closely. "There must be more to yer reasonin' than a description."

In truth, he didn't have any other evidence at the moment to lead him to his determination. What he did have, however, was his life experience and gut instincts. Sometimes, those two things proved far more important than simple evidence.

---

Rory had the sneaking suspicion that the sheriff wasn't telling him everything. Magnus MacElroy seemed intelligent enough. Truthfully, he was not at all what Rory had expected.

Magnus was tall, with brown hair and blue eyes, and he carried himself with an air of confidence. Not an egotistical air, mind you. Just a man who knew himself.

"Sheriff MacElroy, ye have our solemn vow nae to share anythin' ye might tell us with anyone else," Rory said. "Nae even the king." He was making the assumption that the sheriff trusted very few people, the king included.

His assumption was proven correct in the sheriff's reply. "Do ye ken how many men have given me their solemn vow over the years, only to break it when it suited?"

"Probably as many men who have betrayed my trust," Rory replied.

"If word were to get out what we have and what we ken, I fear it will either make him change how he attacks or cause him to leave."

Rory gave that much consideration, and he could not fault the sheriff for being cautious. The old saying about loose lips sinking ships popped into his head. 'Twas certainly a morning of adages.

"What *can* ye tell us?" Rory asked. He knew he needed to gain the trust of the sheriff before the man would ever reveal all that he knew.

"Everythin' about the man, according to our victims, is average. He is about six feet tall, with dark hair and dark eyes. But, since the attacks took place at night, it has been difficult to get a better description."

"So, he could be anyone," Alyn said with a shake of his head.

"He could even be in this verra room," the sheriff countered.

Alyn, being of dark hair and brown eyes, came close to drawing his sword. With a hand to his chest, Rory stopped him from lunging toward the sheriff. "He meant no insult," Rory told him.

"I would never harm a woman," Alyn bit out. "And for him to even hint that I would is an insult."

"I meant no insult," the sheriff said drolly. "I was agreein' with ye. It could be any number of men."

Seeing that Alyn was regaining his composure, Rory turned his attention back to the sheriff. "Is there anythin' else? Anythin' else that we could look out for?"

Rory could see the man mentally weigh his options. Worried, he was quite certain, that he might over-share.

"Aye," the sheriff said as he went to the door of his office. "But nae here."

Rory didn't need to ask why he couldn't speak here. Even he knew the king had spies everywhere.

They stepped out into the late-morning sunshine and turned, heading east, with the sheriff leading the way. At the end of the block, they turned right and headed north. Not a word was spoken until they reached the iron gate of the city's cemetery on old Calton Hill. The sheriff pushed open the ornately carved gate and ushered the knights inside.

For a brief moment, Rory wondered if they weren't being led to an ambush. The worry was set aside moments later. They were now standing far enough from the walls that the sheriff felt comfortable enough to speak.

"I have nae proof," the sheriff began in a hushed tone, "but I believe this man has chosen his victims carefully. I believe he watches them over several days, if nae weeks, before he attacks them."

"What leads ye to think that?" Gavin asked as he leaned in a bit closer.

"All of the women were alone at night. Those that were married or had fathers who lived in the home were attacked when the men were away," he replied.

That made sense to Rory as well as to Alyn and Gavin. "He is too much a coward to attack when other men are about," Rory said.

"Aye," the sheriff replied. "And all his victims? They were wee, tiny things. Even the women he chose were of slight stature."

Rory gave the information a good measure of thought. "Did the women have anything else in common? Did they ken one another?"

"Some did, aye. The prostitutes kenned one another, as a matter of course. But the other women... A few of the older women kenned the younger, but we can find no common thread that binds them all together."

"Had any of them noticed if they had been followed in the days prior?" Rory asked. "Any encounters with strange men?"

The sheriff grunted. "'Tis Edinburgh. Strange men abound everywhere."

Rory waited patiently for the man to answer the actual question.

"As far as I ken, none have reported anythin' out of the ordinary."

"As far as ye ken?" Rory asked for clarification.

"The young girls are far too traumatized to answer many questions. The women are much the same way."

Another point that made sense with Rory. He tried to put himself in the victim's shoes for a moment. He didn't like it, not one bit. He doubted he would have the strength to recover from such an atrocity.

"Mayhap ye should speak to the womenfolk again," Rory suggested. "Mayhap enough time has passed that they can offer ye more information."

"We have tried," the sheriff said, giving Rory a look that said this was not his first day on the job. "But the menfolk, their husbands, they are keepin' their women and daughters under lock and key. To protect them. They will nae let us speak to them again."

Rory could certainly understand a husband's or father's desire to protect. Especially after what had happened to those he vowed to keep safe. He imagined he might feel he'd let his wife or daughter down by not being there to protect them.

"I wonder if they'd speak to us?" Alyn asked.

"Because ye are a knight?" The sheriff scoffed at the idea.

"It could nae hurt to try," Alyn said.

"Nay," Rory argued. "Knight or nae, these men are bound to keep more harm from coming to their women and daughters."

'Twas Gavin who spoke next. "What about the prostitutes?"

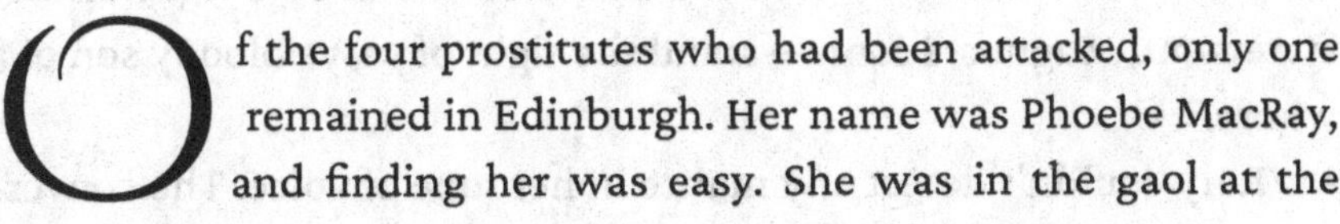

Of the four prostitutes who had been attacked, only one remained in Edinburgh. Her name was Phoebe MacRay, and finding her was easy. She was in the gaol at the moment, arrested two days prior for severe intoxication in public and starting a brawl.

"Ye might want to brace yourselves," Magnus told the trio as he led them down the corridor to the actual gaol. "This is one hard woman."

The corridor itself was well lit, the stone floor slightly damp from the rain that sometimes seeped in through the tiny windows. The sounds of their footsteps were muted due to the low ceiling and tight confines.

The closer they drew to the iron door that led to the cells, the more dank and musty the air became. It became even worse after Magnus opened the heavy door to allow them into the gaol itself.

Rory wanted to retch. The cloying stench of feces, urine, vomit, and heaven only knew what else hung in the air, thick and oppressive. The sense of despair and hopelessness was just as oppressive.

Magnus stopped in front of the first cell to their right. The light from the torch on the wall barely made its way into the small, dark space.

Rory's eyes strained to catch a glimpse of the hard woman Magnus had warned them about. He caught the sound of shuffling from the rear of the cell.

"What the bloody hell do ye want now, Magnus?" The voice, low and raspy, came from the far corner. "Ye want a free tumble?"

"Nay," Magnus replied, his tone firm but his voice low.

"Good," she said. "Because I only give out free tumbles to the blokes I like."

Magnus smiled then and gave a quick glance at the three men standing with him. "I ken, Phoebe." To the men he said, "Phoebe dinnae like me much."

"Bah!" She cried out from the darkness. "That be a right understatement, Magnus. I cannae stand the sight of ye, ye bloody son of a whore."

Rory couldn't detect any malice in her tone of voice. The conversation seemed almost playful, as if the two of them shared a secret they didn't want anyone else to know. He didn't think her too hard. Just the opposite, in fact.

"And if the three of them are here for a free tumble, they can bloody well leave and go straight to hell."

While Gavin and Alyn chuckled, Rory took offense. "My lady, we would never dream of taking that which is nae freely given. We are men of honor—"

She stopped his speech about honor by throwing a bucket against the bars. It crashed with a loud clang before rolling back to the floor. The contents splashed onto the dirty stone floor. Rory hadn't seen the object until it was too late. Some of the liquid sloshed onto his boots.

Disgusted, he took a step back.

"Calm down, Phoebe," Magnus chastised. "That is nae way to treat one of the king's knights."

A loud cackle burst through the darkness. "If he is a knight, then I am the bloody queen of the fairies."

Magnus shook his head, growing more disgruntled as the moments passed. "Phoebe, we would like to ask ye some questions."

"Go ahead, ask yer questions," she replied. There was just a hint of mirth in her voice.

"We want to talk about the man who attacked ye last year."

A deathly silence rent the air, stretching for what seemed an interminable length of time. "Phoebe?" Magnus wasn't certain if she had heard him.

"I said ye could ask yer questions, Magnus. I dinnae say I would answer them."

"Phoebe, this is important," he said, attempting to hide his frustration.

"Och!" she exclaimed. In mimicry fashion, she said, "Phoebe, this is important." She paused briefly before continuing on with what could only be described as a tongue lashing of biblical proportions.

"What about what is important to me, ye filthy bastard? Where were ye when I was forced to the streets as a girl of twelve? Where were ye when I was forced to sell my body for a few scraps of food? Aye? Ye have no answer, do ye, Magnus MacElroy. Important to *ye?* Where were ye the night that madman attacked me and left me for dead? Was that nae important to ye? And when I came here, seekin' help, did ye or yer men help me?" She took in a deep breath of air. There was no mistaking her fury. "Nay, I was turned away. Yer man said 'twas no less than I deserved for bein' a whore. Important to ye? Ye can rot in hell."

Rory was quite certain he heard her choking back tears. It truly tugged at his heart to hear her pain—pain that was disguised as anger and bitterness.

"Phoebe, ye ken I was nae here when that happened. Had I kent—"

"What would ye have done?" she challenged. "Would ye have sent yer men to scour the streets, lookin' for that animal? Nay, I think nae. Ye were too busy suckin' on the king's teat."

Rory stepped forward. "Lass, I am so sorry for what happened to ye. I truly am. We—my comrades and I and the sheriff—we want to catch this man and bring him to justice."

"Justice for whom?" she bit out. "Justice for the innocents who were attacked?" She grunted her derision. "Nae a one of ye bloody bastards cared until he started attackin' the innocent wee lasses. Justice? Nae, there will ne'er be justice for me."

"We seek justice for all of ye," Rory said.

She fell silent again. Rory was quite certain she was either plotting their deaths or, hopefully, giving some thought to what he had said.

"What do I get in return for helpin' ye?"

Rory, Gavin, and Alyn glanced at one another. Gavin shrugged his shoulders with uncertainty.

"We will pay the bailer to let ye out." 'Twas Alyn who suggested that.

Magnus's eyes grew wide with surprise. "Ye may want to rethink that," he said.

"Deal!" Phoebe said. She shot to her feet and came to the bars.

For the first time, Rory and his friends could see her face. Rory imagined she had been rather beautiful in her youth. Tiny lines surrounded her eyes, that were at one time blue but were now rummy and bloodshot. Her hair was the most shocking shade of silver that Rory had ever seen. If she would wash and comb it, it might be quite beautiful.

The brown dress she wore was old and tattered, much like she was. Around her shoulders, she wore a shawl that at one time might have been a deep russet. 'Twas hard to discern, what with the stains and holes scattered about it.

God only knew how old she was.

She smelled much like the gaol itself. That, Rory supposed, was what happened when one was forced to live the kind of life Phoebe lived.

"Get me out of 'ere, and I shall tell ye whatever ye wish to ken."

———

Not only had they paid Phoebe MacRay's bail, she somehow managed to talk the three men into a room at an inn, a bath, and a new dress. Now, the three men were waiting at the inn, sipping on ale while they waited for Phoebe to join them.

"We are spendin' quite a bit of money on an auld whore," Gavin quipped.

"Dinnae call her that," Alyn said. His brow was furrowed and his lips drawn into a hard, fine line.

Gavin was more than a bit surprised by his reaction. "But that is what she is, aye? An auld whore. And a smelly one at that."

"I wager ye yer sword and yer wages for the rest of the year that she is nay an auld, smelly whore by choice." Alyn was quite serious.

Gavin, not wanting to cause an argument between them, raised his hands in surrender. "I reckon ye are right, Alyn."

Gavin had known Alyn since they were weans. Raised within the same clan, their mothers were as close as two women could be without sharing a bloodline. His friend had always had a soft spot in his heart for those less fortunate. A good and honorable trait, Gavin believed.

Although Alyn could be a drunkard and a lech most days, he always had a coin or two for the downtrodden. On more than one occasion, Alyn went without so that he could help someone in dire straits.

"I agree with Alyn," Rory said after taking a swig of ale. "We need to show her the kind of respect and kindness she has nae seen in a good, long while."

"If ever anyone has shown her at all," Alyn replied.

Gavin resisted the urge to roll his eyes. "I cannae believe we had to pay twenty-five groats to get her out of the gaol."

Even Rory had thought that amount more than excessive. "That is nearly a year's wages," he replied.

"Magnus *did* try to warn the two of ye," Gavin reminded them.

"But I dinnae believe it could be anywhere near that amount," Rory said.

"What does it matter?" Alyn asked. "If what she tells us can help us catch this fiend who is running amok, rapin' and killin' women, then it will be worth the cost."

"Aye," Rory said with a nod. "Let us hope that is the case."

Gavin kept his opinions on *that* matter to himself. Silently, he believed that Phoebe would partake of her bath, don her new clothes, and quietly skip away without telling them anything.

He was proven wrong moments later when he caught a glimpse of the woman in question heading right for their table.

Had Rory and Alyn not recognized the new, green woolen gown they had purchased two hours before, they wouldn't have recognized the woman wearing it.

Rory blinked twice and rubbed his eyes as if he couldn't believe what he was seeing. She all but floated across the floor as she headed their way.

"Jesu," Alyn whispered. "Is that her?"

"Aye," Rory replied.

They stood as soon as she reached the table. "I clean up good, aye?" she quipped sarcastically.

"Ye look verra nice," Alyn said.

Gavin swallowed back a retort while Alyn offered her a seat. "Are ye hungry?"

"Aye, I am," she replied, taking a seat betwixt Rory and Alyn.

*I am glad I paid the extra siller for her bath and soaps,* Rory thought to himself. He doubted he could have sat so closely to her had she not bathed. 'Twas remarkable what a difference a bath and fresh clothing could make.

Alyn gained the bar maid's attention. When it came time for Phoebe to make her request, access to anything stronger than cider to drink was denied by all three men.

"Nay," Rory told her. "Magnus made us promise nae to let ye drink anything stronger than cider."

"Magnus MacElroy is an arse," Phoebe argued.

"Be that as it may," Rory began, "I gave him my word."

"Besides, we dinnae have the coin to pay for another one of yer drunken escapades," Gavin added.

Rory and Alyn each shot him an angry look. Gavin shrugged his shoulders and sipped at his ale.

"We will *all* have cider," Rory told the bar maid. She gave him a sweet smile and headed off to the kitchens.

"Are ye mad?" Gavin asked incredulously. "I have nae had cider since I was a wean."

Phoebe rolled her eyes in disgust. "Let the poor man have his ale," she said. "I dinnae want to listen to him carry on like a spoiled child the rest of the night."

Gavin took offense and was about to give her a piece of his mind. Rory stayed the upcoming argument by reminding him why they were here to begin with.

"I dinnae ken if we should talk here," Phoebe said, leaning over the table and whispering.

"Where should we speak?" Gavin asked. "Mayhap in a church?"

She gave him a piercing glower. "If it be quiet and no one else is about to hear us, then aye. We could speak in a church."

"Are ye worried we will be overheard?" Alyn asked.

"Of course I am," she replied as if he were an idiot. "When ye do work for the king, do ye speak of it out in the open where all the world can hear?"

Duly chastised, they agreed. "We will eat then find somewhere safe to speak," Rory said. "But we cannae tarry long. I want to catch this bloody bastard as soon as possible."

---

There were very few places in Edinburgh where one could talk without the worry of prying eyes. Even the shadows had ears.

Thus, Rory and the group went to the one place they felt comfortable enough to speak openly: the same cemetery Magnus had taken them to.

'Twas long after the midnight hour when they finally reached their destination. Only a sliver of a moon offered any light. The air was damp and cold, made worse by the strong breeze. Around them, the leaves rustled, and the wind whistled, adding to the eeriness of the location and time.

Huddled together, they spoke in low whispers. Phoebe shivered, either from the damp night air or from the memories of what had happened to her.

"I dinnae see his face," she told them.

"Then, what help can ye be?" Gavin said through gritted teeth.

"Wheest," Rory reprimanded him. "Let her speak."

"He's a bit of a high-strung fellow, aye?" Phoebe asked mockingly

"High strung?" Gavin asked, raising his eyebrows, clearly insulted.

"Aye," she replied. "I have kent less skittish and less stubborn mules than ye."

"Now, listen—"

"Will the two of ye stop?" Alyn interjected. "We will get nowhere with the two of ye arguin' like cats and dogs."

They fell silent, however their anger was unabated.

"Please, go on," Alyn directed to Phoebe.

"As I was sayin', I dinnae see his face." She paused to see if Gavin was going to make another comment. Satisfied he would remain silent, she went on. "But I can tell ye he was nae too tall, nor was he too short."

"We already ken that," Gavin said through gritted teeth.

Phoebe ignored him. "What I can tell ye is that he had dark hair."

"How do ye ken that?" Rory asked.

"The moon was shinin' that night," she said. "His face was cast in shadows, but the moon light glinted off his hair."

"Did anything about him seem familiar?" Alyn asked.

"Aye, but I cannae remember how I might ken him."

Gavin snorted derisively.

Having reached the end of her patience, Phoebe balled up her fist and hit him right in the jaw.

"What the bloody hell," Gavin asked angrily as he rubbed his jaw with the palm of his hand. "What did ye do that for?"

"Just because I whore for a livin' dinnae mean I have let every man in Edinburgh mount me like stallion to a mare." Oh, she was angry; of that, there could be no doubt. "And just because I might recognize someone dinnae mean I recognize him from the way I make my livin'."

If there had been more light, they would have seen Gavin's face turn purple with rage.

"I may be a whore, but I have feelings, you bloody arse!" She grabbed a fistful of skirt and began to walk away.

"Phoebe, please," Rory said as he placed a gentle hand on her shoulder. She paused long enough to shrug his hand away.

He turned his attention to Gavin. "If ye dinnae wish to hear what the lass has to tell us, then leave, Gavin. If ye do wish to listen, then ye should show her some respect."

"Aye," Alyn added bitterly. "Dinnae be so callous."

Gavin was just as furious with his two friends as he was with Phoebe. He, too, had just been insulted. Phoebe had hit him and cursed him. Yet his friends were inexplicably taking her side.

Without uttering another word, Gavin spun on his heels and left.

Rory sighed his frustration. "I am verra sorry, lass."

"He will be better on the morrow," Alyn offered. "He sometimes needs time to think before he realizes he was wrong."

Summarily appeased by the kindness the two men were showing her, Phoebe drew her new shawl more tightly around her shoulders. "As I was sayin', there was somethin' about him that was familiar. But what it was, I cannae say."

"That's all right, lass," Alyn said. "What else can ye tell us?"

"He smelled..." She paused, trying to find the right word. "...odd."

Rory chuckled softly. "How do ye mean? Did he smell foul or odiferous?"

"Nae," she replied with a shake of her head. "I ken this might sound strange, but he almost smelled like roses."

"Roses?" Alyn's eyebrows lifted in surprise. "So, he smelled like a woman?"

"Nae quite, but verra close. 'Twas a blend of roses and somethin' else I cannae describe. But if e'er I was to smell it again, I'd remember it."

Rory and Alyn gave her description a good measure of thought and consideration.

"He was clean," she added. "He was nae like some of the raga-muffins I usually meet on the streets. And he was clean shaven."

"Can ye think of anythin' else?" Rory asked.

She was silent for a long while. "He came up from behind me, ye ken. He pressed a dirk to my throat..." Her words trailed off.

"I have tried verra hard to forget that night," she said after a lengthy moment of silence. "I ken what most think of me, like yer friend. But I am still a woman, ye ken. I still have feelin's."

"We ken that, lass," Alyn replied, his tone soft and warm.

"I ken there are men out there who take whatever they want and damn the consequences," she said. "But that night was different."

Rory hated to ask his next question but felt he must. "Different how?"

"He absolutely terrified me."

# TEN

J ust when Muriale thought her sister could not surprise her further, she did just that.

When Muriale stepped into the bedchamber to change for dinner with the king, Orabillis was already there. What surprised Muriale to no end was the fact that Orabillis looked stunning.

She wore the dark, emerald-green wool gown that their mother had chosen for her before they left. The long sleeves were trimmed in gold thread, as was the bodice and hem. Intricately stitched amongst the gold were lavender and burgundy flowers.

Her hair was beautifully plaited around her head. A simple silver circlet crowned her head. From that flowed a long, gauzy, green veil that trailed to the floor.

Around her neck, she wore her gold necklace with a pretty blue sapphire-colored stone at the center, which their mother had given her when she turned six and ten.

"I have never seen ye lookin' so...so beautiful!" she exclaimed.

For the third surprise of the day, Orabillis blushed, her cheeks flushing bright pink at the compliment. "Only for our king would I wear such a thing," she replied.

Oh, she tried to sound insulted by the compliment, but Muriale didn't believe it. "I shall look like a mud pie next to ye this night," she quipped with a smile. 'Twas a genuine and sincere compliment.

"Dinnae press the issue," Orabillis warned. "Besides, I have my *sgian dubhs* and dirks well hidden."

Muriale laughed. "Ye realize ye will be searched when we enter the castle, aye?"

Orabillis shrugged. "They will only find the ones I want them to find."

A sudden rush of worry washed over Muriale. "Please tell me ye are nae plannin' to do anythin' foolish this night."

"Of course nae," she replied with a roll of her eyes and a shake of her head. "I can assure ye they are for protection only."

Muriale didn't have the time or the inclination to inquire just what or whom Orabillis thought she might need to protect herself from. They'd be in the castle, under constant guard by the king's own soldiers.

"Verra well," Muriale said as she stepped to her trunk. "But dinnae say I dinnae warn ye."

---

Alysander doubted there was a man in all of Scotland who could be more proud of his daughters than he. Both young women looked regal and stunning, dressed in their finest gowns.

"Ye are too beautiful this night," he jested. "Can ye smudge some dirt on yer faces or tear the hem of yer dress so ye look *less* beautiful?"

As all good daughters do, they giggled slightly and rolled their eyes as if he were serious, even if, for a brief moment, he might have meant what he said. He was ever watchful of his children, especially his older daughters.

"Red John waits for us below stairs with our mounts," Alysander said. "Grab yer cloaks, for the castle can be rather drafty at times."

Muriale and Orabillis glanced at one another. Was their father truly concerned about their comfort? Or was he merely trying to keep prying eyes from looking upon them?

A lysander and his daughters arrived at Edinburgh Castle just in time to be escorted to the grand gathering room. Neither young woman had ever seen the likes of the castle before. Grand and opulent didn't seem words strong enough to describe the place.

E dinburgh Castle was far more grand than either Muriale or Orabillis could have imagined. Made of dark-gray stone, 'twas more massive and imposing than they had realized.

Once they were through the gate, young men appeared from seemingly nowhere to tend to their mounts. Two guards were waiting to escort them inside.

They were all searched for weapons by more guards who were waiting just inside the main entry. Of course, as Orabillis had assumed, they didn't find *all* of her weapons. Only the dirk she had in her belt and one *sgian dubh* in her pouch.

The guard who discovered the weapons gave her a fierce glower as if to ask, "How dare ye?"

"I never travel unprepared," she explained, offering him a most apologetic (albeit false) apology. "Force of habit, I suppose."

Once the guards were satisfied that they had no more weapons, four more men appeared to escort them into the main dining room.

'Twas as opulent as it was huge. Tall, vaulted, beamed ceilings, with two massive fireplaces on either end of the room, and there were plush carpets adorning the floors.

Muriale stared in wide-eyed wonder, as her eyes weren't sure what they should look at next. The beautiful tapestries that adorned the walls? The large, black iron chandeliers that hung from the ceiling? Or perhaps the long table that was set for thirty but could hold another dozen if needed?

"Close yer mouth," Orabillis whispered. "Else they will think us simple-minded folk who have never been anywhere."

Muriale closed her mouth and said, "But we have nae been anywhere before," she politely reminded her. "Have ye ever seen the like?"

"Nay, but we need nae let anyone ken that," Orabillis replied. "Now, please, act like ye have more sense than God gave a goat, aye?"

Orabillis never cared what others might think of her. Their opinions simply didn't matter. Unless, of course, they were praising her about her skills with the sword, arrows, or knives.

But tonight? Nay, tonight she *did* care. They were in the castle and about to meet the king himself. Oh, she didn't admire the man, not really. Like most folks she knew, she thought him a weak man. However, he was their king, and he had her allegiance. As far as she was concerned, they would never be able to repay the debt owed to him for saving her mother and father's lives.

Standing tall and straight, she did take the chance to glance around the room. But, unlike her older sister, she wasn't about to stand with mouth agape, ooh-ing and ah-ing over the decor.

But her mouth *did* fall open only moments later, when she caught a glimpse of someone standing on the other side of the room. Two someones, actually.

"Good Lord Almighty," she exclaimed in a harsh whisper. *It cannae be.*

# CHAPTER
# ELEVEN

Rory and Gavin noticed the two young women at almost the same time they had noticed them. Their reactions were much the same as Orabillis's.

"Good Lord Almighty," Gavin exclaimed. He swallowed hard. "Are they—"

"Aye, they are," Rory replied before he could finish the question.

Gavin was mesmerized by the young woman with blonde hair, wearing the emerald-green gown. She very nearly stole his breath away.

Yesterday, when they'd been following the two lasses, Gavin had been intrigued mostly with the one who was wearing a tunic and trews, her golden locks twisted into a braid that cascaded down her back. There was something awfully provocative about the way her sword swayed with her hips when she walked.

But, now, he almost hadn't recognized her. Oh, she'd caught his eye all right, what with the silver belt hanging just so around her slender waist.

When she had turned ever so slightly to look about the room, his heart skipped more than just a few beats. As a knight—as a man—he'd seen plenty of beautiful women in his life. Now, they paled in comparison to the beautiful young woman across the room. The one who was now shooting daggers at him with her eyes.

Just what he might have done to earn that glowering look, he couldn't say. It amused him nonetheless. And, try as he might, he couldn't resist smiling at her any more than he could quash the laughter bubbling up from his stomach. Oh, she was a fierce thing; of that, there was no doubt. If the way in which she had dressed yesterday wasn't enough proof, then the fire in her eyes certainly was.

Gavin knew he shouldn't have been nearly as amused as he was. He simply couldn't help it. He decided then and there to take that fierce, piercing glower as a challenge.

*I will have ye before the night is over.*

He had no way of knowing then just how wrong he was.

---

Rory's heart skipped at least a dozen beats when he first caught sight of the beautiful damsel in the burgundy gown. No matter how hard he tried, he could not take his gaze from her.

He had recognized her from yesterday. He, Rory, and Alyn had been searching the streets for the madman. They were looking for anything out of the ordinary, anything that might feel off, in any sense of the word.

They'd seen the two young women, wandering the streets, undoubtedly new to the city. They'd gone around the same block three times, in search of what or whom, neither he nor his friends knew.

It wasn't until the pretty brunette bumped into the tall man with dark hair that worry began to creep in. There was something not quite right about the fellow. His first instinct—and 'twas an odd one, at best—was to race across the street and knock the man on his arse. Had it not been for his training and the fact that they were on a mission, he might have done that very thing.

So, instead of acting like a fool, he watched he stranger *and* the lasses. There was something about her, something in the way she carried herself, the way she walked with purpose, even if she was lost. He was drawn to her like a moth to a flame.

Rory soon realized the man was doing his best *not* to appear out of place or that he was following the two pretty lasses. Mayhap, to someone with no experience in spying or espionage, he looked like an ordinary bloke. However, Rory's keen eye quickly picked up on the fact the man was watching and following the two women.

When the man ran into them a second time, Rory knew he was up to no good. He was about to follow the man when Alysander McCullum appeared.

Rory hadn't wanted to stop following the young women or the dark-haired man. But he couldn't very well refuse Alysander's offer to catch up over ale.

They left Alyn to continue without them. It turned out the man was a pick-pocket. Alyn had watched the thief steal pouches from two unsuspecting individuals. 'Twas Alyn who also confronted the man and divested him of his ill-gotten gains. According to Alyn, he told the man to leave the city at once and not to come back. "I think I put the fear of God and us into him," Alyn remarked this morn. "I dinnae believe we will have to worry about him again."

"She is stunnin', aye?" Gavin asked, his eyes still focused on the blonde in green.

Rory cleared his throat, his eyes darting away from the comely, brown-haired lass. "Which one?" His voice caught in his throat like a boy on the cusp of manhood. Thankfully, his friend made no mention of it.

"The beautiful blonde in the green dress," Gavin said.

Relief washed over Rory. He'd sworn an oath to his two friends, long ago, that they'd never let a woman come between any of them. Their friendship meant more to them than anything or anyone else.

But, for the briefest of moments, Rory was more than tempted to put that promise aside, just for a chance to talk to the stunning brunette in burgundy.

---

"Girls, there is someone I want ye to meet," Alysander said, his eyes crinkling at the corners with a braw smile as he extended each of his hands for them to take.

They all but glided across the wooden floor, heading towards the two men they were convinced were spies. Muriale's heart began to pound against her breast. Why she felt like a lamb being led to the slaughter, she couldn't rightly say. It could be the way the dark-haired man was staring at her as if she were a delectable treat he wanted to devour.

Uneasiness crept into the pit of her stomach. Aye, he was a handsome man. Tall, with muscles that seemed to want to escape the tight confines of his tunic and trews.

"Lads," Alysander said with a proud, fatherly smile. "Allow me to introduce ye to my daughters."

Muriale couldn't find her voice. She thought it might be lodged deep in her belly and was dancing happily with the butterflies who had just taken up residence.

"This is Muriale," Alysander said, nodding in her direction. "And this is Orabillis," he said, repeating the gesture. "Ladies, these are two old friends of mine. Rory MacLeod and Gavin MacKendrick."

There was something akin to regret that flashed in the brilliantly blue eyes of one Rory McLeod. It had flashed so briefly that Muriale wondered if she hadn't imagined it.

The one named Gavin was staring at Orabillis with such intensity that it began to make Muriale feel uncomfortable. She was surprised he wasn't drooling.

"'Tis a pleasure to make yer acquaintance," Rory said as he bent at the waist.

Muriale gave a slight curtsey and replied, "'Tis my pleasure as well."

Gavin didn't utter a word. He simply continued to stare with that same, hungry-wolf look about him.

One glance at Orabillis, and she knew she wasn't the least bit impressed with Gavin MacKendrick. If looks could kill, the man would be dead by now.

Oddly enough, the intense glare that caused most men to quake in their boots or divert their gaze wasn't working on the young ginger-haired fellow. Nay, he looked amused.

Before Orabillis could do something foolish, such as gut the ignorant Gavin, a loud voice boomed from the other end of the room.

"His Majesty, Robert Stuart, the High Steward, King of Scotland."

---

Robert II did not fit the image of the one Muriale had created in her mind. From what she had learned over the years, she had expected to find a small, fat, lazy man who might wheeze when he walked. She had also expected a high-pitched voice and crooked teeth.

He was none of those things.

An average-looking fellow, of average height and build. A gold crown sat upon his brown hair. His dark eyes carefully scanned the room as if he were looking for someone in particular.

That someone was Alysander.

The moment Robert's eyes landed on his cousin, his previous look of disinterest faded, replaced with a warm and affectionate smile.

He crossed the room in a few long strides. Muriale and Orabillis were in full curtsey, and the men were bowing at their waists.

"Alysander." Robert said his name with much warmth. It was not the nasally, high-pitched voice Muriale had imagined.

Alysander stood, looking equally as pleased to see Robert. "My liege," Alysander said. "'Tis good to see ye."

"It has been far too long," Robert replied before turning his attention to the two young women. "Ye may rise, ladies," he said.

Muriale didn't know if it was appropriate to look the man in the eye or not. Suddenly, she was nervous and excited at once.

"I take it these lovely creatures are the daughters ye wrote me about?"

"Aye," Alysander said. "Two of the five I am blessed with," he chuckled. "Muriale, Orabillis, I present to ye the King of Scotland."

---

*A*s if the man needed an introduction, Muriale thought to herself.

"Ye are just as beautiful as yer father wrote," Robert II said with a smile.

"Thank ye, yer majesty," the girls murmured in unison.

"I agree," came the voice from one of the men standing behind them. Muriale was quite certain that voice belonged to Gavin. Probably because he seemed far more bold than Rory.

"Ah," Robert said, turning his attention to Rory and Gavin. "Ladies, have ye met my knights?"

*Knights?* Muriale was confused. *Why on earth would knights have been following us yesterday?* A sudden chill tickled at her spine. *Mayhap they were spyin' on us for the king? Mayhap he had caught wind of Orabillis's oftentimes loud and almost-always unkind comments as they pertained to their king?*

She hoped this was not some ruse for the king to get his hands on her family for anything they might have said in the past.

"Alysander was just introducing us," Rory said.

Another chill tickled, this time across her skin. There was something about his voice, deep yet soft, like a warm caress against her skin.

She knew the sensation as soon as she felt it. 'Twas something she hadn't felt since Patrick's death. Guilt plagued her heart, tugging at old memories of the man she had loved more than her own breath. 'Twas as if her heart were saying, "How can ye be so cruel as to be attracted to this complete stranger, when Patrick isn't yet cold in the ground for a year?"

"I cannae believe ye knighted the three of them," Alysander said with much good humor.

*Three? Is the third so small he hides in the pocket of Rory or Gavin?* Muriale nearly choked on her own jest. *Truly, Muriale, get a hold of yerself.*

Robert found the comment highly amusing, as did Gavin and Rory. Muriale had no earthly idea what they found so humorous. A quick glance at her sister revealed that she, too, was just as confused.

"They are good men," Robert said. "I am forever in their debt."

Muriale was impressed. The men must have done something spectacular and noble to be knighted *and* to have their king say he was indebted to them. Her curiosity was piqued, and she found herself quite eager to learn what it was, exactly, they had done.

Orabillis finally found her voice.

"Would ye like to explain why ye were followin' my sister and me yesterday?"

---

It had been some time since she'd seen men looking as astonished as the four surrounding her. Orabillis had asked the question for two reasons.

One, she was curious as to the why of it all.

And, two, she wanted the ginger-haired fellow, the one with the smug smile and arrogant bearing, to know that mayhap they weren't as good at being knights as they might like to believe.

"What are ye goin' on about, Orabillis?" her father asked. His gaze darted between his daughters and his friends.

"Yesterday," Orabillis began to explain, "these two friends of yers were following us, for over an hour. I should like to ken why."

"We were nae following *ye*," Rory said.

Orabillis gave him a look that said she did not believe him.

"We were followin' the dark-haired man who bumped into Muriale," Gavin said.

Muriale was completely taken aback. "I dinnae understand," she said.

Orabillis did understand. "I told ye I dinnae trust him," she politely reminded her sister.

"As well ye should nae," Rory said. "He was a pick pocket."

Muriale's brow furrowed. "But he dinnae take anythin' from us."

Orabillis laughed. "Of course nae. If he had, I would have kent, and I would have done somethin' about it."

Gavin chuckled rather a bit too loudly for her liking. "Ye? What would ye have done other than scream or clout him over the head with yer shoe?"

Alysander hung his head.

Muriale began to retreat. As she did, she whispered, "Orabillis, remember where we are."

"I ken where we are," she replied with a raised brow. Looking Gavin in the eye she said, "'Tis a pity the fool dinnae try anything. I can assure ye that, had he, ye would nae be asking such a question or making such a ridiculous comment."

Gavin tried to respond, but she wouldn't allow him to. "I will disregard yer insult, Sir Gavin. But, tell me, is it ignorance or arrogance that makes ye ask such daft questions?" She gave a quick shake of her head and quickly added. "Never mind. I think I ken the answer."

Robert had never been more entertained. Throwing his head back, he laughed loudly, causing everyone in the room to look their way. "Och!" he said, once he got his laughter under control. "Alysander, ye dinnae tell me what a treasure ye have in this one!" He was, of course, referring to Orabillis.

To Gavin, he said, "I think ye have met yer match, young man. I do, indeed."

There was no more time for discussion on the matter. Robert's attention was stolen from them when he saw his wife, Euphemia, enter the room.

Robert left the group but returned shortly with his wife on his arm. A beautiful woman, with golden-blonde hair and bright-blue eyes, she was dressed regally in a crimson silk gown, the sleeves and bodice trimmed in wide swaths of gold silk. Upon her head she wore a jewel-encrusted crown, with a long, gauzy veil that, to Muriale, seemed to be made from thin strips of gold. It sparkled and shimmered in the candlelight.

"My queen," Robert said, "I should like ye to meet my cousin, Alysander McCullum, and two of his daughters, Muriale and Orabillis McCullum."

While the sisters curtsied dutifully, the queen gave each of them a warm smile. "Robert speaks very highly of ye, Laird McCullum. And I was so sorry to hear of the loss of yer brother Connor. It pained Robert as well."

"Thank ye, yer grace," Alysander replied.

"Yer wife, is she here?"

"Nay, yer grace. She is at home with our four younger children."

"I should hope to have the chance to meet her someday," Euphemia said.

To Muriale, the woman sounded genuine and sincere, and she liked her immediately. "Are ye ladies enjoying Edinburgh?" Euphemia asked.

"Aye, yer grace, we are," Muriale answered demurely.

Orabillis remained silent, simply smiling and nodding. She was not one to lie, and Muriale was quite certain she wouldn't want to lie to their queen. Therefore, silence was best.

"I myself much prefer the countryside," Euphemia said. "I find the city too loud and crowded."

"My sister and I prefer the countryside as well, but it is rather exciting seeing Edinburgh and your grand castle." She didn't wish to insult her king with her true opinion of the city.

Euphemia seemed please with her answer, offering her a warm smile. Leaning in more closely, she whispered, "I myself cannae wait to leave this city. 'Tis far too busy, and it smells worse than a pig pen."

Muriale drew her lips inward and swallowed hard in order to stifle her amusement. Orabillis, however, was not thusly inclined. She did giggle, a bit more loudly than Muriale thought was proper, considering where they were and whom they were speaking to. While Muriale's cheeks flamed red with embarrassment, their queen seemed more than just pleased with Orabillis's response.

"I think ye and I shall get along most splendidly, lass."

Before Orabillis could offer any response, one of the king's men approached and whispered in his ear. "That is dinner," Robert said to the group before turning to the rest of the guests in the room. "To the tables!" he shouted jovially. "Let us feast and be merry this night."

Alysander started to escort his daughters to the table, but Robert stopped him. "I should like yer daughter—" He paused, having forgotten her name.

"Orabillis," Alysander replied.

"Yes, Orabillis. I should like Orabillis to sit near me this night. Gavin? Ye shall sit beside her."

Alysander didn't look too pleased by this.

rabillis was reaching the end of her patience as far as Gavin MacKendrick was concerned. The more the man drank, the more arrogant and obnoxious he became. Not only was he gloating about his multiple conquests with the opposite sex, he also bragged about his skills on the field of battle.

'Twas only out of respect for her father as well as her king that she did not react or respond to the man. Quietly, she ate her meal and did her utmost best to simply ignore him. His arrogance, however, was making that more and more difficult.

"Ye are a bonny thing," Gavin said, offering Orabillis what she had to assume was a smile. On him, it looked like a sneer.

*Thing.* She wasn't a thing, she was a woman. She counted to ten, willing her anger to settle, before she responded. "Was that meant to be a compliment?"

He laughed. "Aye, it was."

She gave a slight nod and sipped at her wine. Oh, there were so many things she wanted to say to him. If the circumstances were different and her king wasn't but a few steps away, she'd have given him a tongue lashing right before she knocked him on his arse.

"Tell me, lass," Gavin said as he shoved a rather large piece of pheasant into his mouth. "Why were ye dressed as a man yesterday?"

Muriale glanced up from her meal when she heard that question. Their father's ears also caught the question. He sat taller in his chair, his senses on heightened alert.

Orabillis took in a deep breath before answering. "I was nae dressed as a man," she politely informed him.

"Ye were wearin' a tunic and trews," he pointed out.

"Aye, but those were made for me, nae for a man. Therefore, I argue, I was nae dressed as a man."

Gavin laughed, quite loudly and drunkenly. "Ye ken what I think?" His speech was slightly slurred and his eyes glassy and red.

No, she didn't, and she didn't truly want to know.

"I think ye want to *be* a man. I think ye believe ye'd make a better man than most."

She closed her eyes and counted to ten before opening them again. Orabillis glanced at her sister. She looked positively horrified. Either with what the man actually said or what Orabillis might say in return. Mayhap 'twas both.

Gavin wasn't making it easy for her to keep up her I-am-naught-but-a-lady facade.

"I have absolutely no desire to be a man," she replied calmly.

Gavin leaned in, close enough that she could feel his breath on her cheek. "I think ye lie," he accused.

"I believe ye are too into yer cups, Sir Gavin," she replied with a quirked brow.

"I am nay so into my cups that I could nae best any man here," he declared with a grin.

"What about any woman?"

---

Muriale loved her sister. Truly, she did. While she might not always understand her way of thinking or agree with her on certain issues, she still loved her. She'd been quietly watching and listening to the interaction between Sir Gavin and Orabillis. Thus far, Muriale had been quite proud of her for holding her tongue and not kicking the man's arse for his insults.

But Sir Gavin had gone too far. Even Muriale knew it. And if she were to be honest at the moment, whatever happened next would be no more than the man deserved.

Gavin had thrown his head back and laughed quite loudly at Orabillis's question. "Aye," he finally replied after catching his breath. "I can best any man *or* woman here."

"Oh, I have no doubt you could best anyone here as it pertains to drinkin'," Orabillis returned in a whisper.

Now they were looking directly at each other, Orabillis and Sir Gavin. What happened next would undoubtedly be written in the texts and tombs of history.

# TWELVE

"For the sake of Christ, Orabillis! How could ye do it?"

Alysander was still fuming and pacing the small confines of Aunt Forvelith's home an hour after they left the castle. Seeing their father angry was nothing new to either of his daughters. Each of his children, more specifically his four eldest daughters, had done things that would make any father turn purple with rage. His daughters, however, never quite seemed to understand why he was so bloody furious.

"What would ye have had me do?" Orabillis asked, keeping her tone as calm and polite as possible.

Alysander stopped in his tracks, raked a hand through his hair, and stared at her as if she'd lost her mind. "What would I—" Stunned with her question, he could barely speak. "I would have had ye sit the bloody hell down when I told ye to."

Muriale was growing concerned for her father's well-being. If his face turned another shade darker, she worried he'd have an attack of the heart. "Da, Mum is nae here," Muriale interjected, "so I will take it upon myself to be the voice of reason right now. I truly think—"

She immediately stopped speaking when she saw the hard scowl her father was sending her way. Truly, she only had his health in mind.

Turning his attention back to Orabillis, he said, "Ye embarrassed and humiliated one of King Robert's knights." Alysander had been repeating those very words for the past few hours. Muriale was quite certain her father was in a complete state of disbelief.

"He embarrassed himself," Orabillis argued. "I cannae help it if the man was too drunk to make a sound decision."

The twitch in Alysander's jaw intensified. "Ye could have let him win." His words were clipped and hard.

Clearly affronted by what her father just suggested, Orabillis shot to her feet. "And dishonor our name? Why should I let someone best me at anything, simply due to their station or title? Ye raised me better than that!"

Her point did very little to ease his anger, but even Muriale could see that the fire in his eyes was dimmed, albeit slightly.

"Orabillis, there is a time and place for everythin'," he reminded her, his voice softening, but only a bit. "And tonight was neither the time nor the place for your antics."

"Antics?" Orabillis nearly screamed, balling her hands into fists. She shook her head, disgusted with her father and the entire conversation. Standing ramrod straight, she looked her father directly in his eyes. "I dinnae realize until now that ye were ashamed of me."

She gave her father no time to respond. Turning on her heels, she thundered to the bedchamber and slammed the door.

"Orabillis!" Alysander called out to her, but it did no good.

Forvelith, who had been politely hiding in her bedchamber, finally stepped out at the slamming of the door. As she stepped into the light of the dining area, she tightened the belt on her robe. "I think ye owe yer daughters an apology."

Bewildered, Alysander asked for clarification, in a not-so-polite fashion.

"Alysander, ye have been yellin' and stompin' yer feet for over an hour now. Yellin' at Orabillis for a crime she dinnae commit."

"Ye have no idea what she did, Auntie," he argued.

"I've been listenin' for over an hour. She accepted a challenge from a very drunk knight, and she won. Thus, this poor king's knight is summarily humiliated and ashamed. Am I correct?"

"Aye," he admitted sheepishly.

"Ye are upset because of how Orabillis made the knight feel."

Alysander snorted. "Of course I am."

"But did ye ask Orabillis how *she* felt when the knight insulted *her*?"

"He dinnae insult her, Auntie. He challenged her. There is a significant difference in the two."

Forvelith tilted her head ever so slightly. "I think mayhap ye are wrong, Nephew. I am nae one to interfere with how someone raises their children, but in this instance, I fear I must speak up."

"Auntie, ye simply cannae understand. Orabillis is—"

"A very kind, sweet young lass who is still tryin' to find her way in this world," Forvelith interrupted. "And, if memory serves me, she is *exactly* what ye made her to be."

If he raised his eyebrows any higher, they'd be sitting on the top of his head. "How *I* made her to be?"

"Have ye nae encouraged her to learn to protect herself? Was it nae ye, according to the letters ye have sent to me all these years, the one who gave Orabillis her first quiver and bow? Was it nae ye who, from the time she was six, allowed her not only to *watch* the men train but also allowed those men to train her?"

"That is beside the point."

Alysander's attempt to argue was quickly quashed.

"Nay, lad. I think that is precisely the point." With a shake of her head, she stood up to return to her bedchamber. Before she left, she had one final thing to say. "Alysander, I think ye need to speak with Orabillis." She paused and corrected herself. "Nay, I think ye need to listen to yer daughter. I think ye will find there were more reasons for her to accept the man's challenge than what ye might realize."

At the doorway to the hall that separated the living quarters from the bedchambers, Forvelith stopped and turned to say one more thing. "But, please, wait until the morrow. I cannae listen to any more arguin' this night."

Muriale had no words of wisdom or advice for her father. She agreed with her aunt completely. Deciding he needed to think about things without interruption, Muriale kissed his cheek. "Good night, Da," she whispered, then she left him alone.

There was much Alysander had to think on. More precisely, he needed to find a way to get his daughter to understand why she shouldn't have done what she did. He also needed to find a way to soothe his old friend's feelings.

It seemed too monumental a task to do sober. Thus, he poured himself a large dram of whisky and sat by the fire. Aye, he had much thinking to do.

Many secret meetings and liaisons had been held in the dark hallways of Edinburgh Castle over the years. If the walls of the hallways, the alcoves, and the tiny nooks and crannies of the massive place could talk, it would undoubtedly lead to the fall of civilization as they currently knew it. At the very least, countless reputations would be destroyed.

Today, however, Rory and Alysander weren't plotting to overthrow any kingdoms or other political maneuvers. But by the time Alysander was done explaining his visit, Rory wished they had been.

'Twas all he could do to keep from laughing at his very concerned friend.

"And now, none of them are speakin' to me," Alysander said, blowing out a breath of frustration. "And Orabillis refuses to apologize to Gavin."

Rory could remain silent no longer. "Have ye lost yer mind?"

Alysander was more than a bit stunned by the question. "Dinnae tell me ye disagree as well?"

Rory shook his head in dismay and let out a long sigh. "Orabillis did somethin' no one else has ever been able to do, man."

Patiently, Alysander waited for an explanation.

"Gavin is like a brother to me," Rory said. "I would lay down my own life to save his, and he would do the same. However," he took in a deep breath before going on, "he is one of the most arrogant men I have ever met when it comes to women and his fighting skills. Now, 'tis nae to say his braggin' is nae justified, for he is quite skilled. Almost as skilled as I." He smiled then, quite mischievously. "Orabillis knocked a bit of that arrogance out of him last night. Apologize?" He shook his head. "Nay, if anything, she should be knighted."

"Please, God, dinnae tell her that!" he exclaimed. "The last thing my daughter needs is that idea put into her mind. She is already almost too much to handle as it is."

Rory laughed at his friend's distress. "I shall take it to my grave," he said, his hand placed over his heart. "Now I have my own request to make."

"What is it?"

"Dinnae ever make her apologize for besting anyone, especially nae Gavin MacKendrick."

Alysander wasn't quite convinced yet that that was the proper course of action to take. "But she did insult him."

Rory rolled his eyes in frustration. "Well, Gavin needed to be insulted. He needed to be knocked down a peg or two, ye ken? His arrogance was beginning to get a wee bit out of control. I have tried, as has Alyn, to talk some sense into the man but to no avail."

"Alyn seems a good lad," Alysander said. While he had known Rory and Gavin since they were weans, he had no idea who this Alyn fellow was.

"He is a good man," Rory replied. "A bit soft hearted at times, but he is still a good man. And a hell of a warrior as well. Now, quit trying to change the subject. Whatever ye do, please, dinnae make Orabillis apologize."

Alysander scratched his jaw as he contemplated the situation for a moment.

Rory slapped a hand on his old friend's back. "Trust me, Alysander. What yer daughter did last night was spectacular." He truly meant it. He then added, rather sarcastically, "It brought tears to my eyes!"

Alysander looked heavenward and shook his head. "I doubt Gavin would agree."

"I would nae worry about Gavin's opinion," he replied. "Besides, the king was most amused by it."

I n hindsight, Alysander realized he should have done his thinking with a clear head, one unmuddled by the affects of too much whisky.

He was missing his wife today, more so than usual. Moirra possessed a levelheadedness that he could certainly use right about now.

He had wakened that morn, fully prepared to listen to Orabillis. And after, he would explain to her why it had not been such a good idea to accept a drunken knight's challenge.

Now, she wasn't speaking to him. Neither were the other women residing over the dressmaker's shop.

"Orabillis, if ye would just listen to reason," he said, doing his best to sound far less frustrated than he was. "I am quite certain ye had yer reasons for doin' what ye did. However, ye need to understand—"

Apparently done with listening to him, she returned to her bedchamber and shut the door rather impolitely.

*Aye, I could certainly use my wife's good counsel,* he thought as he stood in front of the closed door. He was about to leave, when he heard the latch click. A moment later, the door opened. Muriale took one look at him and shook her head as if she were ashamed of him. Then she shut the door.

"I dinnae ken why ye are so mad at me!" he shouted to the closed door.

It flung open a moment later. Orabillis stood there, in her stockinged feet, her robe tied tightly around her waist. "Because ye are an eejit," she said before closing the door again. This time she locked it.

"Young lady, dinnae use that tone of voice with me!" he shouted at the door again. "I will nae stand for disrespectful attitudes."

He was met with stone-cold silence.

"Ye cannae go the rest of yer life without speakin' to me," he said, lowering his voice a tad bit. "I am yer father, Orabillis."

No response from either daughter.

He was getting nowhere in a hurry.

Realizing they weren't ready to speak to him just yet, he decided he would leave. Mayhap he would have better luck smoothing things over with Gavin.

And, hopefully, upon his return, his daughters' anger would have subsided enough to have an intelligent conversation on the matter.

———

Gavin was quite certain the bells to St. Andrew's cathedral had decided to take up residence inside his skull. 'Twas the only plausible explanation for the throbbing pain coursing through his head.

Opening his eyes was a feat in and of itself. They felt as heavy as the iron in his sword. He regretted opening them the moment the sunlight pierced them. His head swam and spun as if he were caught in a whirlpool the size of Inverness.

"Are ye alive?" Rory asked from somewhere across the room. Gavin didn't have the courage to open his eyes again. Instead, he slowly rolled to his stomach and buried his head into his pillow. *Mayhap I will suffocate and end my misery,* he thought to himself.

Even thinking hurt.

He tried to remember the events of the prior evening but drew a blank. The last thing he remembered was sitting next to a very comely lass, enjoying a fine meal. What happened after that, he couldn't have said even under the threat of death.

Someone outside their bedchamber decided then that it was a good time to take a battering ram to it. The sound thundered inside his head, blending with the clanging church bells. *This is it,* he mused. *I will die this day; I am certain.*

A familiar voice was shouting from the doorway. "Gavin, I should like to speak to ye."

'Twas Alysander, the bloody bastard. 'Twas odd that he felt compelled to be angry with his longtime friend. But he couldn't determine why. He couldn't remember. He could barely take in a breath without the overwhelming sensation of being tossed about a boat in the middle of the sea.

"He is hungover," Rory said. "Ye might wish to wait an hour or two."

*In an hour or two, I shall be dead.*

"I want to apologize to him," Alysander said.

"Apologize? For what?" Rory asked, sincerely confused.

"For my daughter's behavior last night."

Rory found Alysander's statement highly amusing. To Gavin's mind, the sound was quite reminiscent of standing under a waterfall. Loud. Painful. Obnoxious.

"Will ye please—" He tried to speak but his mouth was as dry as wool. He swallowed, hoping to clear the walnuts and wool from this throat. "Go away."

He heard Rory say something to Alysander. Truly, he wished they'd stop shouting at one another. Moments later, he thought he heard the door slam. Blessedly, he could no longer hear the men talking. However, the pounding in his skull continued relentlessly.

While Rory was correct in that the king sincerely enjoyed Oribillis's display last night, Alysander wasn't sure if that wasn't necessarily a good thing. Robert was known for odd indulgences. No one knew that better than Alysander, for they were cousins and had spent many summers together in their youth.

"Verra well," Alysander said. "I shall leave the matter alone. For now."

"I suggest ye leave it alone for good," Rory said with a smile.

Wanting to change the subject, Alysander said, "I find myself rather thirsty," he said. 'Twas a veiled suggestion to seek out a nearby tavern.

"I fear I cannae join ye today," Rory said. "I have things I must do for Robert."

"Anything that I could help with?"

It would be good to have an extra pair of eyes and hands to help find the killer and rapist roaming the streets. And with Gavin out of commission for at least today, he could truly use the help. If it had been anyone else besides Alysander making the offer of assistance, Rory would have politely declined. "I doubt Gavin will be up and about before nightfall," he replied.

'Twas then that Alysander smiled for the first time since what he now referred to as Orabillis's debacle. "Oh, he was not only into his cups, I think he stepped into his own coffin."

"That was the drunkest I have e'er seen the man," Rory admitted. Time was getting away from them, and he still had much work to do. "Come, let us find Alyn, and I will tell ye about our mission."

They left the shadows of the corridor, in search of Alyn. Rory hoped it wouldn't take long to find the man.

A lyn hadn't slept more than an hour or two a night for more than a week. This morn, he was beginning to feel the cold exhaustion settle into his bones. If he didn't get some good sleep soon, he'd end up keeling over dead.

He had spent last night hiding in the shadows near Cowgate. Watching, observing, doing his best not to be seen. Not being noticed was easy when one was able to blend in either with the background or with the good folks of Edinburgh themselves.

A master of disguises was he, a talent he'd received from his father, Darrin Buchanan. Darrin had told his son he was a spy for their previous king. As a child, Alyn believed every word the man said. But, as he grew older, questions began to arise. His father, it turned out, had been a thief. The kind of thief who could sneak into a home or a business, day or night, and take whatever he wanted.

Some might consider having a thief for a father to be an embarrassment. But not Alyn. Thief or not, he loved his father. 'Twas he who taught him everything he knew about life and how not to drown oneself in self-pity or shame. "Be proud of yer work, lad, no matter what work ye do."

If Robert II only knew the truth about the man he had knighted, he would probably have him tortured and hanged.

In the end, it wouldn't matter, he supposed. "None of us get out of this world alive," was something else his father said with much frequency.

The sun was just beginning to break when he heard the sound of shuffling feet heading his way. Slowly, he leaned back against the stone wall and into the shadows.

*Some men hunt for food, some for treasures,* he mused. *But I hunt for something far different. I hunt for revenge.*

# THIRTEEN

Rory hadn't slept well, but not for a lack of trying. Every time he closed his eyes, the vision of one Muriale McCullum was there, looking lovely and sweet. No matter what attempts he made to think of something else, he couldn't escape her.

This wasn't like him, not in the least. He was a calm, rational-thinking man whose entire focus was the service of his king. He took great pride in that fact, as well as his ability to push away any distraction, no matter how impressive.

But here he was, lying in his bed, thinking about Muriale McCullum. Everything about the woman was beautiful. From the way her bright eyes sparkled in the candlelight to the sweet sound of her soft voice and everything in between.

More than once, he had found himself lost in thoughts of her, and before he realized it, the morning was half gone. He wasn't a layabout like Alyn or Gavin. Nay, he was always up before the birds and ready to face whatever tasks the day held.

But, now, his mind was consumed with visions of *her*. And, for the life of him, he didn't know what he was going to do about it.

Muriale was beyond tired; she was mentally and physically exhausted and not just from the very late night spent at Edinburgh Castle. She was plum worn out by her sister's seemingly incessant need to rant and rave about their father's behavior and his insistence that she apologize to one Gavin MacKendrick.

In truth, Muriale couldn't blame her sister for being upset. Had she been in Orabillis's predicament, she probably would have behaved exactly as Orabillis had.

However, there was a limit to the amount of complaining one could bear. "I think ye have made yer point," Muriale said as she tried to unclench her jaw. "More than once."

They were in Forvelith's sitting room, warming themselves by the hearth. Their aunt was, as she did every day, working below stairs. While Muriale attempted to concentrate on her sewing, Orabillis was pacing about the room.

"But do ye understand my point?" Orabillis asked as she turned around for what seemed like the hundredth time that morn.

"Aye, I do," Muriale said, her exasperation growing. "As I have told ye repeatedly. I am on yer side, sister. Now, please, sit down, lest ye want to walk a hole into our aunt's floor."

Orabillis let out a heavy breath and shook her hands in an attempt to shed herself of the excessive energy she felt. She sat down in front of the fire but was unable to sit still. She drummed her fingers on the arm of the chair whilst her right leg bounced up and down rapidly.

Muriale could take no more. She tossed her sewing into the basket at her feet and stood. "Grab yer cloak," she said, heading toward the door.

"Why?" Orabillis asked, following behind her. "Where are we goin'?"

"Anywhere but here," Muriale said. "We shall walk until ye are so tired ye cannae be fidgitin' and bouncin' around the apartment."

Orabillis laughed as she grabbed her cloak from the peg by the door. "Ye might want to pack, then, for I fear we will have to walk all the way home before I shed this feeling of anger and frustration."

Muriale let out another heavy sigh. "If that is what it takes to get ye to calm down, then so be it. But might we try a walk around Edinburgh first?"

Her sister shrugged her shoulders. "We can try, but I make no promises."

"That is all that I ask."

---

Thankfully, the sun had decided to make its presence known. The rain they'd woken up to had been blown away by a rather strong breeze from the south. Muriale and her sister now walked quietly down the streets of Edinburgh.

Muriale was grateful for the silence. She and her sister were lost in their own thoughts. It didn't take any great mental acumen to know what her sister was thinking about.

Muriale's own thoughts seemed to scatter like leaves in the autumn wind. With each day spent here, she seemed to feel less and less sad. That realization led to a heavy sense of guilt. Guilt for not having every waking thought consumed by memories and images of Patrick.

Oh, she knew her mother was right in that she couldn't spend the rest of her life mourning the loss of the only man she was certain she could ever love. Still, it hurt to even make the attempt at letting go.

For nearly a year, her grief and despair had been her constant companions. They were comfortable and familiar to her, like old friends or a favorite blanket.

"Where do ye wish to go?" Orabillis asked.

'Twas then Muriale realized they were at a somewhat busy intersection. "I dinnae feel like being jostled about on these crowded streets," she told her. "Mayhap we could keep going in this direction and see where it leads us?"

Orabillis was indifferent on the matter. "Hopefully, it will lead us to somewhere quiet so that I might think."

Muriale quashed a retort she knew would most likely lead to an argument. Instead, she simply smiled and looped her arm around her sister's and continued their forward progression.

The early afternoon sky was a beautiful shade of robin's egg blue. Tiny clouds dotted the sky overhead, moving at a snail's pace. Overall, it was peaceful and serene.

But Muriale didn't feel nearly as peaceful and serene as the weather. With a certainty, her sister was thinking about the events of last night. Muriale's mind was on last night as well, but for entirely different reasons.

One, she couldn't quite shake the image of Rory MacLeod from her thoughts. Aye, he was a handsome man, what with his curly locks of dark hair and bright-blue eyes that seemed to have danced in the candlelight. But there was more to him than that.

And that something more was what was bothering her heart more than anything. It was the simple fact that she had found herself enjoying his company. In many ways, he was like Patrick. He had a good heart. Of that, there was no doubt. He seemed an honest young man, with a good bit of common sense.

What startled her most was the fact that Rory MacLeod had made her laugh. Not just a slight giggle sprinkled here and there but an honest to goodness, full belly laugh. And he had succeeded in making her laugh several times throughout the evening.

Patrick had never made her laugh like that before. That in and of itself wasn't a bad thing. Patrick had made her smile. He'd made her feel loved and cherished and special. Without a doubt, he had loved her more than anything.

But he had never made her laugh like Rory MacLeod had.

Muriale suddenly realized they were walking up a rather big and tall hill. "Where are we goin'?"

"I have no idea," Orabillis admitted. "But turn around."

From their current vantage point, they could see many of the city's streets. Not too far in the distance, they could see the castle looming large and vast. Its walls seemed to embrace the world below it.

"'Tis magnificent," Muriale whispered in awe.

Orabillis nodded her agreement. "Are ye feelin' better?"

Confused, Muriale tilted her head, her brows furrowed. "Me? We took this walk for ye."

Her sister pursed her lips and nodded her head before looking away. Her expression said there was something she wanted to say, but for some reason, she didn't.

"What is it, Orabillis? What is on yer mind?"

"I worry about ye, sometimes, is all. I just want to ken that ye are well."

Understanding set in. "Ye mean have I stopped mournin' Patrick." 'Twas a statement of understanding, not a question.

Orabillis remained silent as she looked out at the horizon.

"I will never stop mourning Patrick's loss, if that is what ye meant." Muriale told her.

She was met with more silence, which was an oddity itself when it came to her sister. The silence stretched on until Muriale began to grow uncomfortable.

"I wish ye would just come out and say whatever it is that is on yer mind."

After a long moment, Orabillis finally turned her attention back to her. "What was it about Patrick that made ye love him so?"

Muriale wasn't prepared for that question. She had to think

about it for only a brief moment. "He made me feel special. He made me feel loved."

"But how? How did he do that?"

"It wasn't just one thing," Muriale began to explain. "He would do little things, like bring me flowers or hold my hand when we walked around the loch."

From Orabillis's expression, she couldn't quite grasp the concept.

Muriale sighed and tried to find the right words to help explain it to her. "I liked him first, as a friend. He was someone I could talk to about just about anything. And he listened. He never made light of what I had to say. My thoughts and feelings were important to him."

"So, it was more than just a physical attraction?"

Muriale smiled. "Oh, there was that as well. Lord above, I thought him the most handsome man I had ever seen." 'Twas nothing short of the truth. Just thinking about him, even now, made her stomach flutter.

"How did ye ken? I mean, how did ye ken that ye loved him?"

These seemed awfully peculiar questions coming from her sister. Never had Orabillis expressed any interest in love or romance. Quite the opposite. She had always poo-poohed it away.

After thinking on her question for a good while, Muriale shrugged her shoulders. "Honestly, I dinnae ken. It wasn't a sudden feeling, Orabillis. It was more a slow realization."

Orabillis turned her attention back to the castle.

Muriale couldn't quite shake the notion that there was much, much more to her sister's questions than simple curiosity. For now, she would remain quiet on the matter. The last thing she wanted was to make her feel uncomfortable, for when Orabillis was made to feel uncomfortable, she often resorted to violence. And last night was all the proof anyone needed to that fact.

After their somewhat-unusual conversation, Muriale had to admit she did feel slightly better. For the first time in a very long while, she was able to talk about Patrick without bursting into tears. The ever-present ache in her heart somehow didn't feel quite so wretched as before.

"Come, Orabillis," she said as she grabbed her sister's hand. "We should get back before Da sends out a search party."

Orabillis giggled. "He only does that for Esa."

"That might be true, but I dinnae wish to make anyone worry."

The truth was she wanted some time alone to think about the revelations she had discovered today.

Together, they made their way down the hill and back to the city. But instead of going directly back to their aunt's home, Orabillis made a suggestion. "We should get a gift for Aunt Forvelith. A way of thankin' her for puttin' up with us."

"I have been workin' on a gift for her: a pretty cloth for her table."

"Ye ken I cannae sew to save my soul from purgatory," Orabillis politely reminded her.

"I could say it is from both of us." Muriale's offer was sincere, if not well met.

Orabillis politely ignored the offer. "She would ken I had naught to do with it. It will nae take long. I promise."

Reluctantly, Muriale finally agreed. If they hurried, there would be time for her to be alone before 'twas time to sup.

They made their way down the narrow, crowded streets. They passed one shop after another, one merchant stall after another. After they began to pass the same shops for a second time, Muriale began to make suggestions. "What about a nice brooch? Or a necklace?"

Orabillis ignored her suggestions. "I will ken it when I see it," she muttered more than once.

It didn't take long for Muriale to suspect something else was afoot.

When Muriale began to suspect that her sister's quest for a gift for their aunt had been nothing more than a ruse, she lost all patience.

In front of a carpenter's stall, Muriale gently grabbed her sister's arm and brought their search to a halt. "Orabillis, we have been going around in circles for over an hour. What are ye truly up to?"

There it was. A flash of something behind her sister's bright blue eyes. She *was* up to something.

"I demand ye tell me the truth."

Rather sheepishly, Orabillis glanced around before leaning in closer to speak. "Are ye nae the least bit curious as to why father's two friends were followin' us around yesterday?"

Muriale closed her eyes and counted to ten before opening them again. "That is what ye are worried over? Why did ye nae just ask?"

"Ye ken?" Orabillis asked, looking quite surprised.

"Aye, I do. I shall explain it to ye as we make our way back to Aunt Forvelith's."

Muriale waited to explain what she knew for two important reasons. The first being that what had been told to her last night was said in confidence. The second was far more appealing, in a way only a sister can share a secret or a bit of gossip with another sister: the wait would drive Orabillis to madness.

Once they were far enough away from the crowds, Muriale began to finally speak. "Do ye remember Rory MacLeod?"

Orabillis rolled her eyes in dismay. "How could I forget him? He is, after all, the dear friend of the man I like to call Satan."

Satan, of course, was Gavin MacKendrick.

"Well, I had the pleasure of speakin' with him as we dined last night."

"I am glad that your experience was better than the one I suffered through."

Muriale carefully made her way around a rather large mud puddle, ignoring her sister's comment. "Rory told me that he, Gavin, and their friend Alyn have been searchin' for a madman."

Orabillis scoffed openly. "All he need do is to glance into a looking glass." She was, of course, referring to Gavin.

Her sister was like a dog on a bone at times. Hell would freeze over before her opinion of one Gavin MacKendrick changed. She would continue to ignore her sister's rants as they pertain to the man. "Apparently, there is a man who has been rapin' innocent young girls," she went on to say. "And, two days ago, they believe he killed one of them."

Orabillis stopped dead in her tracks. "What?"

Muriale took a few steps back, grabbed her sister's arm, and continued down the street. "Aye, 'tis as I said. Anyway, Robert has asked the three of them to find the madman and bring him to justice."

"Why on earth are ye just now tellin' me this?" Orabillis was beyond exasperated.

"Och! I have done naught but listen to ye complain about Gavin since last night. When did I have the chance?"

"Oh, I dinnae," Orabillis began in a most sarcastic manner. "Mayhap over the morning meal? Or perhaps when we were sittin' by the hearth, sewin'? Or mayhap when we began our walk?"

She couldn't understand why her sister was so upset. "Well, now ye ken, aye?" She tried to pull her along the street again, but Orabillis had dug in her heels, quite literally.

"If ye think I am goin' back to Auntie's just to sit and wait for someone to catch this madman, ye are demented."

A sudden sense of dread fell over her. Muriale realized in that moment that she never should have divulged what she knew. "Now, Orabillis—"

"Dinnae 'now, Orabillis' me," she ground out before turning to walk in the opposite direction.

"Dinnae tell me ye plan to search for him yerself," Muriale asked as she raced to catch up to her.

"I do."

"But how?"

Orabillis stopped abruptly and turned back to her sister. 'Twas a most logical question and one that made her angry with her own self.

It wasn't like her to rush into a very serious matter without a plan. *Damn Gavin MacKendrick*, she cursed to herself. She hadn't been thinking clearly since she met the boorish fool.

After giving the matter some thought, she grabbed Muriale's hand and began to lead the way back to their aunt's home.

"What on earth are ye doin'?" Muriale asked as she all but ran to keep up with her sister.

"We are goin' back to Forvelith's, and ye are goin' to tell me everythin' ye ken about this madman."

"But I dinnae ken anything other than what I told ye," Muriale said, her words rushing out.

Orabillis was not convinced. Her sister knew far more than what she was telling her. And if she didn't, she knew exactly whom to turn to for the much-needed information and exactly how she would get it.

Now, if only she could convince her sister.

lysander had heard the rumors since his arrival. Several young women had been raped. One had been murdered.

Hearing those rumors confirmed by Rory and Alyn was still a shock to the senses. And had he not heard it from Rory's own lips, he would not have believed it.

"One man?" Alysander asked before letting out a low whistle. "Are ye certain?"

"It appears that way," Alyn answered.

They were huddled around a tombstone in the middle of the cemetery. The only place, according to Rory, where they could speak without fear of being overheard. 'Twas an odd location, by Alysander's estimation, but he wasn't one to argue over something so unimportant.

"Have ye any suspicions on who could be responsible?"

Rory and Alyn each shook their heads, looking rather displeased and angry. "Nary a one," Rory admitted begrudgingly. "'Tis why we are scourin' the streets each day."

Alysander wasn't sure that was necessarily the best way to go about things. "I dinnae mean to tell ye how to go about findin' him," he began in a low tone.

Rory didn't wait for him to finish. "We are open to suggestions."

"If it were me, I would start at the beginning. Go to the first victim and speak to her."

"We have done that," Alyn said.

"And what did ye learn?"

Quickly, Rory explained what they had learned thus far. The man's height and his unusual scent but naught else.

# FOURTEEN

The sun was just beginning to set in the west before Gavin woke again. If anyone had entered his room whilst he'd been sleeping, he wouldn't have known it.

His head still pounded, albeit not with the same ferocity as earlier, but everything else remained the same. His mouth was still as dry as wool, and his stomach felt as if he had swallowed a barrel full of squid.

It took a good amount of strength to sit up on the edge of his bed. Holding his head in his hands, he made a solemn vow to God. *I shall never drink like that again,* he told himself as he slowly got to his feet.

After relieving his bladder, he went to the wash basin and splashed cold water on his face. Next, he washed his teeth and tried to gargle the taste of stale ale from his mouth.

'Twasn't until he chanced a glance out of the window that he realized how late it was. *Och! Rory and Alyn are goin' to be bloody furious.* While he was sleeping the day away, his friends were out searching for a madman. Guilt pulled at his heart. *Ye are an arse, Gavin MacKendrick.*

If they never forgave him, he couldn't rightly blame them. He knew they would, of course, just as he would forgive them were the roles reversed.

When he caught a whiff of himself, he came close to gagging. *Good God, man! Ye smell worse than death.*

A bath was needed. Mayhap more than one.

As he was searching through his trunk for clean clothes, his thoughts began to turn to the night before. Or partial thoughts, for truly, he could barely remember anything that happened.

His last cognizant memory was of himself, his friends, and Alysander huddled together. Just what they were discussing, he couldn't remember.

After finding clean clothes, he left the bedchamber and headed down the long, cold corridors. With each step he took, it felt as though the sound of his footfalls were echoing off the walls like a hammer on an anvil.

He wanted nothing more than to return to his chamber, climb under the blankets, and wait for the sweet release of death. But he knew God wouldn't be that merciful. It was his own bloody fault.

*I should have listened to Rory and Alyn.* The thought entered his mind, as did the vague memory of his two friends desperately trying to get him to... His memory fell short of what exactly they had been trying to get him to do or not to do.

It wasn't until he reached the doors to the bathing chamber that the vision of a blonde-haired, blue-eyed beauty came popping into his mind.

Then it all came rushing back to him.

Orabillis.

The slap she gave him when he tried to kiss her.

The challenge.

Her acceptance.

And, ultimately, his defeat.

Humiliation and shame crept over his skin first before turning to fury.

"Bloody hell."

It turned out that Muriale knew far more than she realized, much to her sister's barely veiled delight.

Mrs. MacCurdy was in the kitchen preparing the evening meal, paying no attention at all to the two young women. Aunt Forvelith was still working below stairs. Their father would be returning from his business with the king in time to sup with them.

The more Orabillis paced, the more worried Muriale became. She had that look on her face. The look that said she was thinking hard on something. And, knowing her sister as she believed she did, Orabillis was plotting.

"Whatever it is ye are thinkin' of doin', ye can do it on yer own," Muriale said. She picked up her sewing from the basket and carefully draped it across her lap. *Nay, I shall not allow her to draw me into one of her schemes. The last time I did that, she burned the chicken coop clear to the ground.*

Whether or not she was listening or simply ignoring her, it didn't matter. Muriale was determined not to be drawn into any of her sister's plans. Besides, she had much more important things to do.

Such as trying to figure out how she felt about finally moving on with her life.

"They have no good suspects," Orabillis mumbled. "The only thing they ken is that the man smelled like roses and something else."

Muriale continued to ignore her sister and remained focused on her sewing. "Dinnae forget he has dark hair and no beard." Muriale immediately regretted saying anything. Hopefully, Orabillis hadn't heard it.

"Aye, I remember," Orabillis muttered to herself. After more pacing, she stopped and asked, "Have they spoken to any of the other victims?"

"I have no idea," Muriale replied. "And I dinnae ken why ye are so interested."

"Dinnae ye want to catch a killer? A fiend?" Orabillis asked. She was surprised her sister didn't carry the same fascination or desire on the matter.

Muriale sighed as she shook her head. She knew her sister was trying to insult her honor by suggesting she didn't care. Unwilling to argue about honor or right versus wrong, she decided to ignore the slight.

"What can we do?" she asked, rather annoyed with the topic. "We have no experience in such matters. We are only here another week or two. And we have nae the first notion of where to start."

"That is nae what I asked," Orabillis pointed out. "I asked if ye want to catch this man, the man responsible for raping all those poor, young girls and, now, for taking the life of one."

Muriale was insulted by the question. "Of course I want the man caught. What kind of question is that? I simply mean that I dinnae ken what *we* can do."

Orabillis nodded her head as a wry smile formed in the corner of her mouth. "We can talk to his victims."

"But we dinnae ken who the victims are," Muriale pointed out. Truly, her sister wasn't thinking this through clearly. She was, Muriale believed, motivated by her love of intrigue and not by common sense.

"Nay," Orabillis replied with a raised brow and a most devious smile. "But ye ken who does."

---

Absolutely under no circumstance was Muriale going to help her sister with her plans. Aye, she wanted the madman caught just as badly as she did. But to use her feminine wiles to gain information from Rory MacCleod? As far as she was concerned, Orabillis's suggestion was beyond absurd. No matter the honorable reasons behind it, she wouldn't agree.

"Nay." Muriale's tone left no doubt as to her sincerity. "I will nae do it."

"Nae even for the poor women who have already been attacked? Or for the one who has been killed?" Orabillis asked, looking as if she were ashamed of her. "And what of those he will attack in the future? Do ye nae care about them?"

Muriale knew exactly what her sister was up to, and she wasn't about to fall for it. "I will nae behave like a common..." She searched for the kindest words she could think of. "...hussy. I will nae behave like a common hussy in order to glean information from Rory."

Orabillis was incensed and began to pace around the sitting room. "I cannae believe ye would rather allow these poor women to suffer with no justice or let this madman attack—"

Muriale got to her feet and began to smooth out imaginary wrinkles from her blue woolen skirts. Ignoring her sister completely, she headed for the door. As Orabillis continued with her tirade, Muriale grabbed her cloak from the peg and put it on, taking her time with the ties at her neck. Once she felt the cloak was sufficiently tied and smoothed, she finally turned her attention to her sister. "Are ye quite done?"

Orabillis stopped mid-rant, her brows furrowed in a knot of confusion. "Where are ye goin'?" She sounded as confused as she looked.

"To speak to Rory MacCleod," Muriale said as she opened the door. "Are ye comin' with me, or shall ye continue to pace around the room all day like a mad woman?"

"Really, Muriale," Orabillis said as she walked down the street beside her sister. "Ye could have simply said ye would help." Muriale resisted the urge to roll her eyes, choosing instead to affect an air of indifference. "Ye were too busy rantin' and ravin'."

Thankfully, their father had not returned yet, and their aunt was too busy with a customer to notice their departure.

Turning left at the corner, they were heading for Edinburgh Castle. The late-afternoon air was warmer than Muriale had anticipated. It seemed to heat up the awful smells she would never grow accustomed to, no matter how long she stayed.

"I dinnae mind offerin' to help," Muriale said after stepping around a wide puddle. "I simply will nae help as ye suggested."

"Then what are ye goin' to do? How will ye get the names? Are ye goin' to try to sneak into his room and search for information?"

Muriale shook her head in dismay. "Really, Orabillis, ye have the most vivid imagination and penchant for intrigue."

"Well?" Orabillis asked as they stopped at the corner.

Muriale waited for the ox-driven cart filled with hay to pass before she answered. "I plan on speakin' to the man. I will simply explain that we want to help. That mayhap these young women would feel more comfortable talkin' to another young woman."

"And if that dinnae work?"

Muriale sighed in frustration. "Rory is a man of honor, with a keen sense of intellect. It will work."

But, just in case, she sent a prayer heavenward for help.

---

"Nay." Rory couldn't believe these young women were here, at the castle, unescorted, let alone coming to him with such a preposterous plan—and standing in his bedchamber, no less!

Muriale was a lady, for the sake of all that was holy. And he was quite certain she was as pure as new-fallen snow. If she heard even a tidbit of what these poor women had gone through, she would likely die from embarrassment or, at the very least, faint from the disgust of it all.

He wasn't as certain however, about her younger sister. She probably wouldn't bat an eye.

Another worry was what their father would say. Alysander would probably kill him with his bare hands if he knew Rory had accepted his daughters' offer to help.

"Nay?" The lovely young woman was staring up at him as if he had suddenly grown an extra nose in the middle of his forehead.

Her sister looked as though she were ready to stab him in the eye with the dirk he was quite certain she had hidden somewhere upon her person.

"Ladies, I do appreciate yer desire to help." He was choosing his words carefully so as not to upset Muriale's delicate nature.

He soon learned Muriale wasn't quite as delicate a creature as he had assumed.

"Sir Rory, I dinnae believe ye understand our intent," Muriale said as she placed her hands on her hips. He caught a flicker of something in those bright-blue eyes, something he was quite certain was a blend of anger and sheer determination. 'Twas almost frightening, in a very appealing sort of way.

"These young women and their families have all refused to speak with ye, aye?" she asked pointedly.

Rory nodded his affirmation. In truth, his mind was beginning to wander to places he knew it shouldn't. A little strand of her brunette hair had escaped her braid and was tickling her cheek. It took every ounce of strength he owned not to reach out and tuck it behind her ear, just for a chance to caress her skin.

"Women, especially *young* women and little girls, dinnae want to talk to a man about what happened to them, because 'twas a man who hurt them," Muriale said.

"Aye," Orabillis agreed. "I can guarantee ye they dinnae trust any man other than mayhap their da or brothers."

Muriale glanced at her sister and nodded before turning back to Rory. "So, ye see, we *can* help. They will talk to us, Sir Rory."

*Sir Rory.* Why did the way she said his name sound so sexually appealing? Were he not an honorable man, he would toss her over his shoulder and find the nearest priest.

"Are ye even listenin' to me?" Muriale asked. She was now glowering at him, something he found even more appealing. He lied. "Of course I am."

Muriale shook her head in disbelief. "And to think I told my sister that ye were a man of keen intellect and possessing a strong sense of honor."

That stung. He stood a bit taller, shaking the images of their future wedding night from his mind. "I am," he replied drolly. "That is why ye cannae help. If ye heard what these poor little girls had gone through, why, ye would faint straight away."

Orabillis was reaching for the dirk hidden in her sleeve, while her sister broke into a fit of laughter.

Dumbfounded, he asked, "What is so funny?"

---

Once Muriale got her laughter under control, she was finally able to answer. "Ye think me a weak, delicate young woman, aye?" She took two steps toward him and poked a finger into his chest. "Ye have no idea what I am capable of."

Nay, he might have thought he knew all about her from the dinner they shared a few nights ago, but he knew absolutely nothing.

Orabillis was smiling in a peculiar way. As if she were the bearer of a tremendous secret as well as enjoying the interaction betwixt her sister and the knight.

"I am nae weak nor delicate, Sir Rory. I suggest ye never forget that." Her anger was growing by leaps and bounds.

In the beginning, when Orabillis first suggested they hunt for the fiend lurking in the shadows of the night, Muriale truly believed there was naught much either of them could do to help. Now, after hearing Rory MacLeod speaking to them as if they were naught more than two daft women, her fury roiled in the pit of her stomach. He was also falling rapidly in her previous kind estimation of him.

"Yer da would kill me," he said as he crossed his arms over his chest.

Oh, he was doing his best to look fierce and terrifying. Were the situation different, and had she not met him previously, she might have been shaking in her boots right now. But that wasn't the case.

"I can assure ye that my father will see the rightness of our plan," she told him firmly.

"Ye have nae discussed it with him?" he asked, looking rather appalled.

"I am of an age where I dinnae have to ask my father's permission to do anythin'," she replied. "Now, ye can either help us help ye, or my sister and I shall investigate on our own."

She found she rather liked the way he looked taken aback by her statement; stunned, as if she'd just sprouted wings and a beak.

Muriale watched as his eyes darted back and forth betwixt herself and Orabillis. She could see he was mulling over the idea carefully. She had, of course, appealed to his sense of honor in a rather devious way. She was quite certain he wouldn't allow her and her sister to wander the streets of Edinburgh alone whilst looking for a killer.

He pursed his lips and narrowed his eyes as he scrutinized Muriale. She felt an odd tingling sensation trace up and down her spine. There was something about the look he was giving her...

Rory let out a sigh of defeat. "Verra well. But ye will gain permission from yer da first."

Muriale and Orabillis knew that was a feat easier said than accomplished. However, there was too much at stake to allow for any kind of defeat.

"That will nae be a problem," Orabillis said.

Muriale knew she was lying but painted on a smile of victory anyway. "Meet us at our aunt's home in two hours," Muriale said. "We shall begin then."

Rory's expression said he didn't believe for a moment that they would be successful in gaining their father's permission.

Muriale returned his smile and gave him a slight curtsy before she and Orabillis quit the bedchamber.

---

The guard who had escorted them to Rory's chamber was waiting in the hall. Neither sister said a word until after they were nearing the gates of the castle.

"Ye ken we will have to get Da good and drunk before he agrees to this," Orabillis whispered sarcastically.

Neither of them had paid any attention to who might be nearby. Muriale's heart sank when she heard her father's voice coming from behind. "Agrees to what?"

---

Alysander could see the rightness of what his daughters were suggesting. Truly, he could. As their father, he admired their tenacity as well as their sense of right versus wrong.

Having known them for more than a decade now, he knew just how strong headed and stubborn they could be. Especially Orabillis. When she set her mind on something, it would take God coming down from the heavens and speaking to her directly before she would change her mind. The mental image of his daughter arguing with God brought a smile to his face.

Then he thought of his wife. The mother of these two fine, strong, determined lasses, and that smile evaporated in the span of one terrified heart beat.

"Yer mother would kill me," he said. He pursed his lips, shook his head, and crossed his arms over his chest, a stance that he hoped would put the matter to rest. "I fear I cannae allow ye to do this."

"Mother would see the rightness of it," Orabillis said.

Alysander shook his head and made his way through the gates. His daughters were fast on his heels.

"Nay," he said as he walked rapidly down the hill. "Yer mother would have my head on a pike if I agreed to this."

"But ye do see the rightness of it, aye?" Muriale asked as she raced to keep up with him.

"Aye, I do," he agreed rather begrudgingly. But that didn't mean he could approve of what they were asking.

Muriale caught up to him and tugged at his arm. "Stop, please," she pleaded.

A fortnight ago, when he looked into Muriale's eyes, they were all but void of life. It had terrified him so much that he worried she would be dead within a month's time.

Now, his daughter was standing in the middle of the street, pleading with him to listen.

It suddenly dawned on him that Muriale was back amongst the living. The slightest breeze could have knocked him over in that instance of realization. Relief and an overwhelming sense of love exploded in his chest.

*I swore I would do anythin' to get the auld Muriale back,* he remembered silently.

Stuck between the proverbial rock and a hard place, he wished for all the world his wife was here.

"Da, we *must* help these poor little girls and the young women," Muriale pleaded. Her eyes were growing damp as they searched his own. He knew exactly what she was looking for: agreement.

'Twas in that moment that he realized he couldn't deny her this. His only concern for nearly a year had been getting his daughter back. Back to living her life, back to being able to smile and laugh and dance.

He felt his resolve diminish with each beat of his heart. Aye, chances were good that Moirra would kill him, especially if anything happened to either of their precious daughters.

"Verra well," he finally acquiesced. "But ye will nae go it alone."

He watched as her eyes lit up with relief and happiness. She had something far more important to focus on than her own broken heart. Alysander was quite certain that meant her heart was healing. He sent a silent prayer heavenward that she wouldn't revert to the sickly, grief-stricken young woman she had been when they eventually returned home.

"Thank ye, Da!" she exclaimed as she threw her arms around his neck.

He glanced at Orabillis and saw that she was just as happy. However, he was quite certain her happiness was for entirely different reasons. Aye, she wanted this madman caught, but knowing his daughter as he did, she wanted to be in on the kill.

# FIFTEEN

Before Alysander would allow his daughters to help, he lay down several important ground rules. In his mind, they weren't too overly cautious. He simply couldn't allow his two precious daughters to go wandering around the city, looking for a fiend.

"Nay," Orabillis said as they sat at Forvelith's table enjoying their evening meal. "Anyone but him."

The *him* to which she was referring was, of course, one Gavin MacKendrick.

Alysander had suggested Rory and Gavin take turns guarding his daughters. He'd known the two young men for over twenty years. They knew the streets and alleyways of Edinburgh better than most. Besides the men he had brought with him, he trusted his daughters' safety to no one else.

"I will nae allow ye to go alone," Alysander told her.

"Then ask Red John or one of the other men. Anyone but Gavin MacKendrick."

Alysander pursed his lips together in consternation. Why must this daughter of his make things so difficult? If she hadn't done what she'd done at the castle, then they would not now be having this conversation.

"I fear I must agree with Orabillis," Muriale said as she sliced off a bit of ham from the tray in front of her. "I, for one, would rather concentrate on helping find this madman than to keep Orabillis from killing Gavin MacKendrick."

Orabillis smiled rather deviously. "I would do it away from ye. Away from any potential witnesses."

Forvelith rolled her eyes at both young women. "I have to agree with yer father on this. Ye cannae go alone."

"Again, I ask why Red John cannae go with us," Orabillis said.

"Because Red John sticks out like a horse with two tails," Alysander replied. "He terrifies most people due to his sheer size. And he is nae kent for his gentle spirit."

Muriale had to agree. "Da is right. And so is Orabillis. I think Rory might be the better choice. He seems a kind enough man."

Wishing to be done with the argument, Alysander stuffed the last bit of bread into his mouth. "Verra well. I shall ask Rory to assist.

---

"I cannae believe the fathers will nae let us speak to their daughters," Orabillis groused. They were sitting at the Black Boar Inn, drowning their discouragement over mugs of ale. They had been at it for days, with little progress.

They were in a dark corner of the inn, with Muriale and Orabillis sitting across from Rory and Alysander. 'Twas nearing the midnight hour, the inn quiet save for the crackling of the fire in the hearth.

"If we could get beyond their fathers," Orabillis suggested to no one in particular, "I think we would be far more successful."

Muriale agreed, with a simple nod of her head. She was disappointed that they had not made more progress. Her thoughts soon turned to her mother and wishing she was here to offer sage advice.

That is when the idea struck. "We need to speak to their mothers," she said, sitting upright.

She'd managed to draw Rory and her father's attention away from their mugs. Orabillis immediately agreed, slapping her own noggin, "Why did we nae think of that sooner?"

"Do ye really think the mothers will speak to us?" Rory asked.

"Aye, I do," Muriale said. "We might not always tell our mothers *everything*," she began, her enthusiasm growing by the moment. "But when we are truly hurt, truly despondent, aye, we turn to our mothers every time."

———

Muriale, along with Orabillis and Rory, were more than just determined to speak to the young women who had been assaulted; they felt they were on a mission to right the horrible wrongs the fiend had committed. Nothing can make people stronger than believing they are righting a wrong or, as in Rory's case, being on a mission from God and his king.

Muriale had gone into this undertaking with the fervent belief that the victims would rather speak to another female, but that belief began to wane after they had been turned away from the fourth victim's father.

Thus far, their requests had been angrily and bitterly denied, and doors all but slammed in their faces. The menfolk were answering all knocks at doors, barring them from speaking to the victims or their mothers.

Still, Muriale refused to give up.

As they walked down one of the less-crowded streets of Edinburgh, Orabillis let her frustration be known. "Why must men be such eejits?" She hadn't directed the question to anyone in particular, but as the only male in their party of three, Rory felt the need to first laugh then answer the question. "We merely wish to protect those who—"

Gritting her teeth, Orabillis wouldn't allow him to finish what she was quite certain was a most ridiculous statement. "If ye think telling me that men only wish to protect the *weaker* sex answers the question, ye would be wrong—and close to findin' my dirk lodged in yer arse."

Rory threw his head back and laughed again. Orabillis couldn't find the humor in it. Niether could Muriale.

"Pardon me, ladies," he said with a smile. "I ken I should nae laugh. But I am nae one of those men who think women are the weaker sex. If anythin', they are the stronger of the two."

The sisters' responses were an equal measure of astonishment and confusion. Neither could believe they'd just heard a man—any man—voice such an opinion aloud.

Rory smiled at each of them. "'Tis the truth, is it nae?"

They glanced at one another before Muriale found her voice. "We believe so," she said rather cautiously. "But why do *ye* believe it to be so?"

Oh, if he didn't stop smiling at her with such warmth and kindness, she might just swoon. That smile was making her feel all fluttery inside, a feeling she hadn't experienced in nearly a year—a feeling she'd been quite certain she'd never feel again.

But there it was.

Guilt assaulted her heart. She found it difficult to focus on what he was saying, for she couldn't hear his words over her rapidly pounding heart. Plus, she found herself lost in bright-blue eyes filled with such warmth that her legs began to feel weak.

"And that is why I agree," he said as he crossed his arms over his chest.

*Oh, lord above, what did he say?*

She glanced at her sister, who seemed thoroughly and completely pleased with his answer.

"And dinnae ye forget it," Orabillis replied.

Muriale felt ten kinds a fool. She hadn't heard a word the man had said. It must have been something rather amazing, for it made Orabillis smile, which was a rare event, indeed.

"Now, shall we go to the next home?" Rory asked, his smile not faltering in the least.

All Muriale could do was nod in agreement and fall in beside her sister. As they walked, she made a promise to herself to never let her mind or heart get swept away like that again. *Be resolute in all things,* she mused. *Elst ye are libel to lose yer head or yer heart. Or, worse yet, both.*

---

Their luck didn't change until the third day. One father after another had refused to allow anyone to speak to their wives or daughters. The single thread that tied the responses together was that they wanted their womenfolk to forget what happened.

"Do they nae realize that a woman cannae just forget such a thing?" Muriale asked as they were turned away from the seventh home.

"I fear they dinnae," Orabillis replied as she carefully made her way down the dark stairwell. The building was old and smelled musty and damp, with just a hint of desperation hanging in the air.

Muriale led the way, with Rory bringing up the rear. She had just reached the entrance (or the exit, depending on which direction one was heading), when a door to her left creaked open. 'Twas only a crack, just enough to see one bleary, blood-shot eye peeking through. A moment later, the door was closed and bolted shut.

The trio spilled out into the dreary late afternoon. The sound of church bells rang in the distance. Nearby, a dog barked incessantly, the sound of its voice echoing off the narrow alley walls.

'Twas Orabillis who broke the eery silence. "I am gettin' awfully tired of having doors shut in our faces."

Muriale was too focused on getting out of the alley to make any response. Something dark scurried along the wall and disappeared into an even darker hole. She didn't like this narrow, dark alley at all. And, for a long moment, she would have sworn they were being watched.

At the end of the alley, they turned right. Muriale breathed a sigh of relief as soon as they were back on what she considered much safer ground. Cowgate Street was alive and bustling with street vendors and merchants. The cattle had already passed through, if the dung left on the dirty street was any indication.

Rory pulled a bit of parchment from his pouch. "We are nae far from Mairi Hay's home," he said as he perused the parchment. It contained the list of all the victims, as well as their last known addresses.

"Remind me who she is," Orabillis said as she carefully side-stepped a pile of goat dung.

"Aged five and ten," Rory replied. He had memorized each of the victims' names and ages, but he used the parchment to refresh his memory as to where each of them lived.

"Verra well," Orabillis replied. "Lead the way, sir knight."

Rory chuckled as he shook his head but otherwise made no comment. Muriale was overcome with a sudden bout of jealousy. Orabillis certainly wasn't flirting with the man. Why, then, did Muriale's chest tighten? She had no claim on the man, and she was still in mourning. Nay, it didn't make a lick of sense. Ignoring the odd feelings, she followed her sister and Rory up the street.

*My, but he does cut a fine figure of a man,* Muriale mused as she glanced up at him. Broad shouldered and narrow at the hip, with long, well-muscled legs.

*Lord above, I am losing my mind!*

Once again, she found herself daydreaming instead of paying any attention to where she was going. And, once again, she was bumping into a stranger.

But, this stranger, she knew.

"Mr. Desmond!" Muriale exclaimed as she felt two strong hands grabbing her arms to keep her from falling backward.

"My lady," he said with a mischievous grin. "We must stop meetin' like this."

She felt her cheeks grow warm with embarrassment. "I am ever so sorry."

"There is naught to be sorry for, my lady," he said, his grin turning to a smile. "I would rather bump into a comely lass such as yourself than anyone else."

Her embarrassment increased tenfold, and she found herself suddenly mute. Without a doubt, he was flirting with her; she wasn't that naive. While it was rather nice to be flirted with, she felt guilty for liking the attention. *Think of Patrick,* she told herself.

"Muriale? Are ye all right?" Rory asked, her his eyes were entirely focused on Moris Desmond.

"Quite well, Rory," she replied, finally finding her voice.

"It seems Lady Muriale and I keep bumping into one another," Moris said by way of an explanation. "I am Moris Desmond."

From Rory's scrutinizing glower, he wasn't at all impressed with Moris. Feeling the need to explain herself (although *why* would forever remain a mystery to her), Muriale explained how they first met. "So, without Mr. Desmond's help, we would never have found the butcher shop."

"I doubt that," Rory said.

"I shall let ye get on with yer day," Moris said. He bowed slightly to Muriale, then again to Orabillis, before casually walking away.

"Ye cannae befriend every stranger ye come across," Rory said as soon as he was certain Moris Desmond couldn't hear. "Might I remind ye that we are lookin' for a murderer and rapist?"

Muriale didn't care for his chastising tone. "Might I also remind ye that I am a woman full grown? And I certainly dinnae need ye to order me about as if ye were my father, my brother, or my husband."

Rory's face shadowed then, with what could only be described as fury. "I am nae tryin' to be any of those things to ye, Muriale. I have only yer safety in mind."

She didn't like his tone, not one bit. "While I thank ye for yer concern, I might also remind ye that I am perfectly capable of takin' care of myself." She gave him no time to respond, for she was in no mood to argue. "Now, shall we get on with our day? We have more victims to speak to."

---

Mairi Hay was a wee thing, with long, brown hair twisted into a braid that fell down her back and big brown eyes that Muriale was quite certain had once been filled with mirth and happiness.

Now, those eyes were filled with sorrow and deep shame.

All because a madman had decided to take that which didn't belong to him.

They had been here for over an hour, listening and gently prying much-needed information from the poor girl. It was a task that Muriale was not liking in the least.

Thankfully, the girl's father hadn't been home when they arrived. It had taken some convincing before the girl's mother would allow them to enter. Her name was Ella Hay, and her daughter was her spitting image.

Rory stood just outside the door to the small apartment. Mairi was terrified of men now, and his presence made her feel quite uncomfortable.

The women sat around a small table in the dark living area. One fat candle in the middle of the table burned low, occasionally flickering and sizzling.

Mairi sat so close to her mother that she was nearly on her lap.

Ella had one arm draped around her shoulder as she held her daughter's hand with the other. In a corner of the room was a nice-sized bed with a small bed next to it. Ella's youngest daughter, a three-year-old with curling brown locks, was fast asleep on that bed.

"I dinnae want him to do to another girl what he did to me," Mairi said. Her voice was so soft, a whisper really, and Muriale had to strain her ears in order to hear her.

"That is our hope as well," Orabillis replied. "We want to stop him as much as ye do. But we cannae do that without yer help."

Mairi nodded her head as she swiped tears away with a bit of linen. "I cannae sleep at night now," she admitted. "I keep seein' him comin' through the window."

"Which window did he come through?" Muriale asked.

Mairi gave a slight nod over her right shoulder. Muriale glanced in that direction. A long, heavy curtain had been pulled open, the area devoid of anything other than a small, empty table near a window.

"She used to sleep there, with her sister," Ella said. "But, since that night, the girls now sleep next to us. Mairi sleeps on a pallet between our bed and the wall."

Muriale's heart cracked just a little more. The poor girl had cocooned herself into such a small place in order to feel safe. But she didn't feel safe; of that, Muriale was quite certain.

The candle sizzled again, flickered, and cast dark shadows on Ella's face. The poor woman looked grief-stricken for her daughter.

"So, he came through the window," Muriale said, directing the conversation back to what had happened that night.

Mairi nodded and sniffled, her eyes focused on the tabletop. "I dinnae what time it was," she said. "The sun was nae up yet."

"Did he say anythin'?" Orabillis asked, keeping her own voice just as low and soft as Mairi's.

"I woke to his hand over my mouth and a knife at my throat," Mairi murmured. "He told me that if I made a sound, he would kill my family and make me watch while he did it."

Tears slowly fell from her lids, leaving little trails along sallow cheeks. Muriale wanted nothing more than to find the madman and kill him with her bare hands. Without a doubt, Orabillis was feeling the same way.

Muriale hated making the girl relive that night but believed it was necessary in order to help find this deranged man. "Did ye leave out the window?"

"Aye," Mairi whispered. "We climbed down the back stairs. All the while, he had the knife poking into my back."

'Twas difficult to listen to what happened next. Muriale wanted to weep on behalf of Mairi.

"Did ye get a look at his face?" Orabillis asked.

"Nay, 'twas too dark."

"Can ye remember anythin' at all about him?" Muriale asked.

Mairi thought for a while before answering. "He smelled verra clean. And he didn't sound like he was from here."

After exchanging a glance with her sister, Muriale asked, "What do ye mean he dinnae sound like he was from here?"

"His accent reminded me of my mother's uncle. He lives way north of here."

Ella sat taller in her chair as she studied her daughter closely. "Are ye sure, lass?"

Another affirming nod from Mairi. "Aye, Mum. I am. But I am nae sayin' 'twas Uncle James."

"Of course nae." Ella smiled as she gave her a slight hug. "But he sounded like him?"

"Just his accent," Mairi qualified. "He smelled different too. Like he had just bathed in some good-smelling soap."

They refused to make the girl relive the attack itself. Not even Orabillis was that cruel. After talking for another quarter of an hour, Muriale believed they wouldn't learn much else. Besides, the poor girl looked shattered with exhaustion.

"Thank ye, Mairi. Ye have been verra helpful," Orabillis said as she slowly got to her feet.

"I would recognize his voice again if I heard it," Mairi said. "And that smell. That, I will never forget."

*I imagine that would be somethin' I could nae forget either.*

Muriale thanked the women and asked if they might call on them again if the need arose.

"Ye would have to make certain my husband is nae here," Ella said as she walked them to the door. "He has nae been the same since this happened. None of us have. But Gerald... He wants to keep her wrapped up and protected. And he wants blood."

"So do we," Orabillis replied as she stepped out into the hallway.

Before Ella could close the door, Mairi lifted her head to speak again. "There is one more thing."

"What is that?" Muriale asked.

"He took a lock of my hair."

M uriale and her sister exchanged confused glances, neither certain they had heard the girl correctly. "What did ye say?" Muriale asked as she stepped back to the table.

Mairi turned her gaze back to the top of the table. "I was ashamed to tell ye."

Her words tugged at Muriale's heart. She sat down next to her and placed a gentle hand on her shoulder. "Lass, there is naught to be ashamed of. Ye did nothin' wrong. The fault lays entirely with the man who hurt ye."

Orabillis sat back down and agreed with her sister. "Aye, Mairi. None of this is yer fault."

Tears formed in Mairi's eyes again. Her mother stood behind her, rubbing her shoulders in hopes of comforting her.

"Tell us about the hair," Muriale whispered. She had no idea if it held any significance at all, but she felt it important to have as much information as possible.

"When he was done," Mairi began, her voice so low that Muriale and Orabillis had to lean in to hear her. "He took his knife and cut off a bit of my hair. He said, 'a token to remember ye by.'"

Muriale's blood ran cold. It took every ounce of energy at her disposal not to gasp in horror or to begin cursing aloud. 'Twas bad enough this bloody bastard had raped this poor young woman. But to take a "token" was beyond the pale.

"Then what happened?" Orabillis asked.

"He left." Mairi said. "He walked down the alley as if naught was wrong, whistlin' all the way."

*Whistling?* Good God in heaven. The man was beyond insane; he was deranged.

They spent a few more moments with her but learned nothing else. Once again, they thanked Mairi and her mum.

Neither sister spoke a word until they were in the hallway.

---

Rory stepped aside to allow the women to exit the apartment.

"What did ye learn?" he asked as he led the way down the stairs.

"That he smelled clean," Muriale replied. "And he has a northern accent."

Rory stopped mid flight and turned to look at them. "Phoebe MacRay told us the same thing about his smell."

"Who is Phoebe McRay?" Muriale asked.

"One of his first victims. We spoke to her days ago. But she dinnae mention the accent."

"Did she also happen to mention if he took a bit of her hair?"

Rory stopped and spun around to look at them. "What?"

"Aye," Orabillis said. "He took a lock of her hair. Told her 'twas a token to remember their time together."

"Jesu," he whispered as he shook his head in disbelief.

"Apparently, he was nae concerned about bein' caught," Muriale said. "For he walked out of the alley, whistlin' all the way."

Rory's eyes grew wide with disbelief. "He what?"

"Aye," Orabillis said. "He whistled."

From his expression, he was having much difficulty making sense of that bit of news. "One would think he would run or at least be as quiet as a church mouse so as nae to draw any attention to himself."

"We are dealing with a lunatic, remember?" Muriale said.

They continued down the stairs and out onto the street. "According to the girl, the man's accent reminded her of her uncle," Orabillis said. "According to the mum, her brother lives up near Dunbrun."

Dunbrun was a small village in the upper northwest part of Scotia, at least a week's ride by horse. 'Twas one more piece of a puzzle that was growing more difficult to put together.

"I want to talk to Phoebe again," Rory said. "But 'tis almost time to meet yer da."

"Hopefully, they will have learned somethin' as well," Orabillis replied.

Muriale sent a silent prayer heavenward that they would soon catch this man.

---

The pub was nearly empty, save for the group who was searching for a rapist and murderer.

They sat at the back of the pub, crowded in around a small table. With Red John present, there was little room for anyone else.

Rory sat between Muriale and Orabillis. Alysander and Red John, along with Gavin, Danial Gray Beard, and Ardin, were spread around the table as well.

Muriale and Rory had just finished filling the others in on what they had learned from Mairi Hay.

Orabillis was eerily quiet. But if looks were capable of killing, Gavin MacKendrick would be a dead man. Her glowers and glares were enough to make a man's blood run cold, but Gavin either didn't notice or chose to be wise and make no comment.

"We were able to speak to another victim," Alysander informed them as he sipped on a mug of ale.

"Who?" Rory and Muriale asked in unison.

"Catriona McPherson," he replied.

Rory's eyebrow raised in confusion. "But I thought she left after she was attacked?"

"So did we," Gavin answered. "But she has since returned. Apparently, she didn't care for how cold Inverness can get."

"Who is she?" Orabillis asked, her curiosity piqued.

"Catriona is a prostitute," Gavin said.

"Please, nae in front of me daughters," Alysander said.

Orabillis and Muriale rolled their eyes almost at the same time. "Da, we ken about prostitutes," Muriale politely informed him. "What did ye learn?" She directed her question to Gavin.

Red John chuckled mischievously. "We learned she has one of the foulest mouths on anyone I have ever met. She made even *me* blush a time or two."

Alysander glanced at him, giving him a look of warning that said he should mind his tongue in front of his daughters.

"We asked her about how he smelled," Gavin said. "After Phoebe had mentioned it, we thought we should make certain we are only dealin' with one man."

Muriale and Orabillis looked aghast. "Good lord! Please tell me we are nae dealin' with more than one madman," Muriale exclaimed.

"We still think 'tis just one man," Gavin told her. "Phoebe said the same thing about the way he smelled. But she didn't mention any accent."

Muriale let out a frustrated breath. "Did she mention if he took a lock of her hair?"

Several pairs of confused eyes looked back at her. Quickly, she told them what they had learned from Mairi Hay, including the 'token' and the whistling.

Red John's jaw was clenched so tightly Muriale was surprised his teeth didn't break under the pressure. Ardin and Danial Gray Beard looked just as furious.

"He actually took a lock of her hair?" Ardin seethed. "That is disgustin'."

No one disagreed with him.

"What kind of sick man are we dealin' with?" Danial asked.

"A deranged lunatic," Orabillis replied. "A bloody deranged lunatic."

Alysander gave her a quick glance that said, "Mind yer language." Orabillis wasn't the least bit sorry for her choice of words. She had a few more but didn't want to set her father into a seizure of the heart by speaking them in front of him.

"At least we ken now what to ask the women when we speak to them," Rory added before taking a pull of his ale. "Were ye able to learn anythin' else?" He directed that question to Alysander.

The three men shook their heads in response.

"Alyn is out now with the sheriff's men. They are stayin' to the shadows in hopes of finding the man."

"I, for one, dinnae like the idea of waitin' for him to strike again," Orabillis said. "There must be more we can do."

"We are warnin' everyone we meet to keep their doors and windows locked," Alysander said.

"I dinnae think this deranged madman is worried about locked windows or doors," Muriale said.

Rory voiced his agreement. "How many men does the sheriff have on the streets?"

"Ten," Alysander said. "With Alyn, that is eleven."

"That is nae many men to keep watch over a city as big as Edinburgh," Orabillis said. "Mayhap, instead of tryin' to talk to more victims, we should take to the streets with Alyn and the sheriff's men."

"Absolutely not," Alysander said firmly.

"But—"

"Yer da is right," Gavin said. "'Tis too dangerous for women right now."

"I can take care of myself," Orabillis said through gritted teeth.

"I am sure ye can," Gavin said. "But it is still too big a risk to take. We cannae have ye and yer sister roaming the streets at night. Ye would need someone with ye, and that would diminish our already weak resources."

Muriale interjected her own opinion in hopes of quashing what would most likely be a bloody argument betwixt her sister and Gavin. "I agree," she said. "Orabillis, I ken we can take care of ourselves, but we dinnae want to pull men from the search to watch over us."

"We dinnae need men to watch over us," Orabillis retorted. "The two of us together are far stronger than anyone gives us credit for."

"I ken that," Muriale agreed. "However, I still think we need to keep tryin' to talk to the victims."

Orabillis was unconvinced. "I would rather we nae take the risk of him killin' again, sister."

"Neither would I. But we must think logically about this."

"Logic?" Orabillis asked with wide eyes. "I dinnae think this madman is thinkin' with logic."

Alysander couldn't listen to another moment of their arguing. "No more," he said, his words clipped and firm. "'Tis late, we are all exhausted, and we have much work to do on the morrow." He pushed away from the table, a sure sign that he was finished speaking on the topic.

CHAPTER

# SIXTEEN

It had been another long, exhausting night, just one of many he had experienced of late. Bone tired, he could think of nothing else but finding his bed and sleeping for the next sennight.

But there was much that needed to be done before he could rest. No one ever said revenge was easy. It was bloody hard work.

Yet it was a sweet dish, meant to be savored and relished.

These women didn't know what a catch he really was. They couldn't possibly imagine all that he could offer them. The happiness he could bring them. They were too haughty, too high and mighty to pay him any notice, let alone to get to know him.

So be it. The fault lay entirely at their own pretty feet. Had they just given him a chance... But, nay. No one ever gave him a chance. Not once since the day he was born.

Getting even with those who wronged him was his only goal in life now. Getting even and proving to all the world just what a cunning and intelligent man he was. And what a loss it was to those women who would nae even give him a second glance.

Aye, 'twas their loss, not his.

M uriale was up before the sun. She hadn't slept well at all. Her dreams had been invaded with images of Patrick, the many victims, and even Rory. Little swatches of faces—some angry, some filled with anguish—but nothing that she could piece together to make any sense of.

All that she knew when she opened her eyes that morning was that these victims were counting on her to help. To help find this man and instill some justice to him on their behalf.

Orabillis was equally eager to bring this entire ordeal to an end. She didn't linger in bed or grouse about getting up at such an early hour.

They were dressed and out the door long before their aunt woke. They decided it best to let her sleep and not wake her to tell her they were leaving. Forvelith knew the importance of what they were working on and supported them fully in their mission.

" I am only moments away from walkin' up to every man I see, sniffing him for the 'odd yet clean' smell and listening for any accent." Orabillis was growing more and more impatient as the hours passed.

Rory chuckled with the image of her doing just that. Alysander looked as though he were actually contemplating the idea.

"All right," Muriale said as she sat taller in her seat. "We have to come up with a new plan."

"And what do ye suggest?" Orabillis asked, visibly frustrated.

"We ken we want to speak to the mothers, aye? But the menfolk will nae allow us entry. So, I think we should start keeping watch over their homes. As soon as one of the mothers leave, we will follow after her and see if we can talk to her, away from the menfolk."

Alysander and Rory exchanged glances with one another. "That might nae be such a bad idea," Alysander said.

"It certainly could nae hurt to try," Rory said. He turned his attention back to Muriale and grinned. "Ye have a devious streak to ye, lass."

Muriale smiled and shrugged her shoulders. "Sometimes, women have to be devious."

Orabillis let out a quick breath of frustration. "Will the two of ye stop with yer doe eyes at one another and get back to the topic at hand?"

Duly chastised, Muriale's face burned crimson. Rory pretended he hadn't heard Orabillis's comment.

Alysander's brows furrowed as if he had just now noticed the budding relationship between his daughter and Rory McLeod. His eyes darted back and forth between them with a good deal of uncertainty.

"What time shall we start on the morrow?" Orabillis asked.

"At day break," Rory answered as he pulled his list of names from his pouch. He studied it for a few moments before adding, "We will start with Hazel MacCory. She lives nearby with her parents and younger siblings."

---

The men were giving the matter much thought when Gavin and Alyn came bursting through the door. They scanned the room until they found Rory then rushed to the table, looking angry and upset.

"What is it?" Rory asked as he and Alysander got to their feet.

"He has struck again," Alyn said. "He has killed another little lass."

uriale felt her heart crack and her stomach fill with rage. She reached out for Orabillis's arm to steady herself. One quick look at her sister, and she knew Orabillis was just as furious as she was.

In a matter of moments, they were all rushing out the door into the dark night. She and Orabillis were following behind the men, listening intently to every word that was said.

"She was found less than an hour ago, in an alley a block from her home," Gavin said.

"Her name is Alyce McDermott, and she is only ten years old."

Muriale felt the fury increase with this news. For a moment, she wanted to scream and curse and begin a door-to-door search for the man responsible.

"Good lord," Alysander muttered under his breath.

"Magnus sent us to find ye," Alyn said as they led the way down the street.

"Who is Magnus?" Orabillis asked.

The men came to an abrupt halt. Apparently, Rory and Alysander had forgotten the two young women were with them.

"And who are ye?" Orabillis asked, directing that question to Alyn.

"Who are ye?" he returned, looking a bit perplexed.

Alysander decided 'twas best to get the situation with his daughters under control. "Muriale, Orabillis, I want ye to return to Forvelith's."

"Nay!" Muriale argued. "We want to help."

"Who are they?" Alyn asked to anyone who would listen. He was, of course, referring to Muriale and Orabillis.

"Alyn, these are Alysander's daughters," Rory answered.

He was surprised. Grinning widely, he looked at Orabillis. "Are ye the one that Gavin has been complainin' about for days now?"

Orabillis shot a glower towards Gavin. Muriale gave her no time to answer.

"We dinnae have time for this right now. We can introduce ourselves on the way."

Rory stepped in front of her. "Ye are nae goin' with us," he told her.

Muriale quirked a brow, amazed at his audacity. "I dinnae listen to ye, Sir Rory. I am goin'."

"Nay," Alysander said before turning to Gavin. "Will ye please escort me daughters home?"

Gavin looked appalled with the idea. Alyn, however, was eager to help. "I will do it," he volunteered with a wide grin.

Muriale and Orabillis began to argue against that notion. They wanted to help.

"Girls," Alysander said in his firmest tone. "This is nae time to argue. I give ye my word we will tell ye everythin' upon our return. Now, go. Alyn shall take ye home."

Muriale knew they'd simply be wasting valuable time by arguing. With her father's word, she relented and agreed. Orabillis wasn't quite as keen on the idea.

"We will get that one to tell us what he kens," Muriale whispered into her ear. She gave a nod towards Alyn as she pleaded for her sister's understanding.

"Verra well," Orabillis agreed. Before leaving, she shot an angry glare at Gavin, simply because she felt like it.

Moments later, her father and his friends were heading one way, whilst the fellow named Alyn was escorting them home.

"What did ye say?" Muriale asked in utter disbelief. They were standing in their aunt's sitting room, by the fire, and had just finished their formal introductions to one another.

Alyn appeared confused with his brows narrowed. "I said my name is Alyn Buchanan."

It took several long moments for the name to sink in. And not because she hadn't heard it before. How could a Buchanan be knighted? And how in the hell was one now standing in her aunt's home, looking as innocent as a newborn lamb?

"Are ye related to the Buchanan clan up near Inverness?" Orabillis asked.

Muriale took note that her sister was feigning an air of nonchalance, all the while preparing to reach for the dirk in the sleeve of her tunic. Depending on how the young man answered, she was probably planning his imminent demise.

"I think my da was," he said as he took the seat offered to him by Forvelith. "If we are, it would be very distantly."

Muriale wanted to pull his eyes out of his skull. She didn't care how distantly he might be related to those she hated with every fiber of her being. He was one of them, as far as she was concerned.

"So, ye have nae been that way?" Orabillis inquired.

"What? To Inverness?" Alyn asked quizzically. From his expression, he couldn't understand why they were so interested in his travels. "Aye, I have been to Inverness a few times."

"But have ye visited yer father's family?" Orabillis asked.

Alyn scratched his jaw and gave the question a brief measure of thought. "Nay, I dinnae believe that I have. Why do ye ask?"

Muriale couldn't contain her anger any longer. "Because the bloody bastards killed my betrothed, my uncle, and five of our best warriors."

lyn had lied to the two young women, and for good reason. He knew exactly what his father's brother had done the year before.

He was ashamed to acknowledge any part of his bloodline that had to do with Harold Buchanan, his uncle. Alyn despised his now-dead uncle, with a passion.

Even if his father was a thief, he was still a better man than Harold Buchanan could have ever hoped to be. 'Twas because of him that his father left the clan and came to Edinburgh. It had turned out to be a blessing in disguise.

Although he had had nothing to do with the deaths of the men Muriale mentioned, he still felt guilty. Not because he had been involved but because of the blood that ran through his veins. "I am so verra sorry, lass."

He didn't know what else to say.

"Sorry?" Muriale challenged angrily. "Is that all ye have to say?"

Alyn could very well understand her pain and suffering.

"I would rather gut ye than talk to ye," Orabillis said most seriously. "But I am nae in the mood for cleanin' up the blood and hidin' yer body."

One look into the young woman's eyes was all he needed to know she was speaking the truth. Suddenly, he didn't feel quite as safe and assured as he had earlier. An odd sensation, considering who he was.

He cleared his throat as he searched for a way to deescalate the current situation. "Ladies, I dinnae blame ye for yer anger, but I was nae involved in the attack. I am a Buchanan by name and, unfortunately, by blood."

"That is good enough for me," Orabillis said. She was leering at him, undoubtedly plotting his imminent death.

Slowly, he stood to his full height. "Unlike the Buchanans ye have kent, I am a man of honor. My word is my bond. I take my duties as one of Robert's knights verra seriously. Ye have my word that I would never bring any harm to either of ye. I have been sworn to protect ye, and that is what I plan to do."

M uriale wanted nothing more than to run her dirk across Alyn Buchanan's throat. She didn't care that he had no real connection to the Buchanan clan. He was one of them.

"Yer word?" she asked dubiously. "Ye should nae be allowed to breathe the same air as us," she bit out angrily. "Ye are a Buchanan, and that is all I need to ken."

Alyn let out a long, steady breath. "I shall wait in the hall," he said as he headed toward the door. "Make sure the windows are locked."

"As if ye care what happens to us," Muriale said. "I would nae be surprised if ye are nae the fiend who has been killin' and rapin' these women."

Alyn took great offense to her insult. A tick began to form in his jaw, and his eyes narrowed to slits.

But something flickered in those eyes of his, something Muriale couldn't name. Was it fear? Or mayhap 'twas naught more than frustration.

As angry as he was, he refused to respond in any way that would add credibility to her already disgusted opinion of who he was.

He quit the room without saying a word.

CHAPTER

# SEVENTEEN

'Twas all Alysander could do to keep from screaming.

In the dark alley, standing with Rory, Gavin, the sheriff and his men, and countless onlookers, Alysander swallowed back curses and tears. The only light came from the lit torches two of the sheriff's men carried.

Alysander's heart ached for the child as well as for her father.

The poor man was inconsolable as he attempted to get to his child. It took three of the sheriff's men to hold him back. "Let the sheriff do his work," one of the men told him.

"Alyce!" His voice was deep and filled with grief and fury. "Alyce!"

*This could be one of my daughters,* Alysander thought to himself as he stared down at the mangled body of ten-year-old Alyce McDermott.

"Please, I must take her home," Alyce's father cried out. "She needs to go home."

Magnus MacElroy was crouched down, examining the poor girl's lifeless body, taking mental notes of all that he saw. From Alysander's perspective, the sheriff was intently focused on the child and her injuries. But how he was able to block out the cries of her father, he had no earthly idea. Those cries were gut wrenching.

"Soon, John. Soon," the tallest of the sheriff's men was telling him. "I promise ye can take her home soon."

Some of the fight was diminishing in the poor man. He looked utterly defeated and despondent. John McDermott finally looked up at the man who had been talking to him. "What will I tell her mum?"

Alysander closed his eyes and took in a deep, steadying breath. He prayed that he would never have to utter those words himself.

'Twas then that he made the decision to send his daughters home. Edinburgh was far too dangerous for young women or girls. He would not risk their safety any longer. Guilt filled his gut. He had allowed his two precious daughters to help find a killer.

Now that he saw with his own eyes what this madman was capable of, he knew he could no longer allow them to help.

On the morrow, he would be sending his daughters home. He would remain to help Rory, Gavin, and the others find this brutal killer of innocent little girls.

---

After taking mental notes of the latest victim, Magnus finally allowed John McDermott to take his wee one home. Someone had been kind enough to provide a clean sheet with which to wrap the little girl in.

"Fergus, Seamus," Magnus said as he watched John lift his daughter's lifeless body into his arms. His jaw flexed tightly with barely restrained fury. "Ye go with John. The rest of ye, fan out and start talkin' to everyone who is here right now. Then knock on every door. Someone, somewhere, must have heard or seen *somethin'*."

His men quickly fell in to do as he had directed them. As soon as John McDermott and the others were out of ear shot, Gavin, Rory, and Alysander stepped forward. Huddling in closely, they began to speak in hushed, angry tones.

"We must find this man as soon as possible," Gavin said through gritted teeth.

Rory nodded his agreement. "Edinburgh cannae go on like this for much longer. The people are getting angrier with each passin' moment that this fiend is nae caught."

"Tell me somethin' I dinnae already ken," Magnus said bitterly. "I am doin' everythin' that I can. I have nae slept more than two hours a day since this began, and neither have my men."

"But there must be somethin' more we can do," Gavin ground out.

Magnus let out a frustrated breath as he raked a hand through his hair. "Aside from tearing this city down, brick by brick, I am out of ideas."

Rory crossed his arms over his chest as he stared down at his boots. "We have been tryin' to talk with the other victims," he began. "But their fathers and husbands still refuse to allow it. They will nae even speak to Muriale or Orabillis."

Magnus was confused. "Who are Muriale and Orabillis?"

"My daughters," Alysander answered. "But I am sendin' them home on the morrow."

"Home?" Rory asked, stunned with his friend's announcement. "But why? We still have more women to try to talk to."

Alysander shot him an angry glare. "Because this city is nae safe for any lass. I will nae take the risk of this madman gettin' to one of them."

Rory continued to argue in favor of the two young women stayin'. "We need their help, Alysander. Even ye agreed with our plan."

Magnus held up a hand to bring the argument to a halt. "Pardon me, but what plan?"

"What does it matter?" Alysander asked rhetorically. "They are goin' home on the morrow."

Magnus was undeterred. "Regardless of where they will be goin' on the morrow, what *was* yer plan?"

Rory answered the question, ignoring the glares his friend was giving him. "We—that is, Muriale and Orabillis—believed that mayhap the women would be more apt to talk to another woman."

Magnus glanced briefly at Alysander before turning back to Rory. "And?"

Rory shook his head in frustration. "The fathers and husbands refuse to allow anyone to speak to their daughters or wives."

"All of them refused?" Magnus asked, growing more curious by the moment.

"Those that we spoke to have. There are still three we have nae asked yet."

Magnus was silent for a long moment as he thought about the so-called plan that had been put into place. He liked the reasoning behind it and found he wasn't totally against the idea. What he couldn't comprehend was the fact that the fathers and husbands were refusing to allow their wives or daughters to speak to anyone.

"Mayhap 'tis time to be a little more forceful on the matter," he said, breaking the silence. "We must talk to these women."

Alysander's lips pursed into a hard line as he shook his head. "Ye can do it without the help of my daughters."

"How old are yer daughters?" Magnus asked.

Alysander refused to answer the question, so Rory took it upon himself to answer it. "Muriale is nine and ten. Orabillis is six and ten."

"And they volunteered to help?" Magnus asked.

"'Twas their idea," Rory replied.

Gavin finally decided to add his own opinion to the conversation. "I think Alysander is right. They need to go home."

"Ye only say that because of the humiliation Orabillis inflicted upon ye last week," Rory said.

Gavin's face turned red with anger. "Nay," he argued. "I say it because 'tis true. Edinburgh is nae safe for any young woman or little girl. Were they my daughters, I would have sent them home long before now. And I certainly would nae have allowed them to help find a madman."

Alysander looked pleased to have Gavin's agreement on the matter of sending his daughters home, even if he didn't quite believe the reasons he gave for agreeing. Aye, he might care about their safety, but Alysander couldn't help but feel that Rory's assessment was also correct.

"We need to go back to each and every woman, lass, and child and demand to speak to them," Magnus said. "Otherwise, we could be waitin' for months before we catch this man."

"I, for one, would like to see this end now," Rory said.

"Again, ye can do it without the help of my daughters," Alysander repeated.

"Nae every man here has the option to leave the city," Rory told him. "Some dinnae have anywhere else to go."

If he was hoping to appeal to Alysander's sense of honor in order to get him to change his mind, he sorely miscalculated. "I would gladly give them shelter at our keep," Alysander said. "But I cannae risk my daughters' lives. I will nae do it, and I will nae allow them to do it."

"I dinnae ken who we get to help," Magnus said. "But, one way or another, we will catch this madman, with or without aid from your daughters."

Muriale was equally as furious as her sister. Her father wanted to send them home.

Days ago, she would have jumped at the chance to go home. She'd been homesick since the day they left.

But now, the desire to help find this madman was stronger than her desire to go home. For the first time in nearly a year, Muriale felt as though she had a purpose to her life.

"Nay," she said, standing to her full height. "I will nae leave."

Her father's determination to send them home was readily apparent in his piercing glare and pursed lips. "I will nae argue with ye. With either of ye," he said. "'Tis too dangerous here. I will nae risk either of ye to this fiend."

"We are quite capable of taking care of ourselves," Orabillis replied firmly. She was now standing beside her sister. A united front against their father.

"I ken that," Alysander said, although his tone was lacking in sincerity. "But I am still sending ye home."

"I will nae go," Muriale reiterated. "I will stay and help until ye catch this murderer."

The argument continued for nearly a half an hour before their Aunt Forvelith returned home.

"What is the matter now?" she asked. The room had gone eerily silent the moment she'd stepped inside.

"Your nephew is attempting to send us home," Orabillis said, with a nod toward their father.

Forvelith's brow furrowed with confusion. "But why?" she asked, directing the question to Alysander.

Quickly, he gave her his reasons. Logical, sensical reasons. He braced himself for what he assumed would be an onslaught of protests from his most favored aunt.

"I agree," Forvelith replied. "'Tis nae safe here."

Muriale and Orabillis were stunned. They had not anticipated Forvelith's response. Each of them had expected her to side with them. "Aunt Forvelith!" Orabillis exclaimed with wide eyes. "How can ye agree with Da, when ye have nae listened to our reasons for staying?"

Forvelith smiled warmly at her. "I am sure yer reasons for stayin' are just as valid as yer da's reasons for sending ye home." She crossed the room, heading for the kitchen. "But I still agree with yer father. Edinburgh is nae safe."

Muriale couldn't remember the last time she'd felt so betrayed.

"But ye have done naught but support us, Auntie. Certainly ye can see that we must continue."

"Let the men continue with this search," Forvelith replied. She looked tired and worn out, something Muriale hadn't noticed until this very moment.

"We are just as capable as the men," Orabillis argued. "They need our help."

"I understand that ye want to help. But there comes a time when a woman must stand aside and allow a man to do the job."

Orabillis was as astounded as she was insulted. "Do ye truly believe that only men are capable of finding this lunatic? That we, as women, are too mild and meek and might faint at the mere idea of coming across this madman?"

Forvelith's patience was wearing thin. "Of course nae," she bit out angrily. "Were it anyone but a madman rapin' and killin' these poor little girls, I would argue on yer behalf. But that is nae the case. I dinnae believe ye understand just how dangerous this situation is."

Incredulous, Orabillis headed for her bedchamber. "I do understand how dangerous this is. I have personal experience with just how dangerous a man can be."

With that, she slammed the door hard, rattling the walls in the process. Aye, if anyone understood just how dangerous men could be, it was Orabillis.

---

Alysander wasn't so much angry as he was disappointed. There wasn't any time to send his daughters away. As soon as word reached Robert's ears of the most recent death, Alysander and the three knights were summoned to Castle Rock.

The sun was just beginning to peek over the horizon by the time they entered Robert's private chambers. One quick look, and Alysander knew the man hadn't slept and was furious.

"Why have ye nae found this man yet?" Robert asked. With his hands clasped behind his back, he was pacing to and fro in front of his bed.

"My liege, we are doin' everything we can to find him."

Robert stopped in his tracks and glowered angrily at Rory. "Apparently nae all, for ye still have nae caught him!"

"We have men combin' the streets, sire. Day and night. We are also tryin' to speak to the victims."

Robert unclasped his hands, his anger not ebbing in the least. "Tryin'?" His lips pursed as if the word was bitter on his tongue.

Rory was smart enough to understand 'twas a rhetorical question. His friends also understood therefore remained mute.

"I want every available man workin' on this madman's capture."

Alysander closed his eyes and held his breath for a long moment. He knew what was coming. "My liege," he began, choosing his words carefully. "I want to send my daughters home today. I can remain behind, of course, to assist. My men can escort them home."

Robert pinned him in place with an angry scowl. "Is there some other emergency I am nae aware of? One that requires yer daughters to leave the city?"

"The city is nae safe, as we all well ken. I would like to get my daughters safely away while we hunt for this madman."

Robert shook his head in disgust. "I am sure every mother and father in this city would like to get their daughters safely away, cousin. Unfortunately, they dinnae have that option." With raised brows and set jaw, he asked, "Are yer daughters, perchance, sleepin' in a barn?"

"Nay, yer grace. We are staying with my aunt."

Deep down, Alysander knew that he wouldn't be able to change his mind. However, he felt the need to at least make an effort so that, later, when his wife was killing him, he could truthfully say he tried. "If I could, I would take every female out of the city to safety, yer grace. But I can only protect my own daughters."

His king actually threw his head back and laughed, albeit with much sarcasm. "I have met yer daughters, Alysander. The younger one, Orabillis, I do believe she would kill anyone who tried to do her or her sister any harm."

'Twas a compliment, but Alysander couldn't allow his fatherly pride to get in the way.

"She very nearly killed Gavin a sennight ago," Robert said. For a moment, he did sound rather proud of that fact. "If I had a hundred men like her, we could sack England."

Rory was smiling before he realized he was doing so. One furious look from his king erased that smile in an instant.

Gavin, however, looked mad enough to bite nails in half. He didn't need to be reminded of his humiliation. He stood a bit taller, making a grand attempt at not looking offended or angry. He was failing on both accounts.

"Alysander, ye have brought a dozen able-bodied men with ye, am I correct?"

"Aye, my liege, ye are." He felt the walls of his carefully laid plan to get his daughters out of the city begin to crumble. "Three left the day we arrived, to go visit family nearby."

They were interrupted by one of the king's pages entering the room. He was escorting the sheriff inside.

"Where in the bloody hell have ye been?" Robert barked.

Magnus waited until he was in line with the other men before kneeling before their king. "My apologies, yer grace," he said before standing. "I was speakin' with the lass's parents."

Some of the heat left Robert then, his shoulders relaxing ever so slightly. He was a father and could well understand the current hell the girl's family must be going through.

"What have we learned?"

"The family lives above their shop. They are bakers, yer grace. They have four sons and a daughter." He stopped and corrected himself. "*Had* one daughter. Her name was Alyce."

Robert raised a brow to indicate he would like his sheriff to get to the bloody point and quickly.

"Apparently, the killer came in through a window at the rear of the apartment, just as he has done previously with some of the other girls."

For nearly a half an hour, Magnus gave his king all the information he had. He also divulged what Alysander, Rory, and Gavin were able to ascertain from those victims they were able to speak to.

"What do ye mean he smells clean?" Robert asked incredulously. He looked to Alysander for answers. "What does that even mean?"

Alysander cleared his throat before replying. "I think it means that the man dinnae smell like one might expect from a monster. The women also noted that it was an odd, clean smell."

"Cologne perhaps?" Gavin asked, interrupting the conversation.

"I am nae sure," Alysander replied, momentarily forgetting he was in the presence of their king. "But that is a distinct possibility. I dinnae ken why we dinnae think of that before."

"There is only one place in all of Edinburgh that I ken where one could purchase cologne," Rory interjected.

"Charles Mayhew's shop. 'Tis right off Cowgate," Magnus quickly added. His face was alight with hope and possibilities.

"He has the stuff imported from France and Italy," Rory added. "Ye can also get French silk, fine Italian leather, and the like."

"He will nae be open for a few more hours," Gavin said.

"We will nae bloody wait a few more hours," Magnus said as he headed toward the door.

"Excuse me." Robert's loud voice broke through the chatter going on betwixt the men.

Abruptly, they all stopped to face their king. Each man looked sheepishly embarrassed for having forgotten not only where they were but in whose presence.

Each man quickly apologized to Robert, bowing at their waists and begging their king's forgiveness.

"If ye have any problems getting this Charles Mayhew fellow to cooperate," Robert began in a firm voice, "bring him to me. I have no qualms about how I might extract information from the man."

After leaving the castle, Alysander sent Red John to gather all their men. While he did that, Alysander immediately set out to his aunt's home to give them all an update. There was very little time to waste and no room for any arguments. With every one of Alysander's men busy helping to find the madman, he had to trust that his daughters would do as he said. 'Twas a futile hope, but he had so few choices at the moment. He couldn't very well send his daughters home without escort.

"I must have yer word that ye will nae leave this building," Alysander said. He was standing at the door, arms crossed over his chest and his feet firmly planted.

"I give ye my word, Da, that we will nae leave. Unless, of course, we need to run an errand for Aunt Forvelith."

He was about to speak, when Muriale stopped him. "Da, we will nae leave after dark. I do believe we are relatively safe durin' the day, dinnae ye agree?"

After careful consideration, he said, "Verra well. Only durin' the day and *only* if ye are runnin' an errand for Forvelith."

"Dinnae worry, Da," Muriale said. "Ye have my word."

"And I dinnae want ye goin' anywhere near Cowgate, understand?" He hoped that neither of the young women would make any inquiries as to why they shouldn't go near it.

"Aye, Da. We will avoid it like the plague."

He glanced at both his daughters before turning to his aunt. "I mean it, Forvelith. Dinnae let them go wanderin' about the city."

"Ye have my word," Forvelith replied most seriously. "They will be under my constant watch."

Only partially satisfied with the answers and promises he had received, he opened the door to leave. He suddenly felt ill at ease. "Girls," he said as he paused to look at each of them. "I need ye to understand how serious this is."

Muriale tilted her head, her eyes narrowing with concern. "I do, Da. Truly."

There was no time left to speak. He had to meet Rory, Gavin, and the sheriff soon.

Without uttering another word, he quit the room, slowly closing the door behind him.

———

"Why does he nae want us near Cowgate?" Oddly enough, 'twas Forvelith who asked that question.

"I was wonderin' that verra thing," Orabillis said.

Orabillis began to pace about the room, lost in thought, undoubtedly plotting something dangerous.

Forvelith remained standing betwixt the dining area and the kitchen. Muriale sat on a stool by the fire, doing her best to pretend she wasn't the least bit interested in anything other than her sewing.

"Do ye think they might ken who the man is?" Forvelith asked to no one in particular. "Mayhap that is why he dinnae want us near Cowgate street."

Orabillis paused her pacing. With her brow furrowed, she studied her aunt closely for a long moment. "Have ye suddenly developed the ability to read a person's mind?" she quipped. "For I, too, was thinkin' that verra thing."

"Well, 'tis the only thing that make sense," Forvelith replied.

Without looking up from her sewing, Muriale said, "Did ye mayhap stop to think there is another victim down that way?"

Forvelith and Orabillis stared at one another for a brief moment.

"I doubt it," Forvelith said. "Else he would have said so. Besides, he killed last night, aye? I doubt he would kill again so soon."

"Well, we are dealin' with a madman," Orabillis said. "I doubt he has a limit to the number of young women he will rape or kill."

Forvelith nodded her agreement. "Aye, that is true."

"He has raped more than a dozen women that we know of, and has now killed three," Orabillis said, thinking aloud.

"Aye, but what about those we dinnae ken about?" Forvelith asked.

"What do ye mean?"

She scoffed slightly at the question. "Nae all women who are attacked or hurt report it to anyone," Forvelith said, as if everyone in the world knew it.

That piqued Muriale's interest. She sat her sewing aside and spun around. "I had nae thought of that," she admitted. She shuddered with the thought of there being more women out there who had been hurt by this man.

Silence fell between the three women. Muriale began to grow angrier and more frustrated. *How many has he actually hurt?*

"I dinnae understand why ye would nae tell someone," Orabillis said.

Forvelith thought it a strange question. "Shame? Humiliation? Fear?" she replied. "Besides, there are some who believe that any woman who is raped was askin' for it. Mayhap she was out alone after dark. Or mayhap she wore somethin' revealin'."

Orabillis's eyes grew wide with horror, and she suddenly felt quite young and naive. "Nae," she said disbelievingly. "Certainly that cannae be true."

"I keep forgettin' ye have nae been far from home before," Forvelith said with just a hint of pity in tone and expression.

Orabillis chose to ignore the pity staring back at her. "Why are men such eejits?"

"'Tis nae just men who think such things. Women are equally as guilty."

Muriale left her seat to join her aunt and sister's discussion.

"Regardless of what those fools think, we need to catch this madman. No girl or woman is safe right now."

"We?" Orabillis asked. "Dinnae ye just swear to our father that we would nae leave the house?"

"Nae. What I promised was nae to leave after dark."

"Yer point bein'?"

Muriale smile rather deviously then. "I cannae help if it gets dark *after* I leave."

---

Rory MacLeod hadn't slept well since meeting the beguiling Muriale McCullum. She was ever present in his thoughts and even more so in his dreams.

His plight was made worse these past several days when he was forced to share almost every waking hour with the beautiful woman. Mayhap *forced* wasn't the correct word. Nay, he'd volunteered for the duty and went along like a lamb to the slaughter.

Until her arrival, he had sincerely believed his entire life would be spent in service to king and country. There would be no time for frivolities such as taking a wife and having a family.

But, now, that was all he could think of.

Muriale had unwittingly turned his entire world upside down.

He didn't have time for such things, especially now, when he considered the task at hand: finding a madman.

Now, he found himself in a position he had never believed he'd be in. And he didn't like it.

He'd fallen in love.

He knew 'twas so the moment Alysander said he'd be sending Muriale and her sister home, to keep them out of harm's way. The sense of loss at the mere thought of her going away had nearly knocked him to his knees.

And when Robert denied Alysander's request to send his daughters home, he could have danced a jig.

He didn't dance. It wasn't in his nature to do so. However, he realized in that moment that there was naught he wouldn't do for Muriale or for the chance to be with her, even if it was only for a few more days.

That was another realization that irritated him to no end. *This is nae like me.*

"Are ye even listenin' to me?"

Gavin's voice broke through his quiet reverie.

Rory cleared his throat before answering. "Honestly? I was nae. Was it important?"

Gavin shook his head in frustration. Too mired in his own worries, he didn't even ask Rory where his mind was. "I said I cannae wait to catch this madman. The sooner we do, the sooner they leave, and I will never have to lay eyes on Orabillis McCullum again."

Rory grinned. He'd known Gavin since they were weans. They'd grown up together and were as close as brothers.

And not once in the past twenty-five years had any young woman gotten under Gavin's skin like Orabillis McCullum had.

Plainly put, he'd finally met his match.

"What do ye find so amusin'?" Gavin asked as he stomped down the street. They were on their way to meet the sheriff at the gaol.

"Ye must admit she is a beautiful lass," Rory said.

Gavin stopped and looked at Rory with a look of horror. "Beautiful? Have ye recently taken a blow to yer head?" He shook his head in disgust.

"I think ye are just angry because she bested ye in front of the king."

"She dinnae best me!" He exclaimed. "I was drunk. I guarantee ye that, had I been sober, it would have been *me* bestin' *her.*"

Rory didn't care to argue his point further. And if he ever admitted to his friend how he felt about Muriale, he'd never hear the end of it.

*B*loody hell!

*He hadn't meant to kill her. But she wouldn't stop crying! If she had only listened and done what he told her to do, she would now be alive.*

*Truly, it wasn't his fault she was dead. Nay, they wouldn't be able to blame him for her death. She had no one to blame but herself.*

*Of course, her parents would mourn her passing, as any good parents would do. And they would probably cry for justice on her behalf.*

*But where was the kindness or justice for him? Nay, no one even glanced his way, let alone offered even a drop of tenderness. If only the women had been kinder to him, well, Edinburgh would definitely be a far different place.*

*There hadn't been any other option for him. If they wouldn't give him what he needed, he would take what he wanted.*

*As for the little girl, Alyce. Oh! She had been a bonny little thing! But, alas, she couldn't quit her crying long enough to save her own neck.*

*If only she had listened.*

*If only she hadn't looked at him with such horror.*

*He had tried to explain to her why he was doing what he was doing, but she didn't listen.*

*Truly, he hated killing her. He didn't want to kill anyone. All he wanted was to exact his revenge on all the women who had done him wrong over the years.*

*And the little girls, well, if he ruined them now, they wouldn't grow up to be snooty, arrogant wenches.*

*If only she had listened.*

# EIGHTEEN

Charles Mayhew didn't like being woken in the middle of the night. Whoever was pounding on his front door was going to be in for a rude awakening themselves.

With his sword in one hand, he made his way down the stairs and across his shop. He hadn't bothered to tie his robe shut. It swirled behind him as he stomped across the floor. "Stop yer banging!" he shouted angrily.

He doubted he could be heard over the noise they were making. "Charles Mayhew!" A deep voice boomed from outside.

Angrily, he leaned his sword down against the wall so that he could remove the wooden bar. No sooner had he lifted the latch than the door was flung open from the outside.

Momentarily stunned, he jumped back, leaving his sword behind.

"What in the bloody hell is goin' on?" he shouted at the group of men who were now barging into his business. Scanning the group, his eyes quickly found the sheriff amongst the crowd.

Now he was as confused as he was angry. "MacElroy? What in the bloody hell are ye doin' here at this hour?"

"We need to talk to ye about yer colognes," Magnus said as he stepped to the front of the crowd.

"My colognes?" Charles was incredulous. "Have ye lost yer mind? Come back after I open, and we can talk all ye want to about colognes."

"Nay, we will talk *now*," Magnus said. "'Tis about the madman rapin' and killin' innocents."

Mayhew's bushy eyebrows raised in abject surprise. "Certainly ye dinnae think *I* am that man!" He was clearly insulted. "Get out of my shop now."

Magnus took in a deep breath. "Calm down, Charles. We dinnae believe 'tis ye."

Charles stuttered and stammered his reply. "I would think nae!"

"But I think ye might ken *who* this madman is."

"Me?" He was back to being insulted and stunned. "I can assure ye, Magnus, that I dinnae share my company with men of that ilk."

"We think he might be a customer," Magnus explained.

"Ye cannae blame me for who I might sell cologne to," Charles argued. "'Tis nae like I can ask my customers, 'Are ye a killer or a rapist?'"

Magnus had reached the ends of his patience. "Will ye just shut up and listen?"

Taken aback by the sheriff's harsh tone, Charles Mayhew stood a bit taller. Before he could voice any further arguments or opinions, Magnus said, "Let us go into the back and talk."

He didn't wait for Charles's agreement or permission. With Rory, Gavin, and Alyn right behind him, Magnus headed to the back of the shop.

Bewildered, Charles stood frozen as a statue.

Magnus pulled open the curtain that led to a small room Mayhew used as an office. He paused then turned and looked at the bedraggled man. "Well?"

Magnus felt a headache forming at the base of his skull. Frustration and lack of sleep formed into a rather large knot.

They'd been speaking with Mayhew for over an hour. Thus far, the man was of very little help.

"If I knew the scent, then I could tell ye who might have purchased it," Charles told him for the fifth time.

"Do ye sell a lot of colognes?" Rory asked. He was standing in the doorway, arms crossed over his chest, one leg crossed over the other.

"Believe it or nae, I do," Charles replied indignantly. There wasn't a doubt in anyone's minds that the man didn't want to be here talking to anyone. He was growing tired and quite weary of all the questions.

"But how many *men* do ye sell it to?" Rory asked. He, too, was growing tired and was quite eager to get out of the shop.

Charles was seated on a small table across from Magnus. He turned to glance over his shoulder, looking rather annoyed. "As I have told ye a dozen times already, I sell dozens of bottles each week to dozens of people—men and women."

Magnus let out a slow breath as he scratched his temple with a crooked index finger. "We ken that ye have a successful business, Charles. What we would like to ken is if any of the men you sell yer scented water to seem out of place or odd. Do any of them have an accent that would make ye think they are from the far north?"

"And as I have told ye repeatedly, nay. No one stands out to me."

Gavin was clearly just as frustrated as everyone else. "I say we just take all the bottles of cologne and have our victims smell them."

Charles jumped to his feet, appalled at the thought. "Ye cannae just take all my colognes! I will nae allow it."

Alyn put a hand on the man's shoulder and shoved him, hard, back onto his seat. "Easy on, Mayhew. We are nae tryin' to steal from ye. We are simply tryin' to find a killer."

Magnus looked up at Gavin. "That might nae be a bad idea, MacKendrick."

Gavin raised a brow in question.

"But instead of takin' the scents, we should bring the women *here*," Magnus said.

Every set of eyes in the cramped space looked at him. Clarity dawned in the three knights.

"But will their menfolk allow them to come here?" Rory asked.

Magnus got to his feet. "They will nae be given a choice."

After a lengthy discussion on just how they might help capture the madman, Muriale, Orabillis, and their aunt decided it would be best to try to sleep. Exhausted, Muriale fell into the bed and slept like the dead. Orabillis was equally exhausted and fell asleep before her head hit her pillow.

They were awakened a few hours later by their aunt. Normally, both young women would have groused and complained and begged for more sleep. But there was much to do this day.

Hurriedly, they rushed to get dressed. Muriale chose to wear her green woolen gown. After washing her face and teeth, she twisted her hair into one long braid that fell down her back.

Orabillis decided it might behoove her to dress a bit more femininely, only because most people were put off by a woman in tunic and trews. If she made herself a bit more presentable, she might have better luck gaining cooperation.

However, she had enough weapons for ten men hidden under and within her dark-blue gown. Dirks, knives, and *sgian dubhs* were tucked into her woolens, her boots, the pouch at her waist, and even the sleeves of her dress.

Typically, Muriale would have rolled her eyes and made some off-hand comment on her sister's need to overdo things, but not today. She had a few weapons of her own strategically placed upon her person. They were, after all, on the hunt for a very dangerous man.

"I wish I could come with ye," Forvelith told them.

"Ye have a business to run," Muriale said with a smile. "But I promise we will come back or send word, should we need ye."

Concern was etched into her brow. "I am suddenly overcome with guilt," she admitted.

"Guilt?" Orabillis asked.

"Aye. I promised yer da that I would nae let ye get into any trouble."

A grin spread across Orabillis's face. "We are nae goin' to get into any trouble, Auntie. We are merely going back to the butcher's for ye."

A lie was a lie was a lie. All three women fervently believed that lying was a sin. However, they each also believed Alysander had left them with no other choice.

"Now, ye remember where ye are goin'?" Forvelith asked as the girl's donned their cloaks.

"Aye, to the butcher's," Orabillis said with a mischievous grin.

"And then to see Phoebe MacRay."

While Muriale didn't know all the names of each of the victims, she had memorized a few. One of those names, her aunt Forvelith had recognized as one of her clients: Phoebe MacRay.

"Ye just tell her I sent ye," Forvelith told them for at least the fifth time. "She will help ye if she kens who ye are."

"Aye, we ken," Orabillis said as she opened the door. "And I promise ye, I will nae let anything happen to Muriale."

Forvelith smiled wanly. "Or yourself."

Orabillis gave her a wink. "Or myself."

Phoebe MacRay had managed to stay out of the gaol for a fortnight. She'd done her best to avoid the sheriff, his men, and the three bloody knights who had come to see her all those many days ago.

Phoebe was old enough and wise enough to know that the world was neither a safe place nor a fair one. It was filled with all manner of people, some who wished to do naught but bring harm and pain just for the sake of it and others who wouldn't say shite if they had a mouthful of it. She despised most people but none more so than the elite arses who looked down their noses at her.

'Twasn't her fault she lived the way she did. Orphaned at age eight, she was shuffled off to an orphanage in Inverness. At age three and ten, she married the first man who had asked her.

A year later, they were living in Edinburgh and looking forward to a quiet life together. Then the fool up and died on her a few years ago.

With no family or friends she could rely upon, she did whatever she could to survive. Eventually, that meant selling her body to strangers.

Circumstances or fate, whatever one might choose to call it, had made her a hard woman. No longer did she lie awake at night, wishing for someone to rescue her, for someone to whisk her away from this city and this life.

Hope was a pointless feeling. Hope didn't feed you or keep a roof over your head.

Hope was for fools.

Even the madman who had attacked her had told her so. "Dinnae scream. Dinnae make a sound. Dinnae hope that I will stop or spare yer life. Hope is for fools, dinnae ye ken."

What did it matter? He was just one more man. Just one more man who used her for his own pleasure and purpose. That was how she had to look at it, or else she'd lose her mind.

He hadn't killed her. There were days she wasn't sure if that was a blessing or a curse. Usually, her thinking leaned towards the latter.

Try as she might, however, she couldn't shake the memory of that awful night. To this very day, she could still feel his hands wrapped around her neck. She could still hear the sound of his voice. And his smell. 'Twas burned in her memory. She'd carry that all the way to the gates of hell.

Hope was for fools.

Heaven was only for the righteous.

Phoebe let out a heavy sigh as she lay on her pallet. She shared a small, dank, dingy room over a tavern with seven other whores. One small room with one tiny window and a leaky roof. They barely had room to move, which oftentimes made for harsh words and arguments.

Crammed in like the cattle the farmers brought down Cowgate Street, they all were. She hated this place, but 'twas better than sleeping in an alley. Lord knew she'd done enough of that over the years.

"Sophie! Quit yer snorin'!" 'Twas Mable Smith yelling again. She and Sophie were like sisters; they loved and protected one another, but most of the time, they fought.

Mable took her pillow and hit Sophie in her chest with it. "I said stop yer snorin'!"

Still half asleep, a bleary eyed Sophie bolted upright. "What the bloody hell are ye on about?" Her voice was scratchy with sleep.

"Because ye were snorin' again, ye auld whore."

Sophie grunted and rubbed her eyes. "Says ye."

"Says everyone from here to Inverness and back!" Mable shouted. "Ye snore like a drunkard."

"But I dinnae drink. Ye ken that."

"Shut up and go to sleep!" 'Twas Claire Montgomery's voice calling for quiet.

"I was asleep until Mable woke me," Sophie politely pointed out.

Phoebe found their conversation almost amusing. Almost. "Will the lot of ye shut yer gobs?"

"Och! Ye have woken the queen," Mable said. Her voice dripped with sarcasm.

Most of the whores she knew referred to her as the queen. Phoebe had never been able to figure out why. She was a whore just like the rest of them. Never did she put on airs or pretend she was better than any of them.

Soon, everyone was awake, arguing and cursing like the auld whores they were.

Their arguing stopped abruptly when a knock came at their door. Everyone turned in unison, as if there was a rabid bear trying to gain entry.

Another soft rap came moments later.

"Who do ye suppose it is?" Sophie whispered.

"I doubt it's the sheriff," Mable whispered back. "He pounds on the door as hard as he pounds on Claire," she cackled softly.

"The landlord?"

Phoebe let out a heavy sigh, tossed her blanket aside, and got to her feet. "I swear, ye all are daft." She had to climb over Margie MacCoy to get to the door.

"What if it's the fiend!" Sophie exclaimed in a loud whisper.

Phoebe rolled her eyes. "He dinnae knock."

"How do ye ken?" Sophie asked. She wasn't the brightest of lasses.

Phoebe ignored her and opened the door. She was quite surprised to find two very pretty young women standing on the other side.

The last time Phoebe saw her roommates move as quickly as they did at the sight of the two young women was when the sheriff and his men came to raid the alley where they worked. The only difference now is they didn't look terrified. Nay, they were staring at the women as if each of them had three arms and legs apiece.

"Who the hell are ye?" Phoebe asked, not the least bit interested in their answer. *Probably some good Christian women come to save the poor, downtrodden whores from a life of sin.*

The pretty brunette answered with a warm smile. "I am Muriale McCullum. This is my sister Orabillis."

"If the nuns sent ye, ye can go back and tell them they can shove hot coals up their arses," Phoebe said as she tried to close the door.

Muriale giggled. "The nuns have nae sent us."

Phoebe gave them a quick look up and down. "Ye dinnae look like whores lookin' for work. I think ye'd be better off with the king's soldiers. This is nae a place for ye."

Muriale and Orabillis smiled at each other. "We're nae here to find work."

"Then, be gone with ye," Phoebe said as she tried to close the door.

"Forvelith Carruthers sent us."

———

Muriale had chanced a glance over the woman's shoulder. She could just make out shadows of women in the darkness. As soon as she mentioned Forvelith's name, hushed whispers and murmurs broke from within.

The room was dark, save for one lonely, dust-filled shaft of light coming in through the broken window. The smell coming from within burned nostrils, but she refused to show them any pity. Not because they didn't deserve it but because she didn't want to insult anyone within.

"We are here to see Phoebe MacRay," she said.

More murmurs of surprise filtered in through the dank, musty air.

The woman who answered the door gave them another up-and-down glance. There was so much distrust in her sad, blue eyes.

"I am Phoebe MacRay," she said. "And, again, I ask ye what the bloody hell ye want."

Orabillis tilted her head to one side, her brows furrowed with curiosity. "'Tis a conversation best done in private."

"I have no time for the likes of ye," Phoebe said as she once again tried to shut the door.

Orabillis leaned in and whispered into the woman's ear. "'Tis about the bloody bastard who attacked ye."

Understanding set in as Phoebe stood to her full height. A moment later, she grabbed her cloak from the peg by the door and hurried out into the hallway.

"I dinnae want to speak here," she said as she headed toward the staircase.

Neither sister said a word as they followed Phoebe down the stairs and out into the morning light.

---

Muriale didn't like being in the cemetery, even if it was during the daylight hours. There was something eery and spooky about the place. The trees swayed as the wind howled through the leaves, adding to the sensation.

The three women stood near a small headstone made of granite. The tall green grass swayed to and fro in the gentle breeze.

"So, Forvelith is yer aunt?"

"Aye," Muriale replied. "She is my father's aunt."

Phoebe pursed her lips together as she studied each of the women closely. "I have never seen ye at her shop."

"We are nae from Edinburgh," Orabillis said.

"Why did Forvelith send ye to me?"

"We have been helpin' to find the man who attacked ye," Muriale said. "We thought mayhap ye could help us to find him."

Phoebe shook her head in dismay. "I already told those three knights everything I ken."

"We ken that," Muriale said. "But we were hopin' ye might talk to us. Ye ken how men can be."

Phoebe took in a deep breath, her lips drawn into a hard line. "What the bloody hell is that supposed to mean?"

"All I meant was that every woman over the age of ten can tell ye that, sometimes, men only half listen," Muriale said, hoping to calm the woman's ire.

Orabillis snorted a giggle. "On a good day, men are naught but eejits."

Phoebe quirked a brow, still uncertain just what she should make of these two young women.

"Do ye remember telling Rory about the way the man smelled?" Muriale asked, steering the conversation back to the matter at hand.

"Aye, I do," Phoebe replied.

"Would ye recognize it if ye were to smell it again?"

Phoebe crossed her arms over her chest and glowered. "Why?"

"Forvelith told us that there is only one place in all of Edinburgh where one can purchase scents."

Phoebe chortled in derision. "Charles Mayhew's shop."

"Ye ken him?"

She quirked a brow. "There is nae a whore in Edinburgh who dinnae ken Charles Mayhew."

Muriale and Orabillis exchanged curious glances.

"And, before ye ask, he was nae a customer," Phoebe said. "I would eat mud before I let that man climb on top of me."

"I'm afraid I dinnae understand," Muriale said.

"He is one of those high and mighty, self-righteous pigs who thinks he is better than anyone else. 'Tis because of him that we cannae work near Cowgate anymore."

"How did he manage that?" Orabillis asked.

"He hired some of the sheriff's men to run us all away," Phoebe replied. Venom all but dripped from her tongue. "The bloody bastard. I still have the scar on my arms from those bloody sons of whores."

"A scar? From what?" Muriale was appalled and not certain she wanted to know the answer.

"Charles Mayhew had them whip us."

The sisters looked positively mortified.

"Aye, that's right. They had horsewhips. Beat the bloody hell out of us and warned us ne'er to come near that part of town again. Poor Mable could nae sit for a week."

Instantly, Muriale found herself despising Charles Mayhew, even though she'd never set eyes on him. Anger bubbled up in the pit of her stomach with the images of those poor women being beaten. *I hope there is a special place in hell for the likes of those men.*

Muriale was beginning to second guess their original plan. Mayhap it wasn't such a good idea to ask Phoebe to go to the shop and see if she could identify the scent.

"I hope Charles Mayhew and his men rot in hell," Phoebe said. "I only wish I could be the one to send them there."

"Ye will have to beat me to it," Orabillis said firmly.

Niether Phoebe nor Muriale doubted she meant what she said.

---

"I ken that ye already talked to Rory, Gavin, and Alyn, but we would like to ask ye a few more questions," Muriale said. She would get around to mentioning a possible visit to Mayhew's shop after.

"Did he by any chance take a lock of yer hair?"

It was clear she was confused by the question. "Nay," she said, drawing the word out slowly.

Muriale twisted her lips into a knot of frustration. Mayhap the taking of the hair was not as important as she previously believed.

"But he did take my bracelet," Phoebe said. "The bloody bastard."

"Yer bracelet?" Orabillis asked.

"Aye. 'Twas nae worth anythin' to anyone but me," she replied. "Just a bit of leather twisted together. It had been my da's."

Muriale and Orabillis exchanged glances with one another. Another token, perchance?

"He cut it clean from my wrist," Phoebe said. "Told me he was takin' it as a token of our time together."

Muriale and Orabillis were stunned, their eyes opening wide with astonishment. "Did he whistle when he left?"

"Nay, he just sang a bawdy tune, the bloody bastard."

***

*A man who rapes women—kills some but nae all—takes a token, then whistles or sings as he walks away? To say the least, Muriale was perplexed.*

"Madness only makes sense to the mad." Orabillis was thinking aloud and having just as much difficulty sorting out all the information.

Phoebe laughed her agreement. "Ain't that the truth."

A gust of wind came up, wrapping skirts around legs. A storm was coming up from the south. "We better leave before we get caught in the rain," Muriale said. She received no argument.

They walked Phoebe back to her home, at a brisk pace. The usually crowded streets were thinning out. It seemed they weren't the only ones who didn't want to get caught in the rain.

"I wish I could be there when ye catch this madman," Phoebe

said. "Och! What I would nae do to have a chance to kick him in his bollocks."

Muriale couldn't stop herself from laughing, not just at what Phoebe had said but how she had said it. The woman was a force to be reckoned with.

"There is something ye could do to help speed up that process," Orabillis said.

"What would that be?"

"Ye could go to Charles Mayhew's shop with us."

Phoebe came to an abrupt halt, nearly colliding with Muriale. "Are ye mad?"

"Hear me out," Orabillis said. "Ye have said ye would never forget the way he smelled, aye?"

Her brow knotted, and she seemed to be bracing herself for something awful to happen. "Aye. 'Tis a smell I will never forget."

"We thought that, if we took ye to Mayhew's shop, ye might recognize the scent."

"So, what do ye plan on doin'? Sniffin' every man in Edinburgh?"

Orabillis chuckled softly. "Nay. But Mayhew might remember the names of those he sold the scent to."

Slowly, clarity began to dawn. "And then ye can round those men up and talk to them."

"Aye," Muriale said, offering her a hopeful smile. "It would help tremendously with our list of suspects."

"Ye have a list?" Phoebe asked with a raised brow.

Orabillis was just as curious. "I was nae aware we had a list."

"We do," Muriale said. "And it contains the name of every man in Edinburgh at this point. If we could narrow that down to even a hundred men, it would be helpful."

"I suppose 'tis a better plan than none," Orabillis said.

Just then, the sky turned gray, the color of slate. They picked up their skirts and headed down the street. Hopefully, they would be able to make it to Cowgate Street before the sky opened up.

# NINETEEN

They were forced out of the rain and into a little bakery a short distance from their destination. Thankfully, they weren't completely drenched.

An older man with arms the size of tree trunks and a chest so broad his neck couldn't be seen stood behind a counter. He had fuzzy gray hair, dark-brown eyes, and a scar over his left eye.

"What can I get for ye," he asked.

"Nothin'," Phoebe said. "We only want out of the rain."

Before the man could argue, Muriale stepped forward. "We would each like one of yer small brown breads, please. And would ye have any butter or jam to go with it?"

"This is a bakery, nae a public house or an inn," he retorted. His eyes were locked onto Phoebe.

"Verra well," Muriale said, offering him her warmest smile. "We will take just the bread. And if it would nae be too much of an inconvenience, kind sir, might we stay here until the rain lets up?"

Carefully, he scrutinized the three women. "One of ye, I ken," he said, looking angrily toward Phoebe. "But ye two... I have nae seen ye before."

"We are here visiting my aunt. Forvelith Carruthers."

His countenance changed from one of irritation to one of delight at the mere mention of her aunt's name.

"Never a finer woman e'er graced God's earth," he said. He actually smiled before turning back to Phoebe. "I feel I should warn ye about spendin' yer time with that one." He nodded in her direction. "She will do naught but ruin yer reputation and get ye into trouble."

Phoebe was about to give the auld man a tongue lashing he would never forget, but Orabillis stepped in front of her.

"I dinnae ken who ye are, baker man, but I will nae have ye talkin' about my cousin, Forvelith's niece, in such a cruel manner." For emphasis, she placed her hand on the hilt of her sword.

"Forvelith's niece?" He was incredulous.

"Aye," Muriale said. "Now, would you please give us our bread?"

Were it not a deluge of rain outside, Muriale would have given the man a piece of her mind and left without doing any business with him. He grabbed a piece of cloth and started to pull the bread from the basket.

Orabillis apparently didn't care about the rain. "Nay," she said, her tone laced with derision. "I will nae do business with a man who insults our family."

He stopped and stared at her, the bit of cloth dangling from one hand, his fist around the loaf of bread. "I dinnae insult ye."

"Nay, but ye insulted my cousin, Forvelith's niece. Ye will nae be gettin' our coin today. I would rather scrounge through a dung heap for a bit of food than to eat bread baked by such an uncaring auld man such as ye."

With that, she spun on her heels, grabbed Phoebe by the arm, and left the bakery.

Stunned, it took a moment before Muriale could move her feet to catch up to them.

A few doors down, they found a tavern for refuge from the rain. Hopefully, no one here would insult Phoebe or Orabillis. Muriale was soaked to the bone.

Puddles of water formed at their feet as large droplets fell from their cloaks. Poor Phoebe had naught but an old worn shawl to keep the rain off. It hadn't worked. She very much resembled a kitten who had fallen into a bucket of water.

"Come, let us get close to the fire," Muriale said. They made their way through the crowded place, with Muriale leading the way.

She didn't notice the men staring at them as they wound their way to a table near the large hearth. There were only a few spots left at one of the long tables.

"I suppose beggars cannae be choosers, aye?" Muriale said as they sat down. The corner was dark and rather cold, but it was better than running through the downpour out of doors.

They weren't left alone for more than a few moments before a short, portly man approached. "Can I buy ye lovely lasses a mug of ale?"

Muriale closed her eyes and prayed Orabillis wouldn't take insult to the man's offer. "Nay, but thank ye kindly," Muriale said.

Phoebe looked confused. Had she been alone, she would have asked for more than a mug of ale. She would have gotten a bowl of stew out of the auld fool before taking him into the alley to return the kindness.

He left, looking insulted. Muriale gave a slow shake of her head. Before she could comment on anything, another man soon approached, a few years younger and a few inches taller than the previous fellow. "Good afternoon, ladies."

"Go. Away." Orabillis's words were firm, clipped, and left no doubt at all to how she felt about his intrusion. "We have our own coin to buy our own drinks and meal."

Taken aback, his mouth fell open. "I was only tryin' to be courteous."

Ever the peacemaker, Muriale said, "That is awfully kind of ye, but we are fine, thank you."

"And we dinnae want any company," Orabillis said.

Insulted, the man walked away, grumbling about ungrateful women.

"Really, Orabillis," Muriale said. "Ye could learn a bit about diplomacy."

"And ye could learn to be less polite."

Phoebe leaned over the table to speak to them. "I dinnae have any coin for ale," she whispered. "Let the next man buy me one, aye?"

"We will pay for yer ale and yer meal," Muriale said. "That is, if anyone comes to take our order."

Phoebe sat back and shrugged her shoulders. "Man or woman, I care nae. I just want a bit to drink and eat."

Muriale's eyes grew wide in horror. Orabillis grinned and shook her head at her sister's response.

"Nay!" she exclaimed, perhaps a bit too loudly. Lowering her voice, she said, "Phoebe, no. That is, I mean, we dinnae expect—" It was a struggle to find the right words. She'd never been in a situation like this before.

"Muriale, calm yerself," Orabillis said, still grinning at her discomfort. Turning to Phoebe, she said, "Ye dinnae have to earn this meal. Remember? We are cousins. And cousins take care of one another."

---

M uriale was still flustered when the barmaid finally appeared. They ordered ale and meat pies, the only thing available to eat.

"I dinnae remember the last time anyone paid for a meal who

dinnae expect anything in return," Phoebe said after the barmaid left. "It had to have been before me parents died."

Muriale felt a pang of sadness for her. "When did they pass?"

"I was eight," she replied. "Was sent to an orphanage in Inverness."

Muriale was confused. "Dear lord! Dinnae tell me ye had to—"

Phoebe smiled and rolled her eyes. "Nay. I dinnae experience my fall from grace until a few years ago, after my husband died."

Muriale couldn't help but feel a tremendous sense of pity towards her. How sad to lose your parents, then to lose your husband. And to be raised in an orphanage, to boot.

"Dinnae pity me," Phoebe said. Pursing her lips, she pretended not to be quite as offended as she truly was.

"I am so sorry," Muriale said.

"She asked ye nae to pity her," Orabillis pointed out.

"I need no one's pity, least of all from ye."

Surprised, Muriale said, "From me? What did I do?"

Phoebe turned to Orabillis, ignoring Muriale's question. "Or ye, *cousin.*"

Orabillis didn't appear at all bothered by the woman's anger. "I apologize."

'Twas as if the two women were having a private conversation that only they could understand. Muriale hadn't felt this dumb in a very long while. "Can ye explain what the two of ye are talkin' about?"

"She is mad that I called her our cousin and Forvelith's niece."

"But why would ye be upset over that?"

"Because she dinnae need us pretendin' she is anythin' but what and who she is."

How was her younger sister so much wiser than she? She felt even more foolish. "I am verra sorry, Phoebe. We only meant to help."

Phoebe snorted derisively. "How could ye ken anythin', raised as ye were."

"I think ye are under the delusion that our lives have been naught but easy," Muriale replied. "Nothin' could be further from the truth."

"Truly?" Phoebe asked, raising one red brow. "Were ye forced to sell yer body just to survive?"

Ashamed, Muriale felt her face grow warm. "Nay, I wasn't'."

"Our lives were difficult in other ways," Orabillis said. "But we will all agree yers was far more difficult. And, for that, my sister and I are most humbly sorry."

"Again, I dinnae need yer pity."

"'Tis nay pity," Orabillis said. "'Tis sorrow."

"Sorrow?"

"Aye. Were ye truly our cousin, yer life would be inherently different. That is what pains me. Ye were nae given a chance or a choice."

They ate their meal in silence. Thankfully, they weren't bothered by any more men wishing to partake of their company.

Muriale paid the barmaid and thanked her for her hard work. She had to stand up in order to look out the window to see if it was still raining.

Unfortunately, it was, but not with the same ferocity as before. "Mayhap we will wait a bit longer before heading out."

"Do ye still wish to visit Charles Mayhew?" Orabillis asked.

"I think we should," Muriale said. "As long as Phoebe is up to it."

"I am," Phoebe replied.

Muriale couldn't help but think the meal had done the woman a world of good. She decided against asking if that was the case.

"But I warn ye, he might nae let me into his shop, the eejit." She shivered as if she were disgusted with the mere thought of seeing the man. "That fool believes he is better than everyone."

Orabillis smiled deviously. "He will nae be thinkin' that by the time we are done with him."

———

Everything Phoebe said about Charles Mayhew was nothing short of the truth. If anything, she might have grossly understated the truth.

Dressed as if he were royalty, with a silk tunic and fine leather trews, the man was as arrogant as the day was long. Rings adorned his fingers, and heavy gold chains draped around his neck. Were he not an arrogant prig, he could be considered a handsome fellow, but his nasty personality made him an ugly man.

"I dinnae care what ye want," Mayhew told them. He was puffing out his chest, his nose lifted as if there was an unpleasant, foul smell filling the room.

Orabillis despised the man the moment he opened his mouth. The more he spoke, the more her dislike of him intensified. "Verra well," she said with a shrug of indifference. "Muriale? Phoebe? Please, send word to uncle Robert that Mr. Mayhew refuses to cooperate. He and Euphemia dinnae leave for another few days."

At the mention of Robert and Euphemia, Mayhew's attitude changed from impudence to doubt. "Are ye tryin' to tell me that our king is yer uncle?" He shook his head in utter disbelief.

"Nay, he is nae our uncle," Orabillis said. "He is our father's cousin. But he does like us to call him Uncle."

From doubt to surprise in the blink of an eye, he stammered, fighting for the correct response.

Muriale and Phoebe played along with Orabillis's ruse and headed for the door.

"Wait!" Charles called out to them.

When Muriale turned around he asked, "Does she speak the truth?"

"Of course she speaks the truth. Are ye accusin' my sister of lyin'?"

He opened and closed his mouth several times as he tried to regain some semblance of composure. After a lengthy moment of stammering, he said, "There is nae need to get the king involved."

Orabillis glanced over her shoulder at her sister and smiled victoriously. Turning back to Mayhew, she said, "I will be sure to let Uncle Robert ken just how helpful ye have been."

---

After more than a half an hour of smelling the different scents Charles Mayhew offered, Phoebe was unable to find the proper one. "My head is beginning to spin," she said. "They are all starting to smell the same."

"I have no more," Charles told her. "This is everythin' I offer."

Muriale and Orabillis were discouraged by their lack of progress. "At least we tried," Muriale said.

"I am verra sorry," Phoebe said. She was just as disheartened as they were.

"Dinnae fash yerself," Muriale told her. "We will still find him. I ken we will."

Orabillis wasn't nearly as certain as her sister. Still, she didn't want Phoebe to feel badly for not being able to find the cologne.

"Like I told the others, I sell a few bottles of scents a week. Sometimes more, sometimes less."

"What others?" Muriale asked.

"The knights that were here. They got me out of a sound sleep before the sun was even up."

Muriale let out a quick breath. "We are of like minds, it seems," she said to Orabillis.

"Apparently so," she replied.

"Would it behoove us to bring in one of the others?" Orabillis asked.

"Nay," Muriale replied. "If Phoebe could nae find it, I doubt they will."

They thanked Mayhew and stepped out into the early afternoon air. The torrential downpour was gone. In its place, just a drizzle. The kind of annoying rain somewhere betwixt an actual raindrop and a heavy mist.

"What now?" Muriale asked.

"I fear I must leave the two of ye," Phoebe said.

"We shall walk ye back to yer home," Muriale said. 'Twas the least they could do after forcing her to spend the last hour in the presence of Charles Mayhew.

Phoebe studied both women for a time. "I have never met the likes of ye before. Well, other than Forvelith. She is one of the few people who ever treat me with any kind of respect."

"I fear I dinnae ken how to treat anyone any differently," Muriale said. "I treat others the way I would like to be treated."

Phoebe snorted with derision. "I wish more people were like ye. What a better world this one would be."

---

*They are getting' too close to the truth. Far too close to discoverin' who I am. If I am nae careful, they will figure it out and thwart my plans.*

*I must be more careful. I have far too much work left to do.*

*I ken they will eventually catch me. Nothing good lasts forever, after all. The thrill of the chase is half the fun.*

*They walk by me, without taking any notice. No one sees me. No one notices. There is something to be said for plainness. Plainness leads to anonymity, which is exactly what I want.*

*I ken I play with death every time I take a lass. But I dinnae care.*

*In the end, we all die. None of us are gettin' out of this world alive.*

CHAPTER

# TWENTY

ith Phoebe left off at her home, they decided to head back to Forvelith's. "I am soaked to the bone," Muriale said. "I would like to get out of these damp clothes."

Orabillis couldn't argue against it. "Mayhap we will see Da and tell him what we learned—or didn't learn, rather."

"I still think 'twas a good idea," Muriale replied.

"Aye, it was. Mayhap this lunatic purchased the cologne from somewhere else."

"According to Forvelith, Mayhew's is the only shop in town that sells colognes." Muriale reminded her.

"But he is nae the only person in all of Scotia who sells it. Mairi did say the man sounded like he was from the north."

Muriale had thought about that but refused to give up on at least making the attempt. It *had* been a good idea, even if it hadn't led them any closer to the man's identity.

The heavy mist began to lift, and gray skies gave way to bluer ones. Still, the glimpse of the sun didn't truly lift their spirits.

They were not far from Forvelith's when Orabillis began to feel

203

that someone was watching them, and she couldn't shake the sensation.

It didn't take long for Muriale to notice her sister's silence and the change in her bearing or demeanor. Orabillis had stood taller, her hand resting on the hilt of her sword as she began to scan their surroundings. It hadn't happened all at once, those changes in her demeanor. If Muriale hadn't known her sister, she wouldn't even have noticed. The hair on the nape of her neck stood up, and a chilling sense of warning traced up and down Muriale's spine.

"What is the matter?" Muriale asked, lowering her voice to a more conspiratorial tone.

"I think someone is followin' us."

Muriale resisted the urge to turn around to check for herself. She was thankful for her sister's ability to sense danger, for she certainly lacked that gift.

"Let us slip into the miller's," Orabillis whispered, "and see what he does."

---

The miller's was a very large, spacious shop. A long counter stood near the back of the space, filled with scales, bags, and various other milling accouterments. Muriale went to the counter, pretending to be interested in the various flours available.

Orabillis pretended to look around near the front of the shop. Patiently, she waited for whomever it was who had been following them to walk by, hoping for a glimpse.

Her patience began to wane after long moments went by with no sign of the individual.

Muriale purchased the smallest amount of flour the miller had to offer before meeting her sister near the door.

"Did ye see anyone?"

"Nay," Orabillis replied. She was more than just a bit concerned.

Mayhap the interloper was waiting for them to exit. She caught a glimpse of the small bag of flour in her sister's hand. "What did ye buy that for?"

"I wanted it to look as though we had intended to come in." Muriale thought it a sound ruse, no matter her sister's opinion.

Orabillis nodded approvingly before leading the way back to the street. As she glanced around, she caught a glimpse of a man to her left.

He was doing his best to feign interest in whatever was displayed in the window of one of the shops. As soon as he saw Orabillis, he turned away rather quickly.

'Twas Moris Desmond.

---

Orabillis led them in the opposite direction. If her instincts were correct, he'd be following them soon enough.

"'Tis that Moris Desmond fellow," she whispered to her sister.

Muriale was confused by that bit of information. "Certainly ye dinnae think he is following us?"

"I certainly do think that," she replied rather drolly. "And I will prove it."

They crossed the street and turned north. At the moment, the streets were nearly deserted. Large puddles were scattered hither and yon, which made it a bit more difficult to traverse the street.

Hanging from the side of the building was a wooden sign swaying in the wind: *Mrs. Keith's Flower Shop*.

Orabillis stopped abruptly to turn to look through the large window, pretending to be interested in the flowers displayed within.

Moris Desmond was right behind them.

As soon as they stopped, he ducked into another establishment.

"He would make a horrible spy," Orabillis quipped.

"Are ye certain 'tis him?"

"Of course I am certain," Orabillis whispered harshly. "And I intend to find out just what he is about."

———

Muriale didn't like the idea that a man she thought to be a gentleman was following them as if he were some sort of spy. While she didn't know anything more about the man other than his name, he had certainly made her believe he was naught more than a nice man.

"I wonder why he is following us." She was keeping her voice low so as not to be overheard.

"Because he is the fiend who has been attacking the young girls," Orabillis ground out.

Muriale didn't hold the same level of certainty as her sister on that matter. Then again, Muriale didn't possess the same ability as she did when it came to these things.

"We should find Da," she said. "He will want to ken about this."

"If he thinks we have found him out, he might make a run for it," Orabillis worried aloud.

"He will only do that *if* he is the lunatic we have been lookin' for."

Orabillis was more than just a bit surprised by her sister's comment. "Why else would he be followin' us?"

It had been intended as a rhetorical question. However, Muriale didn't take it that way. "Mayhap he likes us?"

Orabillis hung her head in shame. "Truly, Muriale. How can ye be so daft?"

"I am nae daft," she replied. "Mayhap he is just shy."

"If Moris Desmond is shy, I will eat my own boot.

Muriale felt herself growing frustrated by the conversation. "Either way, we need to let Rory and the others ken."

The clouds decided at that particular moment to roll in like Highlanders invading England. One moment, the sun was shining, and the next, 'twas nearly as black as pitch.

Orabillis took it as an omen, but she wasn't about to voice that opinion. The wind picked up, swirling their skirts around their ankles, and little waves formed in the puddles that surrounded them.

"I think we should get back to Forvelith's," Muriale said. "The rain will soon be upon us."

"We will be drowned like proverbial rats before we can make it," Orabillis said. "Let us find a tavern or inn to wait out the storm."

The mist soon turned to droplets that splattered all around them. She hated that Orabillis was right, but there was nothing she could do about it.

"Fine," she acquiesced. "But as soon as the rain lets up, we will find Da."

Orabillis nodded her agreement as she grabbed fistfuls of skirt and began scurrying down the street. Muriale was right behind her.

Not for a moment did she take that little nod as anything other than a way to keep her from arguing further.

---

Unfortunately, the rain didn't let up. In fact, it only got worse.

Lightning cracked as the thunder rolled across the city. More than once, the thunder was so loud it shook the walls of the inn, rattling the items displayed on the walls.

Muriale and Orabillis had been inside the inn for more than an hour. There was no sign that the storm would be letting up anytime soon.

"I wish we could get word to Da," Muriale said. "He is goin' to worry."

"I doubt that," Orabillis argued. "He dinnae even ken we are out. He thinks we are still at Forvelith's."

"Then, she will worry." The truth was that Muriale was worried.

Orabillis scoffed at the idea. "Nay. She kens we are smart enough to come in out of the rain."

That might be true, but it didn't offer her any measure of comfort. "But if Da stops to check in on us—"

"Muriale, ye are a woman full grown. Aye, he might worry, but that is what all fathers do. Now, please, quit yer worryin' over nothin'. We are safe and dry, and that is all that matters."

'Twas Muriale's turn to scoff. "Ye are bein' awfully calm about this."

Taken aback, Orabillis's expression was one of surprise. "What is there nae to be calm about?" She shook her head in dismay. "Truly, Muriale. Ye are makin' a mountain out of a mole hill."

Muriale didn't feel she was making a mountain out of a mole hill. There was a very odd *something* niggling away at her nerves. She couldn't name it, couldn't explain it, but 'twas there nonetheless.

"And will ye stop yer fidgitin'?" Orabillis chastised.

She hadn't realized until she pointed it out that she was bouncing her leg up and down nervously.

"What on earth is the matter with ye?"

Muriale let out a frustrated breath. "I cannae explain it," she finally admitted. "But the longer we sit here, the more I get the feelin' that somethin' bad is goin' to happen."

She was sincerely grateful that her younger sister wasn't looking at her as if she had nine heads.

"Dinnae worry about it, Sister. We have a lunatic on the loose. Of course ye are on guard."

She wasn't so certain it was being on guard rather than worrying herself into an early grave.

"What time is it getting' to be?" she asked as a way to change the subject.

"I suspect Mrs. MacCurdy is preparin' the evenin' meal by now."

Muriale puffed out her cheeks and blew. It had been a very long, exasperating day. They had learned quite a few things, even if the facts weren't leading them directly to the killer.

"Why do ye suppose he takes the tokens?" Muriale asked. "And do ye think he takes somethin' different from each of his victims?"

Orabillis had been contemplating that very question. "I dinnae why, but aye, I do believe he takes somethin' from each of them."

"'Tis odd, aye? The way he commits these crimes."

"Odd?" Orabillis shook her head. "'Tis down right lunacy."

Muriale couldn't argue against that. "When we catch him, I would love to ask him why."

"Why does he rape and kill?" Orabillis asked. "I think the answer is the same to all of yer questions: The man is insane."

Muriale had her own thoughts on the matter. "But he cannae be too insane."

Orabillis's brow furrowed. "What do ye mean?"

"Well, he *is* insane. That is certain. But he must also be rather smart, aye? To be able to sneak into these homes and take the women and girls out, unseen and unheard."

"Smart or mayhap just lucky."

"'Tis possible 'tis a bit of both," Muriale replied.

"No matter the why of it all, we must catch this man before he kills again," Orabillis said as she looked into her empty mug. "Else there will nae be many women or girls who have been untouched by him in all of Edinburgh."

That was a horrific thought. Even more horrific was the idea that he might move on to another city before they could catch him.

———

Another hour passed before the thunder and lightning finally began to wane. While Muriale grew more nervous by the moment, Orabillis grew more frustrated.

They were wasting precious time by holding up in the inn. There was a madman on the loose, and she was stuck here, waiting for the rain to cease as if she were worried she'd melt if she got too wet.

"I am goin' to the privy," Orabillis said as she pushed away from the table.

"In this weather?" Muriale asked.

"Well, I dinnae think I can wait until it passes, elst the barmaid will be cleanin' up after me as if I were a bairn nae yet trained to use the chamber pot."

"I dinnae think it is safe," Muriale argued.

"Safe or nae, I cannae hold it in any longer. I will ask to see if they have an indoor privy."

She didn't bother to wait for Muriale to argue against it. "I promise I will be right back."

"I should go with ye," Muriale said as she reached for her cloak.

"I doubt he is out on a night like this," Orabillis said. "'Tis nae a night safe for man nor beast nor murderers. Sit down, and I shall ask about the privy. If 'tis too far away, I will come back to get ye."

With that, she left her sister sitting alone.

CHAPTER

# TWENTY-ONE

Rory, Gavin, and Alysander were huddled together in an alley near Hay Market. 'Twas a gloomy, blustery day, which only added to their disquiet over their lack of progress.

"We have been goin' in circles for too long," Gavin said. "We have men combing the streets, day and night, and it has led us nowhere."

"What would ye suggest we do?" Rory asked. He was just as bothered by the situation as anyone else.

Alysander decided to answer that question himself. "We should go speak to the sheriff again."

"And ask him what?"

"Certainly he keeps a list of names. Names of men who he has dealt with in the past."

"What? Drunkards and pickpockets?" Gavin asked incredulously. "I doubt 'tis a drunkard or a pickpocket committin' these attacks."

"And ye would be right." 'Twas the sheriff speaking as he made his way toward the group. "We do have a list of men we have arrested before," he told them. He blew into his hands and rubbed them together. "'Tis cold today, aye?"

Ignoring his comments on the weather, Rory asked about the list.

"My men and I have talked to nearly every man we have arrested in the last two years."

"Nearly?" Alysander asked with a raised brow.

"Some have died, some have moved away, and some are still in the gaol," he explained.

"What kinds of crimes were these men arrested for?"

"Public drunkenness, thievery, public brawlin', pickpocketing, and the like."

Those seemed petty crimes, to Alysander's way of thinking. "Ye have nae arrested anyone for murder or rape in the last two years?"

"I dinnae say that," Magnus replied. "Believe it or nae, there haven't been that many murders in the past few years. And those that did happen were solved almost immediately, the culprits arrested and sentenced."

"And the rapists?"

"Only one," Magnus answered. "He was let go."

"Let go?" Rory was astonished to learn they had set a rapist free.

"Aye, he was."

When no further explanation was forthcoming, Rory asked for more details.

"The young woman in question came back to us a few days later. She said she had made a mistake, that she had been drinkin' that night and that it was all a misunderstandin'. So, we let him go."

"A lovers quarrel?" Gavin asked.

Magnus shrugged his shoulders. "I dinnae," he replied. "I was in Inverness when it happened. One of my men handled it."

Alysander, Gavin, and Rory glanced at once another in confusion. "But ye have talked to the man in question?"

"Why would I?" Magnus asked as he pulled his cloak a bit tighter. "Damn but it is cold."

"What if the woman was afraid of standin' against the man?" Alysander asked.

It took a long moment before clarity dawned in Magnus's eyes. "Bloody hell."

"What is the man's name?" Alysander asked.

"I dinnae ken," Magnus said. He spun on his heels and began to walk back to his office. "But I will bloody well find out."

Alysander, Rory, and Gavin were fast on his heels.

"Are there any other such instances?" Alysander asked. "Any other complaints where the woman changed her mind?"

"I dinnae ken," Magnus bit out. He was bloody furious with himself for not thinking of it sooner. He paid no mind to the large puddles he was splashing through as he thundered down the street.

"How can ye nae ken?" Gavin asked.

Magnus didn't want to take the time to explain but felt he must in order to save face. "There are men among my deputies who are layabouts," he began as he turned a corner and headed north.

"Then, why do ye keep them?" Rory asked.

"Because they are there at Robert's behest." Robert had quite effectively tied his hands on the matter. He held his tongue on how he truly felt about their king for three reasons. First of all, Alysander was the man's cousin. Secondly, he was in the presence of two of Robert's knights, and they had sworn an oath to the man (though, he imagined they had done so unwittingly). And, lastly, he wanted to keep his head firmly attached to his shoulders.

"How many men?" Alysander asked, referring to those appointed by Robert.

"Seven."

Bewildered, Alysander exclaimed "Among how many?"

"Eleven, if ye include myself."

"So, out of eleven men, there are only four of ye who are trustworthy?" Alysander couldn't believe what he was hearing.

"That about sums it up," Magnus replied. He, too, had received his current position by Robert's grace. But, unlike the other fools, he took his role as sheriff seriously. Also, unlike the others, he had a heart and truly cared about the people of Edinburgh.

"Does he nae understand the seriousness of this?" Alysander asked.

"Ye should ask him. He is nae *my* cousin." As soon as the words were out of his mouth, he regretted speaking them. "I mean—"

"I ken what ye mean," Alysander replied. "And I shall."

Magnus would have loved to witness that conversation.

———

Henry MacGill—Hawk, to all who knew him—was a short, slender man of middle age. What was left of his thinning brown hair he kept swept across his head in the hopes of hiding the loss. 'Twas a miserable attempt to look younger.

Appointed to his current position the day Robert took the throne, the man still had no inkling regarding what it took to be a good deputy. Magnus believed the man couldn't find his way out of a privy, let alone help catch a rapist and killer.

"Hawk, I need ye to think clearly," Magnus told him. He was doing his level best to maintain his composure. The man had earned the moniker not because of any keen intellect but due to the fact he'd been attacked by a hawk as a young boy, and the name had stuck for over thirty years.

"I am thinkin' clearly," he replied in a bitter tone. "And I tell ye, I cannae remember."

Magnus closed his eyes and did his best to calm his nerves before asking his next question. But Rory stepped forward to speak to him instead.

"I would advise ye to think hard—and quickly, man. We have already wasted enough time as it is."

They were trying to get him to remember the name of the man who had been accused of rape nearly two years ago. Unfortunately, Hawk hadn't kept a record of those events, which went against every rule Magnus had put in place the day he became chief. "And I told ye I cannae remember."

Furious, Rory stepped around the man's desk, grabbed him by his tunic and pulled him out of his chair. "Listen and listen well, ye little weasel," Rory was seething mad. "If ye dinnae remember that name and remember it quickly, I shall go to Robert and tell him about yer lack of professionalism. He wants this bloody bastard caught today, and if he learns that ye were too lazy or too stupid to help, he is nae goin' to be happy. Do ye understand?"

Hawk was as terrified as a mouse being chased by a cat. His eyes nearly bulged from their sockets. He stammered and stuttered for a few moments before he finally managed to speak. "'Twas my cousin!" He shouted his admission.

"Yer cousin?" Nearly every man in the small room spoke in unison. Then they erupted into angry curses and accusations.

Magnus was ready to break the man's neck. "Yer cousin?" he repeated in utter disbelief.

Rory let the man go, shoving him back into his chair. Had he not let him go when he did, he might have gutted him.

Magnus took Rory's place in front of the man. "Explain it to me," Magnus barked his demand. "And give me his bloody name."

# TWENTY-TWO

Muriale tried to convince herself that everything was fine. Orabillis was armed to the teeth and had been trainign with some of the best warriors in all of Scotia since she was six years old.

If anyone could take care of herself, 'twas Orabillis.

Still, the thought of her going out into the dark, stormy night alone made the hair on her neck stand up. There was, after all, a madman on the loose.

*If anything happens to her, Mum and Da will never forgive me.*

Deciding 'twas better to be safe than sorry, she left her spot at the table to go in search of her sister.

She stopped by the bar and asked the innkeeper where the privy was.

"Out back," he replied, pointing a thick thumb in the general direction.

Muriale donned her cloak as she hurried down the small corridor. She opened the heavy wooden door and stepped out into the cool evening air. The rain had let up, but heaven only knew when it would start again.

The area behind the inn was as black as pitch. She couldn't see her hand in front of her face. *How on earth had Orabillis made her way to the privy?*

Her question was answered a moment later when something hard came crashing against her skull.

Stars exploded before her eyes as she felt herself falling to the muddy earth. She landed with an *oomph* against something soft but lumpy.

"Muriale, run." 'Twas Orabillis's voice, weak and scratchy.

---

Plunged into darkness, with her head spinning and bile climbing up her throat, Muriale couldn't move. The pain was paralyzing.

She didn't have to ask what happened. Instinctively, she knew she had been clobbered by something hard and heavy. Fear blended with the pain, twisting in her head and her stomach.

If she could retch, she might feel better.

"Orabillis," she whispered into the darkness. The fear enveloping her increased its hold when no reply came. Mayhap she was speaking, but Muriale couldn't hear her due to the pain pounding in her skull.

Moments passed by as she fought to steady her stomach, to find her voice to scream. Still, no sound from her sister or whoever had attacked them.

A sound of scuffling feet echoed in her ringing ears. It was soon followed by a familiar scratching sound. A few rapid heartbeats later, a torch sprung to life.

Still, she couldn't move. She tried. Oh God, how she tried!

The form of a man appeared, cast in shadow from the torch. The only thing she could see was Orabillis's sweet face next to her own.

Using the toe of his boot, the stranger shoved Muriale off her sister. She rolled onto her back, the motion making her dizzy and nauseated.

*Get up!* she shouted at herself. Her body wouldn't listen to her own plea.

Suddenly, the man crouched low and laid the torch on the damp earth. It hissed and sizzled.

There was naught she could do as he picked Orabillis up and tossed her over his shoulder, with seemingly little effort. He bent once again to grab the torch before hurrying away into the dark night.

*Get up!*

---

Ye will nae just lie here and watch him take yer sister away! She was screaming inside her own head. *Ye ken what he will do!*

With every bit of energy she could muster, she slowly rolled over onto her hands and knees. She felt queasy again, and her head pounded relentlessly. But she refused to fall or to fail.

Taking in a few slow, deep breaths, she willed her stomach to settle. The pain she could deal with, but not the nausea.

Lifting her head, she could see the faint glimmer of the madman's torch. Dark, then light, then dark again.

Scrambling to her feet, she took one more deep breath before taking that first step to go after them.

*Ye will nae allow him to rape or kill again.*

---

The opportunity had presented itself, and it was one he simply couldn't allow to pass by. He'd been watching her for some time now, ever since their first encounter. That day, she had looked at him with such anger and hatred, and for no good reason.

He knew immediately she was one of those women who thought she was better than anyone else.

He could also tell she had been born into a life of leisure. Spoiled to the point she often wore tunic and trews, as if she were some warrior goddess from another realm. What with her sword dangling from her waist, her blonde hair perfectly coiffed, and her dirk glinting in the sunlight, what else was a man to think?

Undoubtedly, she could have her pick of any man she wanted. All she need do was to crook her little finger, and they'd all come running like slobbering dogs.

'Twas unfortunate that her sister appeared when she did. Now, she was a kind woman. She hadn't looked at him the same way so many other women did. Nay, she had smiled and apologized for bumping into him. Of course, their encounter had been quite intentional. That was how he sometimes chose his victims: a chance encounter, an accidental collision with a comely lass, just to see how she would respond. If she was kind and apologized, he'd leave her be. But if she was rude or haughty, heaven help her then.

When he was done with her sister, he was going to seek her out.

Muriale. Such a pretty sounding name for such a pretty woman. They'd make beautiful children together.

Excited anticipation traced up and down his spine at the thought. He actually felt a bit giddy about the prospect of making her his wife.

---

K eeping up with the madman wasn't easy. The torchlight kept bobbing in and out of her line of vision whenever the madman stepped behind an obstacle.

Muriale refused to give up, even though the pain pounded mercilessly inside her skull.

She had no idea exactly where they were, as this part of the city was as dark as Fingal's cave. The occasional flicker of a candle in a window let her know she wasn't quite alone.

With the streets deserted, she assumed they were in a residential area. One- and two-story buildings crowded together, with no sign of a business or public house. Just the occasional bark of a dog or the lowing of a cow in the distance.

A heavy mist clung to the air, the clouds overhead pregnant with rain. She didn't care if the sky opened up to drench her to her bones, she had to keep going.

*Blessed Father, help me,* she prayed as she made her way around one obstacle after another. Little privies and pig pens, fences made of stone or wood... All things she couldn't see but could only feel her way around.

*He cannae be a stranger to this city,* she thought. *He hasn't stumbled or tripped. He has been here before. He kens this place.*

With her mind racing, she tripped once again over what felt like loose stones. She landed on her stomach, her chin just inches from the wet ground.

"Damn!" she whispered her curse. Quickly, she got back on her feet. Panic began to set in, for she had lost sight of the torch. Frantically, she pushed forward, her eyes darting in all directions as her heart pounded against her breast.

*Blessed Father, please help me.* She repeated her prayer over and over in her mind.

Blood rushed in her ears as her panic intensified. *Where are they?*

Relief washed over her moments later when she saw the torch flickering again. *Thank ye, God!*

A moment later, the clouds pushed away, allowing the moonlight to light her way. Another answer to her fervent prayers.

———

Rory, Alysander, Gavin, and dozens of other men had spread out across the southwestern part of the city. They had a name and a description of who they believed might be the killer they had been searching for.

Gavin and Alysander went to talk to the young woman who had made the accusation and then recanted. First, however, they would get Muriale and Orabillis. Their hope was that the young woman would be more willing to talk to them than to the men.

Hawk had told them that his cousin was good at disguising himself, a trait he had learned from his father - a well-known Edinburgh thief who had been hanged several years ago. His death was something Homer couldn't quite get over. He hadn't been the same since.

Rory didn't care about the why of it all. His only wish was to get the man off the streets and keep anyone else from being attacked or murdered.

The rain had been relentless most of the day. Their mission was made more difficult by it and added to their frustration.

Unfortunately, Hawk's cousin was nowhere to be found, but Rory refused to rest until he was. There was a chance that this fellow was not the rapist or the killer, an opinion Hawk adamantly voiced. "He is a good man. He would nae hurt a flea, let alone a woman."

If Rory had learned anything in his life, it was that looks could be deceiving. Some people will appear to have a calm and kind presence, but anger them once, and they can transform into someone you don't recognize, in the blink of an eye. Hell, even their king was like that.

Cowgate was nearly deserted at this hour, undoubtedly due to the incessant rain that deluged them throughout the day.

*I hope Muriale is warm and dry.*

He closed his eyes and let out a frustrated breath. Even now, when he was supposed to be looking for a lunatic, Muriale was never far from his thoughts.

When he first met her, he had hoped he was merely infatuated with her, attracted to her physically, simply due to her beauty.

But the more time he spent with her, the more he realized his feelings went far beyond infatuation. And there was more to her than her breathtakingly beautiful looks.

She was a fierce woman with a stubborn streak as wide as the ocean. But she was also extraordinarily kind. He had watched and listened to how she made the victims they spoke to feel safe and at ease. She had been able to gain access to information from them in ways the men hadn't.

Add to that her quick wit, the way her pleasant giggle made him chuckle, her keen sense of right versus wrong, and her levelheadedness, and it was no doubt he would be attracted to her.

Who was he kidding? He was more than just attracted to her. He was quite certain he was falling in love with her.

He shook the thoughts of Muriale McCullum away. Later, after they found the madman, he would take the time to think through his feelings more fully. For now, he had to concentrate on a killer.

Less than a block away, he heard Gavin calling his name.

---

"What do ye mean ye cannae find them?" Rory asked. Worry was quickly filling his heart.

Gavin was clearly concerned. Alysander, however, looked furious. "My aunt sent them out before the noonin' hour, and they have nae returned." Even in the dimly lit evening light, Rory could see the intense anger in his friend's face.

"Why on earth would she send them out?" Rory demanded to know. "Did they nae promise to stay at home?"

Alysander raked a hand through his damp hair as he let out a heavy breath. "They promised nae to leave after nightfall. I should have kent they had agreed far too easily."

"Blast it!" Rory exclaimed.

The mist turned to rain again, the heavy rain clouds turning the twilit sky dark.

Trying to add some calm and common sense to the conversation, Gavin said, "I believe they are each smart enough to get in from the rain."

"What are ye on about?" Rory asked with an edge of frustration to his tone.

"I mean, even we have had to take refuge in an inn or tavern a few times this day. Mayhap that is what they have done." He didn't think it took any great mental acumen to sort it all out.

Rory looked as relieved as Alysander with the idea now planted in their noggins. "Let us split up," Rory said. "Look in every inn, tavern, and public house in the city."

"And when we find them?" Gavin asked.

"Get them to Forvelith's at once," Alysander nearly barked his answer. "And dinnae let them leave."

Quickly, they made plans on who should search where. Each man would take a two-block area from Cowgate to Haymarket. As soon as one of them ran across any of the other men helping to search for the madman, they would have them join in the search for the two missing women.

With the knowledge that the madman usually skulked his way into open windows and took very young girls, Rory felt a twinge of hope. The man was a coward; of that, he had no doubt. Chances were good that Muriale and her sister were safely tucked away in an inn nearby. Besides, if they had run across the madman, there probably wouldn't be enough left of his body to identify.

For a brief moment, he allowed himself to grin at that notion, and it actually lifted his spirits. Muriale was a force to be reckoned with, and Orabillis, he was convinced, was bordering that fine line between lunacy and genius. She could indisputably take care of herself.

*They will be fine,* he told himself as he quickly made his way down the street. *The madman dinnae stand a chance against the two of them.*

# TWENTY-THREE

Orabillis feigned sleep. She had woken not long after the bloody bastard had tossed her over his shoulder. But her head was pounding, and her ribs ached from where he had kicked her after she had collapsed to the ground.

She wasn't necessarily afraid so much as she was infuriated. Not because he had caught her unawares, or had hit her over the head with something heavy, or even that he had kicked her when she was down.

Nay, she was furious with herself for being completely absent minded. She had neither seen nor heard him coming, and the fault lay completely with herself.

But she wasn't without hope, nor did she despair over what his plans for her were. Nay, she was going to get out of this alive and unharmed, save for the bump on her head and the aching ribs. Those would be the last injuries he was going to cause her.

Before this night was over, he was going to be a dead man.

Gavin had run into Alyn near Haymarket street. He quickly filled him in on all that had taken place within the last half hour.

"Jesu!" Alyn exclaimed. "Ye dinnae think the madman has them, do ye?"

"Nay," Gavin replied. "The man is a coward and only goes after the very young or those who are too small to defend themselves."

Alyn nodded in agreement. "Aye, they can take care of themselves. Especially Orabillis, as ye already ken."

Gavin glowered, his eyes turning to slits. Chances were good that, even if he lived to be a hundred and ten, neither Alyn nor Rory would ever let him forget that night. The night Orabillis McCullum humiliated him in front of God, his king, and everyone else in attendance.

"If ye find them, take them home immediately," he said, choosing to ignore his friend's comment. "And send word that ye have them. We will meet in one hour at the Crooked Goat."

They split up, going in opposite directions.

While Gavin believed the women were fine, he was still furious with them. While they were all running around like dogs chasing a cat, trying to find the two women, the madman was left to roam the streets, unimpeded.

'Twas undoubtedly Orabillis's fault. Muriale was by far the smarter of the two and had likely gone along with her sister just to keep her out of trouble.

Orabillis was petulant, spoiled, hard-headed, and obstinate. Aye, she was a bonny lass to look at, but that was the only good quality he could find in her. He was quite certain she possessed no redeeming qualities.

*I feel sorry for the man who has to marry* her *someday.* He chuckled aloud, unable to imagine a man strong enough to handle having Orabillis as a wife.

A lyn had visited a tavern and two inns in the southwest quadrant of the city, and still there was no sign of the two women.

There had been very little let-up on the rain for most of the day, so it was no wonder they would seek refuge from it. At the moment, large droplets fell from the sky, splattering loudly against every surface, including his cowl and cloak.

He didn't mind the rain; 'twas the lightning he was concerned over. Aye, he could handle just about every type of weather—overly warm, frigidly cold, snow, wind, ice, and rain—but the lightning? God could keep that, as far as he was concerned.

The rain stopped as quickly as it started, just as he came upon another inn. The Black Boar Inn sat on the corner of a usually busy street. The sign over the door swayed in the wind, creaking and groaning as if it were protesting the interference. He pulled open the heavy wooden door and entered. The entryway felt small and cramped. In the dim light, Alyn stood in silence to catch his bearings. Water sluiced down his cloak, leaving little puddles of water. His boots, soaked through from all the rain, squeaked and sloshed as he stepped to the second door and pulled it open. The lighting was much improved inside the larger space. Straight ahead was a long, wooden counter and behind that, a small doorway covered with a heavy drape.

To his left was a nearly empty dinning area. To his right, a set of stairs that led to the sleeping chambers above. As he approached the counter, a beefy-looking fellow with dark hair and broad shoulders came through the drapes. He paused for a brief moment as he scrutinized Alyn closely.

Alyn introduced himself to the man. "I am lookin' for a couple of women."

The man chortled. "We ain't that kind of establishment."

"Nay," Alyn replied. "They are daughters of a friend of mine. They have nae returned home yet, and their father is worried."

Another chortle. "Ye should be out lookin' for the man who is rapin' and killin' these poor lasses."

Alyn was in no mood to explain himself or to give more details. "Their disappearance could be related to this madman. Now, please, have ye seen two lasses in here? One has golden-blonde hair and the other, brown."

"Aye, they were here. The blonde-haired one asked where the privy was. The other followed not long after." He gave a nod of his head indicating which direction they'd gone.

"How long ago was this?"

The man shrugged his shoulder with indifference. "Mayhap a quarter of an hour ago. No more than that." Once again, he nodded in the direction of the privy.

Alyn felt hopeful knowing he wasn't far behind the two women. He thanked the innkeeper and started to leave the same way he had arrived: through the front door.

"Ye will nae find them that way," the innkeeper said. "They have nae yet returned from the privy."

For a brief moment, Alyn was tempted to strangle the man for the sheer pleasure of it, the idiotic fool. "Why did ye nae say that before?"

The stout man leaned over the counter and replied, "Ye dinnae ask."

A lyn could have strangled the innkeeper. The only thing that saved the man's life was the fact that Alyn was in too much of a hurry to waste any more time.

On his way to the back door, he grabbed a low-burning torch from a black iron wall sconce. He pushed the door open and stepped into the cool, dark night. "Muriale? Orabillis?" He called into the darkness. Straining his ears, he heard no reply. He called out to them again and was met with the same eerie silence. Naught more than the bark of a dog or the snort of a pig could he hear.

When he stepped forward, his shoe brushed against something hard. Crouching down, he held the torch lower in order to get a better look.

Fear, anger, and dread hit him all at once.

*Orabillis's sword.*

A lyn raced back inside and demanded the innkeeper send someone first to the Crooked Goat and then to the girls' aunt.

The fool refused until Alyn removed his dirk and held it to his neck—what there was of it. "Ye will do as I say, without question. Send word to the Crooked Goat and then to Forvelith Carruthers's home."

"Forvelith Carruthers?" The man was clearly surprised. "She is their aunt?"

Why it mattered, Alyn didn't know, nor did he care. "Aye, she is."

"Bruce! Willem!" The man yelled so loudly Alyn wasn't sure if the rafters would fall down. He was tearing off his apron and shoving Alyn's hand away as if he were swatting at a fly. "Forvelith Carruthers is one of the best women I have ever kent! Had I kent they were her nieces..." He tossed the apron onto the counter.

Two young, spry-looking lads came bounding down the stairs. "Boys! I need one of ye to run to the Crooked Goat and one to Forvelith's home."

They glanced at one another with confused faces but waited patiently for further instructions.

Alyn stepped closer to the young men. "Ye are to find Alysander

McCullum or Rory MacLeod." He gave a quick description of each man. "Tell them that Orabillis and Muriale have been taken. Tell them to come here, to the Black Boar Inn, at once."

"And if we cannae find them?" the taller of the two boys asked.

"Ye go on to Forvelith's home. She has a dress shop—"

"Forvelith?" the boys asked in unison. "She is one of the finest women any of us has ever kent," the shorter boy said.

Alyn resisted the urge to roll his eyes. "Give her the same message and tell her to find Alysander's men. Or, better yet, find Magnus MacElroy, and tell him the same."

The boys nodded, looking most serious, considering the circumstances.

When Alyn turned around, he bumped into the innkeeper, who had donned his cloak and grabbed a sword.

"I need ye to stay here, sir. Tell anyone who comes to help that I have gone out the back way to search for the girls."

He was readily disappointed, his brows furrowing into a hard knot. "I ken these back streets and alleys," he argued.

Alyn had been roaming the streets and the shadows of the alleys for weeks. He was quite certain he wouldn't need the man's assistance.

"I have no time to argue," Alyn told him as he headed toward the back. He could hear the innkeeper rapidly giving instructions to the barmaid.

Alyn was out the door moments later, with a very determined innkeeper hot on his heels.

"My name is Roger," he said as he caught up with Alyn. Alyn was searching the area for more clues as to what might have happened to the two women.

"Watch where ye step, man," Alyn told him. He was crouched low again, carefully studying the ground.

In the mud, he could make out three different sets of footprints. One definitely larger and deeper, indicating they were left by a man. The other two had to belong to the girls.

Upon closer inspection of the area where he found Orabillis's sword, which he now had strapped to his own waist, he caught a glimpse of a few stones, each with dark splotches on them. Cautiously, he swiped his fingers onto the stones and held them close to his eyes. *Blood.*

"And why dinnae ye tell me they were Forvelith's nieces?" Roger asked. He'd been talking nonstop, but Alyn hadn't been listening.

He stood tall, swiping the thick blood onto the hem of his tunic before answering the man.

"Ye dinnae ask."

———

Bruce and Willem—brothers, sons of Roger MacSwain—understood the importance of their mission. While they might not have understood the intricacies, they knew the importance.

Good lads they were, as their father often bragged to anyone who would listen. They adored their father as much as he adored them.

After their mother's death some years ago, Forvelith Carruthers stepped in to help care for and raise the boys. If it hadn't been for her kindness and aye, her stubbornness, lord only knew where they'd be right now. Most likely in the gaol, still trying to cope with the loss of their mother.

They were racing up the road as fast as they could. Splashing through mud and water, their cloaks billowing out behind them.

"The Crooked Goat is only a few streets from Forvelith's," Willem, the youngest of the brothers, remarked.

"I ken where it is," Bruce replied sharply.

At the age of five and ten, Bruce, the eldest, felt responsible for his younger brother. Usually, he was quite kind and generous with his time. From whence his sharp tone came, Willem didn't know.

"I was only tryin' to help."

"Ye can help by runnin' faster," Bruce replied. "This is important."

"I ken it is," he replied, growing more than just a bit frustrated and annoyed with his brother's tone. He was only eleven, but he was by no means a foolish lad.

"Hurry up," Bruce scolded.

"My legs are nae as long as yers," Willem reminded him. "I am goin' as fast as I can."

Bruce ignored him for now. He was far too young to understand exactly what was going on. The two pretty girls who had spent the better part of the afternoon at his family's establishment were missing. They were Forvelith's nieces, and they were in danger.

He had managed to put two and two together and realized, as soon as the knight started speaking, exactly what was going on. The knight was worried that the pretty girls had been taken by the madman who had been terrorizing the city for the past year.

There was naught he wouldn't do to help Forvelith or any member of her family. 'Twasn't just because he felt he was indebted to the kind, older woman. Bruce wanted to be like the knights he had met over the years. Strong, honorable men with unparalleled skill with a sword.

If he could help, at least in some small way, to get this madman off the streets, he would take pride in it.

Lost in his own thoughts, he hadn't realized that he had run right past the Crooked Goat until his younger brother yelled his name. "Bruce!"

Coming to an abrupt halt, he turned to see what his brother was yelling for. Willem was pointing to the sign over his head. *The Crooked Goat Tavern.*

Feeling ashamed, he grunted, made a promise to not get lost in daydreaming again, and headed inside to find the men he'd been sent for.

CHAPTER

# TWENTY-FOUR

Alyn had walked right by Muriale and hadn't noticed. But she had seen him, with the innkeeper. She had been hiding in the shadows, hoping to catch a glimpse of the madman and her sister. She'd lost sight of the torch not long ago and was praying for another glimpse.

Not knowing why Alyn Buchanan was lurking in the darkness in this area of town, she decided to remain hidden. She didn't trust him as far as she could throw him. But why was the innkeeper with him? Were they friends? Allies?

The two men came to an abrupt halt less than a dozen steps from her position. Alyn's torch flickered in the strong breeze, blazing upward, casting a larger area of light around him.

"There!" Alyn whispered angrily as he pointed towards something she couldn't see.

"Go back to the inn, and wait for Alysander, Rory, and Gavin," he ordered.

The innkeeper nodded his head rapidly. He looked intensely worried.

It suddenly dawned on her that Alyn was looking for her and

Orabillis. She felt seven kinds a fool, hiding like one of the king's spies.

The ache in her head was slowly subsiding, and she actually began to feel relieved at seeing him. Even if he was a Buchanan bastard.

Before she could call his name and make her presence known, he was disappearing into an older, decrepit-looking building.

She couldn't yell for him or shout for him to wait; the last thing she wanted to do was warn the madman of their presence.

The innkeeper raced right passed her, mumbling under his breath. Once he had passed by, she got to her feet and followed after Alyn.

---

Alysander, Rory, and Gavin were huddled around a table in the corner of the Crooked Goat. They'd only just arrived and were waiting impatiently for someone, anyone, to appear with word of Alysander's daughters.

"I am growing weary of waitin'," Gavin said. "We should go back to look for them."

Rory agreed. He gulped down the rest of his ale and slammed the mug down hard onto the table. It rattled the empty mugs left behind by his friends.

They had just stood up, when they heard a young voice calling out for Alysander.

"Alysander McCullum!" the lad shouted a second time.

"Here!" Alysander said, raising his arm as he headed toward the lad. Gavin and Rory were right behind him.

The brown-haired boy looked relieved to see him. "The knight, Alyn, he sent us to fetch ye," Bruce said breathlessly.

Worry stabbed at Alysander's heart. "Well?"

"The girls, they have gone missin'. He thinks the madman has taken them."

Willem glanced up at his brother, confusion etched in his face. "He dinnae say that."

"What *did* he say?" Rory demanded harshly.

"He said for ye to come to the Black Boar Inn," Willem answered. "The girls are missin'. He says for ye to come quick."

Bruce stepped in front of his little brother. "Sir, I think he is worried that the madman has taken them. He needs ye to come quickly."

None of the men waited for the boys to add anything else to the conversation. They bolted for the door and headed into the dark night.

———

*What had Alyn seen?* Muriale wondered as she made her way into the building. She was as quiet as a church mouse and prayed her footfalls didn't echo off the stone walls.

The entryway was as dark as pitch and unnervingly still. However, up above, on the landing, she caught the flicker of Alyn's torch.

Stealthily, she made her way above stairs. *He must believe that the killer is in here, somewhere.*

Oh, how she wished she could race up the stairs to let him know she was here and that the madman had Orabillis. But she couldn't take the risk of the madman hearing, if he was indeed somewhere in this dilapidated building. Nay, the risk was too great; too many lives were at stake.

As she made her way up the stairs, she withdrew the dirk from the belt at her waist. She had a *sgian dubh* tucked into each of her boots. This had been at Orabillis's insistence earlier in the day. Later, after she found her sister, she would tell her how grateful she was for her love of weaponry.

One step at a time, testing each stair for loose wood or creaking noises, she was halfway up when she heard a man groan loudly. It was quickly followed by the sound of a body hitting the floor.

Her blood ran cold.

———

As Alysander and his friends made their way down the street, they came across Red John and Ardin. As they ran, they explained the situation to them. Andrew stopped and let out a loud, shrill whistle, and before they knew it, the rest of Alysander's men came running.

Not much longer, the group burst through the door of the inn. A wee lass with curling brown hair was standing behind a counter. Her eyes grew as wide as trenchers when she saw all the men filing in.

"They went out the back not long ago!" she exclaimed. "Ye will need torches," she quickly added.

Some of the men grabbed whatever torches remained in the iron sconces on the wall. They spoke not a word as they made their way out of the building and into the small garden behind the inn.

"Which way to do ye supposed they went?" Rory asked as he held a torch over his head, straining his eyes to see something, anything, that might indicate where they had gone.

Before anyone could answer, a stout, barrel-chested man came running toward them. "Are ye lookin' for Alyn and the lasses?" he called out to them.

"Aye!" Rory shouted back.

"This way!"

They didn't have a clue who the man was, and neither did they care. Rory ran as quickly as he was able, careful to steer clear of the multitude of obstacles in their way.

As he ran, he sent a silent prayer heavenward. *Please, God, let her be all right.*

"I am Roger," the man called out as they neared his location. "We saw him take the lass into an abandoned building only a few moments ago. He sent me back to fetch help."

Worry filled Rory's gut. *The lass? Only one?*

Roger didn't wait to explain it further. He spun on his heels and headed back the way he had come. "We dinnae ken where the other one is," he said, sounding out of breath as well as worried.

"Which one does he have?" Gavin asked.

"I dinnae," Roger replied as he made his way around a pig pen. "We could nae see. He had her tossed over his shoulders like a sack of wheat, the bloody bastard."

The men wound their way through narrow passages, muddy paths, and around squat structures.

"We dinnae ken where the other one is," Roger explained, his breathing becoming more and more labored. He was clearly out of shape.

Another jolt of worry and dread filled Rory's heart. *I will kill anyone who brings her a moment of pain or harm.*

He couldn't know it at the moment, but Gavin was thinking the very same thing.

---

Muriale stood in the shadows, her back firmly planted against the wall near an open doorway. She could just make out a pair of muddy boots lying just inside the door. There was no way of telling just who those boots belonged to, thus she decided it best to proceed with a great deal of caution.

From within the room, she could hear a man's deep voice, one she didn't recognize. "For the sake of Christ, will ye be quiet?" he shouted to or at someone else in the room. "I have just killed a man. I need to think, damn it! I need to think!"

Her heart seemed to fall to her toes and bounce back up again. That wasn't Alyn's voice.

Straining to hear something else, she willed her heart to slow down. She heard muffled moaning sounds coming from within.

"I said shut up, ye stupid whore!"

Muriale took the sound of feet shuffling away from the door as the perfect opportunity to chance a glance inside.

Alyn lay on the floor, blood oozing from his chest, his torn shirt exposing a deep wound near his heart.

The room was empty, save for a dirty mattress on the floor to her right. Ahead, under a window covered with old wood, lay her sister.

She was bound at her feet, her hands behind her back and a filthy length of cloth shoved into her mouth. Orabillis was struggling, undoubtedly cursing her captor to the devil as she tried to figure out a way out of her current predicament.

The stranger had his back to Muriale and was starting to kneel down, seething with fury. "I told ye!" he shouted.

Muriale could only watch in horror as the man lifted his arm and plunged his dirk into Orabillis.

---

M uriale screamed like a banshee as she ran across the room and leapt onto the man's back.

He was so surprised he fell backward, landing on Muriale. "Get off me ye witch! Get off me!"

Muriale wouldn't let loose the tight hold she had around his neck. The dirk she held firmly in her right hand glinted off the candlelight.

Before she could turn the dirk to slice his neck, he rolled over to his stomach. Muriale lost the grip on his neck. They each lunged to their feet at the same time.

She knew him!

uriale might not have known his name, but she remembered him. Weeks ago, she'd very nearly tripped over the man. Orabillis had scolded her that day, for being kind the the stranger with one eye.

His maniacal laughter echoed throughout the small space.

"'Tis good to see ye again, lassie. Although I thought ye were a much nicer lady."

"I am going to kill ye," she told him. There was not so much as a quiver in her voice. She said what she meant and meant what she said.

Her heart was pounding against her breast, but otherwise, she remained calm and composed. She had killed before. She knew how to do it and what to expect afterward.

"Ye?" He shook his head in disbelief as he smiled crookedly. One single brown eye was filled with so much hatred and insanity that 'twas difficult for Muriale to believe.

"Aye," she said with a nod. "I am going to kill ye."

"Bah! Ye dinnae have the stomach for it!"

'Twas Muriale's turn to laugh. "Ye dinnae ken the depths I will go to protect my family, ye bloody son of a whore. I have killed before, and I have no qualms about killin' again."

Foolishly, the one-eyed man threw his head back and laughed. Muriale took that opportunity to lunge forward.

Although she had aimed for his heart, he had stopped laughing and tried to jump out of the way. Her dirk landed only an inch or two away from his heart.

With every fiber of her being, every ounce of strength she owned, she pushed her dirk in through skin, flesh, and muscle before hitting bone. As she held her breath, she pushed and pushed until the dirk could go no farther.

A look of astonishment came over his face as he looked down at the dirk sticking out of his chest. "Ye bloody stabbed me!" He was incredulous.

In one swift move, Muriale bent and grabbed one of the hidden *sgian dubhs* from her boot.

"I told ye I would," she said as matter of factly as if she were speaking to her mum about sewing.

With her *sgian dubh* fisted tightly in her hand, she stepped forward, aiming for his heart once again. And as he had moments ago, he tried to dodge the impending blow.

Instead of plunging into his cold black heart, his angle, the timing of his movements, forced the dirk to go through the only eye the lunatic had left.

He slumped to the floor and keeled over onto his side. The rattle of death was caught in his throat, and a few heartbeats later, he was dead. His heart no longer beat, and his lungs no longer took in air. He would never get an opportunity to hurt another living soul.

A dirk in his chest. A *sgian dubh* in his eye. Blood spilled from his nose, ears, and mouth, as well as his chest.

"I always keep my word."

---

Rory and Gavin had heard a scream coming from the second floor. They took the stairs two at a time and reached the door first. Alysander and Red John were right behind them.

They had arrived in time to see Muriale plunge her *sgian dubh* into the madman's eye. There had been no time for any of them to react. All they could do was watch.

All hell broke loose a frantic heartbeat after the madman collapsed on the floor. Rory wanted to get to Muriale, but his friend was lying in a pool of blood at their feet.

Rory knelt beside Alyn and felt for a pulse. Nothing.

Alyn Buchanan was dead.

Gavin had already stepped over his dead friend's body, pushing past Rory in order to get to Orabillis. She was lying unconscious on the floor, blood oozing from her stomach. He whispered her name softly as he took her hand to feel for a pulse. 'Twas weak, but it was there, and that meant hope. Carefully, he scooped her up and hurried towards the door.

Alysander was being barred from entering the room. Red John and Ardin were holding him back, arms wrapped around his chest. "Wait, Alysander!" Red John told him.

"Let me get to my daughters!" Alysander shouted as he fought against the tight hold they had on his arms.

Gavin pushed past all of them. "We need a healer!" he shouted to anyone who would listen.

Alysander turned as white as a summer cloud. He felt as though his world was spinning out of control. "Orabillis," he whispered her name as he stepped aside.

"She is still alive, but she needs a healer," Gavin told him as he pushed through the throng of men standing in the hallway.

Rory shouted that Muriale was unharmed as he led her out of the room. He thought she was oddly quiet. Undoubtedly in shock.

Alysander was temporarily frozen with fury. "Da!" Muriale cried as she fell against his chest.

Alysander looked up at Rory. "Is he dead?"

"Aye. Alyn is dead, and so is our madman."

Alysander could take very little comfort in that bit of news. He patted Muriale on the back and said, "We must leave at once. Orabillis needs us."

Rory ordered two men to stay with the bodies, whilst commanding another four to go find the bloody sheriff.

After giving the order, he quit the hallway and went after Muriale. There was something important he needed to tell her.

lysander knew that if he didn't send for his wife, she would never forgive him. Red John and four of the other men left immediately to return to their keep and bring Moirra back with them. 'Twas a task that none of them wanted, but it needed to be done nonetheless.

Gavin raced to the castle, with Orabillis in his arms. Only the best of healers tended to the king, and Orabillis deserved only the best.

Thankfully, one of Alysander's men appeared with a horse. Gavin handed Orabillis off to the younger man before climbing atop the skittish mare.

He wanted to be gentle with the lass, to take care not to cause her any distress or pain. But there was no time to be kind. He sat her on his lap, shoved her head against his chest, and kicked the horse into a full run.

"Lass, dinnae die on me," he told her. "I want a chance to get even with ye."

She moaned and mumbled something incoherent. Any sound, any movement, meant she was still alive.

As long as her heart beat, there was hope.

# CHAPTER
# TWENTY-FIVE

A pall had fallen over Edinburgh Castle and clung to it for days. 'Twas as if it had been draped in a heavy cloak of worry and despair.

Muriale refused to leave her sister's side. Although she didn't have the same talent for healing as her sisters Mariote and Esa, it mattered not. She wasn't going to leave her side, not for a moment.

Forvelith arrived early that first morn. She brought clean dresses for Muriale and beautiful night-rails for Orabillis. The poor woman hadn't realized the seriousness of her niece's injuries until she came into the chamber and saw three healers, four nurses, and the rest of her family standing around the bed.

She didn't stay long, for the room was stuffy and quite over crowded. "Alysander," she said as she patted his back. "I am so verra sorry."

He couldn't think, let alone speak. He thanked her before turning his attention back to his daughter.

Alysander rarely left the room. And when he did, it was to pace the hallway outside the bedchamber or to visit the chapel. Never in his life had he prayed as much as he was praying now.

Orabillis had lost a good amount of blood. The wound had been deep, the blade of the dirk nicking her liver and small intestines. The worry over infection was soon proved true when the fevers hit later that afternoon.

For three straight days, those fevers raged, tormenting the young woman. The healers tried everything they could to break them, from covering her with heavy furs to plunging her into a cool bath.

Nothing was working.

When the fever was at its worst, Orabillis would cry out, unintelligible words most of the time. Her skin was the color of ash in a cold hearth, gray and depressing.

Rory and Gavin rarely left the room themselves. Rory was there to offer Muriale whatever help he could. His words of encouragement, however, often fell on deaf ears.

Numerous times, he forced Muriale to step away long enough to eat. Alysander would take her place, holding his dying daughter's hand, whispering kind and inspiring words. He wanted her to know he loved her and that aye, she was his favorite.

At one point, Alysander leaned in close and said, "Robert has sent word, Orabillis. He demands that ye live."

At those words, Orabillis groaned, and her brow furrowed in consternation. Alysander smiled and kissed her brow. He fully believed she could hear every spoken word.

Gavin stayed far away from the bed, watching in silence as people came and went. *If she dies, I will never forgive myself.*

The sheriff came to speak to them on the second morning, letting them know that the killer had been identified. Homer MacGill was Hawk MacGill's cousin. A man who had lost an eye, as well as his mother, before he turned ten years.

While Orabillis fought for her life,

By Robert's order, Hawk was now in the king's dungeon, where he would bloody well stay until the king made up his mind what to do with the lazy fool.

None of the three men truly cared about who the killer was or the fact that Hawk was behind bars somewhere below the castle. They took no comfort in the news but thanked Magnus all the same. He left that morning and hadn't returned.

———

On a bleary, blustery morn, three days after he was killed, Rory and Gavin laid their friend to rest. The funeral was a grand affair, attended by their king, their queen, and their fellow knights.

Trumpets blared, a priest prayed, and eulogies were given. Everyone spoke about what a good man he was, how he always helped the poor and less fortunate. He was a man of honor, with unparalleled skill on the field of battle.

Even Phoebe attended the event, though she stayed to the rear of the church, refusing to come forward to tell him goodbye. She would mourn him in her own way.

Alyn would have hated every moment of it. Rory and Gavin both knew that Alyn would have wanted to be buried next to his father, in a quiet ceremony, with only the two of them in attendance. Not this grand, dandy affair.

But neither Robert nor Euphemia would listen. *He died serving his king and country*, Robert told them. *He was a hero, and we shall bury him as such.*

'Twas difficult to argue against their sovereign. Alyn would have understood. He wouldn't have liked it, but he would have understood.

As soon as the last bit of earth was tossed over their friend, they headed back into the castle.

The three had been inseparable for many years, and Alyn's loss was akin to losing a brother.

"What should we do with his things?" Gavin asked as they entered the bedchamber they all shared.

"I dinnae believe he has any family left," Rory said as he pulled a heavy trunk from the foot of Alyn's bed.

"Mayhap he left instructions on what to do in the event of his untimely death," Gavin suggested.

Most young men their age didn't plan for such events. But, being one of Robert II's knights, death was always a hair's breadth away. Planning for such events was an intelligent thing to do.

Rory puffed out his cheeks and let out a heavy breath. Going through the last belongings of a friend gone far too soon was something he never wanted to do.

Hinges creaked and groaned when he opened the heavy wooden lid. The first thing he saw were Alyn's battle vestments: gauntlets, chainmail, leathers. All clean and shiny, with his initials carved into the leather breastplate.

Showing much care, Rory removed those items and carefully placed them beside him on the bed. Under those were a few tunics, trews, woolens, and the like. One extra sword belt, two expensive looking *sgian dubhs*, and one dirk with an intricately carved wooden handle.

On the bottom was a heavy box made of steel. He realized after his first attempt to open it that it was locked.

"I wonder where the key is?" Gavin asked. It took a while, but they finally found the key, tucked under Alyn's pillow.

Each man doubted there was anything of true value inside the box, but they were still curious as to its contents.

Inside was a heavy pouch filled with gold and silver. "Jesu," Gavin said with a whistle. "I have never kent him to have more than a groat to his name at any given time."

"Neither have I," Rory replied.

The next item was a leather-bound journal. The inscription on the front identified it as belonging to Alyn Buchanan.

"Open it up and see what it says," Gavin said eagerly.

"These may be his personal thoughts," Rory argued. "Mayhap we should nae read them."

Gavin shook his head, grabbed the journal from Rory's hands, sat down next to him, and opened it. A folded piece of parchment fell out and onto his lap. Rory took that and read it aloud.

"If anyone is readin' this, it means I am dead. It is my wish that the gold and silver coins be given to Phoebe MacRay."

"What?" Gavin said, more than a bit surprised at that news.

"I dinnae ken they knew each other well enough for him to leave her his fortune," Rory replied.

"I am beginnin' to realize that mayhap we dinnae ken him as well as we thought." Gavin turned his attention back to the journal and began to read.

"Lord," he exclaimed in a whisper, his eyes open wide in astonishment. "Listen to this:

*I fear I ken who the killer of these innocent lasses is: Homer MacGill, a distant cousin on my mother's side, who has nae been right in his own head since he was a wean. I have no evidence yet, but I believe it in my bones to be true.*"

Rory was bewildered. "Homer was his cousin?"

"Apparently so," Gavin replied before turning back to the handwritten text and reading aloud.

*I will prove it. I only need a few more days. Once I have that proof, I will kill the man with my bare hands. I will then finally have my revenge.*

"Revenge?" Rory said. "Revenge for what?"

Gavin let loose a frustrated breath. "Mayhap if ye would quit askin' questions so that I can read it, we could find out."

Rory wasn't at all embarrassed by his friend's comment. "Just read it."

"*Lorens MacGill, Homer's father, was the man who killed my mum. Kent for bein' a thief rather than a murderer, he killed her on the ninth of July the year of our lord one thousand three hundred and sixty-one. I have been tryin' to catch him ever since. 'Tis only recently that I learned of his death.*

*Kennin' Homer as I do, I believe him to be responsible for the rapes and deaths of all these innocent people. Since I cannae kill Lorens, I shall kill his son. Then I will have my vengeance.*"

Rory let out a long, low whistle. "I never kent that. Nae any of it."

"Neither did I," Gavin said. "I wonder what other secrets the man possessed?"

"I am nae certain I want to ken," Rory replied. "Some things are best left to the shadows."

―――――

Neither man wanted to be away from the two sisters for any longer than they had to.

Orabillis's condition hadn't changed one way or another. She hadn't awakened, had barely stirred or even moaned.

Gavin hated it. He would give anything to hear her at least cry out in pain. Or toss and turn or complain about the concoctions the healers kept shoving down her gullet.

Anything other than the deathly stillness that seemed to echo off the walls. The silence was maddening.

Quietly, Gavin prayed that she would make a full recovery and very soon. Not even on the threat of a slow, painful, agonizing death would he ever admit he had any feelings for the bonny termagant.

*I'd rather be gutted and my entrails fed to the wolves than kiss ye.* He ran those words over and over in his mind several times a day since their first meeting and dozens of times an hour since she was injured.

Nay, he didn't much care for her harsh tone nor for what he considered to be a verra arrogant attitude. Women shouldn't be arrogant. They should be soft, malleable, and warm.

Orabillis McCullum was none of those things.

Still, there was something about her...

―――――

'Twas the middle of the night on the fourth night that Orabillis took yet another turn for the worse. The fever had grown so intense that it threw her into convulsions.

The healer acted quickly, forcing some vile concoction down her throat as he yelled her name. "Orabillis, can ye hear me?"

Alysander and Gavin believed the healer was being far too rough with her.

"Drink this, damn it!" the man shouted as he tried to pry open her jaw.

Alysander tried to pull the healer away, but Muriale stopped him. Holding him back, she said, "Give it a moment, Da. He is tryin' to help her."

Gavin had pulled a dirk from his waist and held it against the healer's throat. "If ye dinnae let go of her now, *ye* will need a healer."

He loosened his grip on her arm and let her fall back against the pillows. The convulsions slowly began to subside, and a long while later, Orabillis's body relaxed into the bed.

Alysander held his breath. Muriale buried her head into his chest as she wept. Rory placed a warm hand on her shoulder, the only thing he could think to do to offer his support.

The healer leaned over the bed and put his ear first against her chest then her face. "She is still alive," he whispered.

Relief washed over Alysander and Muriale. Now she wept tears of relief.

The healer came to speak with Alysander. "If she makes it through to morning, 'twill be a miracle. But if she does, we have hope. I have done all that I can."

"The convulsions..." Alysander couldn't finish his question. Words were lodged in his throat like walnuts.

"It means the fever was verra high," the healer explained. "Sometimes when that happens, it can mean one of two things."

"What things?" Muriale asked.

"Either death is nigh or she could be on the mend. We never ken until one or the other happens."

"But there is hope still, aye?" Muriale asked, pleading for him to answer affirmatively.

"Aye, there is still hope." By the tone of his voice, she wasn't certain he believed what he'd just told her.

"If she does survive, she might not be the same."

"What do ye mean?" Alysander asked, choking on the words.

The healer blew out a slow breath. "Sometimes a fever can get so high that a person dies, or they lose their hearin' or vision or the use of their legs or..." He paused, trying to find the proper words. "...or they cannae think like they used to."

"Ye mean she would be an imbecile?" Muriale came close to gagging on the words. Suddenly, she felt faint and nauseous. *She would nae want that,* she thought.

"That is verra rare," the healer said thoughtfully.

"She is a fighter," Alysander said, his voice cracking. "If anyone can survive this, Orabillis can."

"Aye," Muriale agreed. "Besides, Mum will nae allow her to die."

At the thought of his poor wife having to bury her daughter, Alysander could no longer hold back his tears. He left the room to cry in solitude.

Rory stepped closer. "What can I do?" he asked.

Muriale couldn't look at him; she couldn't look away from her sister. "Pray, Rory. Pray."

---

It had been an awful night, filled with worry, dread, and many shed tears. There was nothing so heartbreaking as the death-watch of someone as young as Orabillis.

In the wee hours of the night, Muriale had wept quietly for a good, long while. Her heart was breaking for her younger sister. There was nothing on earth, not even a direct order from their king, that would take her away from Orabillis. 'Twas sheer exhaustion that finally won out. Unable to keep her eyes open, she laid her head down on the bed next to Orabillis and finally succumbed to sleep.

Rory slept in a chair near Muriale, just in case he was needed. The poor woman hadn't slept in days, refusing to leave her sister's side. In truth, he was there because he loved her and wanted to be as near to her as he could be.

Alysander had all but collapsed, sliding to the floor near the end of Orabillis's bed. He slept upright, with his legs outstretched, his head lolled to one side.

When Rory woke next, it was to the sound of a perfect summer morn taking place outside the bedchamber. Through the window, he could hear birds flittering from tree to tree, a cacophony of different songs floating into the bedchamber. The sun shone brilliantly, and little clouds of dust danced in shafts of light streaming in through the glass.

It was the kind of morn that was filled with hope and promise.

Through sleepy eyes, he glanced first at Orabillis. Her chest still rose and fell but at a terrifyingly slow rate. God in Heaven, how he hated this. The poor girl didn't deserve this, none of this.

Neither did her sister. Poor Muriale was consumed with worry. She had barely eaten a thing since their arrival. Dark circles had formed under her pretty eyes, her skin had gone pale, and when she spoke, her voice sounded weak. If one hadn't known better, they might assume that she, too, was near death's door.

Rory quietly worked the kinks out of his neck, stretching his arms out wide, doing his best not to wake anyone. Other than the bird-songs out of doors and the soft crackle of the fire in the hearth, the room was deathly still.

He leaned back in the chair and closed his eyes. Oh, how he hated the agony Muriale and her father were going through. He wished there was something he could do to take all this pain and suffering away from them, especially from Muriale.

The poor woman had suffered far too much this past year. According to Alysander, the reason he had brought them here to begin with was to help her overcome her grief at losing the love of her life.

Rory still held out hope that Muriale could love again. And love *him* as much as he loved her.

But now wasn't the time to think of such things. Guilt tugged at his heart. *Her sister lies close to death, and ye sit here hoping to win her heart.* He was glad everyone was still asleep, for they couldn't see his face burn red with shame.

He must have dozed off not long after, for the next thing he heard was the door to the bedchamber quietly opening. It was quickly followed by the sounds of rustling skirts.

He chanced a quick glance before coming fully awake. 'Twas one of the nurses coming in to check on Orabillis.

---

The nurse was a short, slender woman with a hawkish nose and big eyes. He rubbed the sleep from his eyes and watched her closely.

Gently, the nurse lifted Orabillis's limp wrist to feel for a pulse. Although her expression was unchanged, she pursed her lips and all but fled from the room.

Rory felt his heart sink.

A nurse rushing out like that could only mean one thing: The poor lass had succumbed to her injuries and passed away.

He couldn't move for a long moment, overcome with sorrow at losing someone so vibrant and so young. He'd only known her for a short while, but that mattered not. He liked her spirit and her zest for life. And for the way she had bested Gavin.

*Gavin.*

Lord help him, he didn't want to tell his friend the news. While the man pretended he didn't give a whit about the lass, Rory knew better.

He also didn't want to be the one to tell Muriale or Alysander the news. He would rather kiss the king of England on the mouth than to deliver that news.

*Let them sleep peacefully for just a little while longer.*

---

Rory hung his head low, his elbows resting on his knees. He prayed that neither Muriale nor her father would wake before the nurse and healers returned. Call him a coward if you wish, but he simply couldn't wake them to tell them that their beloved daughter and sister was dead.

And where in the bloody hell were the healers and the nurse? She had run out of here like her skirts were on fire.

"Water."

His eyes sprung open, believing 'twas Muriale who was speaking. When he saw that Orabillis's eyes were open and heard her repeat the word, he got to his feet so quickly he knocked his chair over.

The crash startled both Muriale and Alysander from their slumber. Alysander leapt to his feet, his hand on the dirk at his waist. His eyes were darting around the room rapidly as he tried to ascertain what was going on.

"Quiet," Orabillis said. Her voice was scratchy, cracking from being parched.

Muriale was stunned. Moving without thinking, she grabbed a cup of cool cider. Rory stepped in to help Orabillis sit up as Muriale raised the cup to her lips.

"Nae to fast," she told her. "Ye haven't eaten in days. It might come back up." Her words came out in a rush of confused excitement and utter disbelief.

Orabillis drank greedily until her sister pulled the cup away. "More," she said.

"Nay, let that hit yer belly first," Muriale told her. "And if it stays down, ye can have more."

Rory gently helped her to lie back down.

"God, I hurt," Orabillis said. Her voice was still scratchy and her eyes only half open.

"Ye have been through a very difficult time."

"How long?" she asked, closing her eyes tightly.

"How long have ye been here?" Muriale asked. "Five days, six nights."

She took a deep breath in through her nostrils and attempted to let it out slowly. Her throat was so dry she began to wheeze before breaking out into a coughing fit.

Just then, the healers and nurses came rushing into the room. Gavin was leading the way. He raced past everyone and went to stand at Orabillis's bedside.

The same healer who had helped her through her convulsions the night before came to her side, pushing Muriale and Rory away as gently as he could. Gavin, however, refused to leave. One look at his powerful glare and the healer knew not to even make the attempt.

Anxiously, Muriale, Rory, and Alysander waited in a dark corner of the room. Muriale chewed nervously on her thumbnail. Alysander kept raking his hand through his hair as he stared at the back of the king's healer.

Rory was more focused on Muriale than her sister. He was worried about the shadows under her eyes and the fact that she had barely eaten or slept in a sennight. As soon as the healer pronounced Orabillis out of the woods, he was going to insist Muriale eat and get some rest.

He resisted the urge to chuckle at the image of *him* trying to convince Muriale of anything. She was just as stubborn as her younger sister. As determined as she was beautiful, as intelligent as she was kind. Oh, he would never be bored with her as his wife.

The sound of the healer's voice tore him out of his quiet reverie.

"God has answered all of yer prayers," the man said as he stood to his full height. Looking first to Muriale then to Alysander, he said, "I believe she will survive," he said before quickly adding the caveat, "But only if she rests and does as we ask."

'Twas a collective sigh from the trio. "Thank ye," Alysander said as he pushed by the man.

He took Orabillis hand in his. "Thank God, lass," he said, his voice cracking ever so slightly. "If ye are nae right as rain before yer mum gets here, I fear I will nae survive her wrath."

Orabillis managed a faint smile, but otherwise did not speak. She simply wasn't strong enough.

Alysander tore his gaze away from his daughter to look up at Gavin. "Thank ye," he whispered. He knew that had Gavin not acted as quickly as he had, Orabillis would not have survived. Aye, they owed a great deal to the healers and nurses, but Alysander firmly believed he owed more to the knight than he would ever be able to repay.

Gavin said nothing as he stood like an ancient guard next to Orabillis. There was a notable frown on his face as he kept staring at the young woman. Was it concern and worry or something else? Alysander had no idea and decided to mark it up to the man being just as exhausted as the rest of them.

Muriale stepped forward and knelt beside her sister. Tears of relief and utter joy trailed down her cheeks. "Och! Orabillis!" she exclaimed with a scratchy voice. "Ye nearly scared me into my own grave, lass." Taking Orabillis's hand into her own, she squeezed it tightly and kissed the back of it. "I would nae have survived losin' ye."

"Wheest," Orabillis murmured. "I am fine. 'Tis naught but a scratch."

Everyone chuckled at the audacity of her statement. Everyone save for Gavin. Nay, he chose that moment to leave. Sliding between the wall and Muriale he quit the room without so much as a by-your-leave.

Orabillis hadn't noticed Gavin's presence or departure at all. She'd been too busy pretending she wasn't in any pain.

But Rory and Alysander had noticed Gavin's rather odd retreat. While Alysander shrugged Gavin's exit as nothing more than a man on the brink of exhaustion, Rory knew better.

*My friend,* he mused, *is verra much in love. And he is terrified to admit it.*

# TWENTY-SIX

By the time Moirra arrived a few days later, Orabillis had improved immeasurably. Believing she was coming to carry her deceased daughter home, she wept the entire day with joy and relief.

Orabillis didn't really want anyone fussing over her. She would have much preferred being left alone to heal in peace and quiet. Her mother, however, rarely left her side.

Mercifully, Muriale, Rory, Alysander, and the others had been able to catch up on much-needed sleep. Those first days after Orabillis had been attacked had been physically and emotionally difficult. Sleep was a luxury Muriale didn't feel she could afford, not while her sister teetered so close to death.

Muriale slept from dusk until well after dawn after her mother's arrival. If she dreamt anything, she couldn't remember. Even after sleeping for such a lengthy time, she still felt tired, and her bones ached. She imagined it would take a week or so before she began to feel like her old self again.

Much to Orabillis's vexation, her family tended to her in shifts, waiting to do whatever they could to make her more comfortable.

"Will ye please leave me be?" Orabillis groused one afternoon. "And if I dinnae get out of this bed soon, I will lose my mind."

"Now, Orabillis," her mother began, using the softest and warmest tone she could muster. "The healers say ye must stay abed another week."

She could take no more. Angrily, she tossed back the blankets and tried to sit up. "I have been abed for over a fortnight," she exclaimed. "No. More."

Moirra tried to gently push her back, but Orabillis resisted. It hurt like the devil, but she didn't care.

"I can see it pains ye," her mother argued.

"Aye, it hurts like hell," Orabillis said through gritted teeth. "But I dinnae care. I just want to sit in that chair by the window." 'Twas a lie, of course. She wanted to do more than sit by a window. But, God help her, if she moved farther than that, she would undoubtedly faint. God help her then.

Her father came to her rescue and her side, giving his wife a pleading look. "We will help ye to the chair." Alysander said.

Moirra finally acquiesced. "But if ye undo all the work the healers did, dinnae blame me."

It took unparalleled strength to keep from crying out in pain as well as to inch her way to the chair. But, once there, she felt victorious, pain and exhaustion be damned.

---

With her sister well on her way to making a full recovery, Muriale was finally able to relax. Her thoughts were no longer consumed with the need to catch a madman or with the agonizing worry over her sister.

Sleep was a welcomed respite to the harrowing and busy last several weeks. Well rested now that her mother was here to assist,

Muriale had time alone to think. And, for the first time in a year, to dream peacefully.

Her heart was no longer filled with sorrow and despair over losing Patrick. Oh, she loved him still and always would. Those feelings would never change.

However, with the passage of time and help from her family, she could now think about her future. And it didn't look nearly as bleak and hopeless as she once believed.

Muriale was finally able to shed the heavy cloak of grief and mourning. Now, she could see clearly that her life had purpose. What that purpose was, she wasn't sure. But she knew it was there, just on the horizon, within reach. Just as it had always been, but she was in too dark a place to see or to even make the attempt to grab it.

On this bright, late-summer afternoon, she and her mother were walking in the gardens at Edinburgh castle. Orabillis was sleeping peacefully (or pretending to, if Muriale's suspicions were correct). Alysander was with Rory and Gavin, training with a dozen other knights in a courtyard on the other side of the grand castle.

"'Tis good to see ye smile again," Moirra said.

"'Tis good to smile again," Muriale admitted. "This past year has been quite a tryin' time."

Moirra quirked a pretty brow. "Tryin'?" She clucked her tongue. "That is an understatement, dear daughter. It has been ugly and terrifyin'."

Muriale couldn't argue otherwise. No matter how one chose to describe it, she was simply glad it was over.

They paused to look at the many roses. Shades of red, pink, white, and yellow swayed in the gentle, sweet-smelling breeze.

"Rory seems a nice fellow," Moirra remarked. She feigned disinterest and quickly added, "So does Gavin."

Muriale knew her mother well enough to know that she wanted to discuss something important but was being somewhat gentle in bringing the matter up. "Aye, mum, Rory is a nice fellow."

"As is Gavin," Moirra added.

Muriale had spent far more time with the two men than her mother had. First impressions can sometimes be deceiving. "Gavin MacKendrick has a short temper and a tongue he cannae hold when the situation requires it. He is also dimwitted."

Confused, Moirra asked for further explanation.

Muriale took in a deep breath before recounting the incident betwixt Gavin and Orabillis, the night they dined with the king.

"The fool tried to kiss her," she said. "He also made some extremely unkind remarks about women and his belief that they are only good for one thing."

"Nay!" Moirra exclaimed, her eyes wide, her mouth open in horror. "Och! What did she do?" She closed her eyes and braced for the answer.

Muriale smiled rather proudly. "She proved to everyone in atten- dance just what a fool he is. She had him pinned to the floor with a dirk at his throat before he realized what was happening."

"Aye, that sounds like our Orabillis," Moirra said. She let out a quick breath. "Please tell me that was the end of it."

Muriale laughed as she shook her head. "We are talkin' about our Orabillis. Of course that wasn't the end of it."

Unsure if she could take the full story standing, Moirra suggested they find a place to sit. In the middle of the opulent gardens were a set of benches carved from limestone and granite.

Once she was settled, she asked Muriale to continue and to hold nothing back.

"When she finally let him up, he challenged her to a weapon of her choice. And, aye, before ye ask, she took the challenge. She chose arrows."

Moirra closed her eyes and took in a deep, steadying breath. "How bad did she humiliate him?"

Muriale drew her lips inward in an attempt to keep from laugh- ing. "So much so that she has won favor with the king, and Gavin despises her."

"Jesu," Moirra whispered. "That is why we are here instead of Forvelith's?"

Muriale nodded. "That is one of the reasons. 'Twas Gavin who carried her out of the building after she was stabbed. He was the one who brought her here. He carried her in his arms even after he was brought a horse. He carried her all the way here. And, according to the maids, he was yelling at the top of his lungs as soon as he reached the gate, calling for the king's healers. He yelled all the way to the chamber she is now in. 'Bring the bloody healers, damn it!'"

Moirra tilted her head slightly. "That dinnae sound like a man who despises a woman."

Muriale shrugged her shoulders slightly. "I would agree. He stayed in that chamber the entire time. He even threatened one of the healers with a dirk to his throat when Orabillis had the convulsions. He felt the healer was being too rough with her."

"Again, I say that dinnae sound like a man who despises a woman. Quite the contrary."

"I am nae sure," Muriale admitted. "Once she was deemed out of the woods, he left, and we have nae seen him since."

Moirra gave that bit of information a good measure of thought. "That is odd, aye?"

"Aye, I find it odd. Mayhap 'twas guilt he felt at her being wounded. Ye ken how men can be. They sometimes blame themselves for events they had no control over."

"This is true," Moirra agreed.

"I remember when I stumbled over my own feet and ended up with a knot on my head. Poor Patrick blamed himself. 'I should have been there,' he said." Muriale smiled fondly at the memory.

Moirra studied her daughter closely for a long moment. "Do ye ken that this is the first time in a year that ye have mentioned Patrick and dinnae fall into a heap of tears and despair?"

"Aye, Mum, I do."

"So ye are back amongst the livin'," she said with a relieved and happy smile. "I am glad to hear it and to see it."

Muriale continued to smile. "It was difficult to get beyond my grief," she admitted. "But ye were right. Patrick would nae have wanted me to wallow in despair all the rest of my days. He would have wanted me to be happy, as I would have wished the same for him."

"I need to put that in my journal," Moirra quipped cheekily.

With her brow furrowed, Muriale asked her to explain.

"After a woman's daughters reach a certain age, they no longer believe their mum is right about anythin'. I like to mark those rare occasions when one of them admits I am nae nearly as ignorant as they once believed."

Muriale couldn't help but laugh at her mother. "I would like to formally apologize on behalf of all my sisters for that mistaken belief."

Surprised, Moirra sat a bit taller. "Och! An admission *and* an apology in one afternoon? Will wonders never cease?"

They laughed jubilantly, something they hadn't done in quite a long time. "Now," Moirra began, "tell me about this knight, Sir Rory MacLeod."

---

Muriale knew what her mother wanted to hear. It was impossible to answer, for she wasn't quite certain what her own true feelings on the matter were.

"He is a good man, Mum. Truly, he is."

Moirra gave her a knowing smile. "But ye dinnae love him."

"Mum, I barely ken the man. And if ye take a moment to think, I have nae necessarily had the time to think about anything other than my sister's survival."

"I think he loves ye."

"Dinnae be ridiculous," Muriale said, dismissing the idea in its entirety. "We barely ken each other. How could he possibly love me?"

In truth, the idea that someone might take a liking to her did, in fact, make her heart skip a beat or two. Yet doubts still lingered.

Moirra smiled warmly as she patted Muriale's hand. "'Tis nice to hear that ye are nae against the idea."

"I dinnae say that."

Moirra was still smiling when she said, "Ye have much improved since bein' here, daughter."

Muriale rolled her eyes. "If by that ye mean I no longer weep uncontrollably all the day long—"

"I do."

"Or that I have finally stopped grievin' myself into an early grave—"

"That, too."

"Or that I have finally begun to live my own life again—"

"Aye, that as well."

"Then, aye. I have much improved since bein' here."

"So, yer mum is correct twice in the same day?" Moirra asked sarcastically. "I truly must find my journal."

<hr>

Orabillis didn't want to admit that she was still in a good amount of pain. To do so would have meant being forced back into the bed, where she was convinced she would die from sheer boredom.

For the first time in an age, she was left completely alone. She sat in a comfortable chair next to the window, looking out at the gardens below. But she paid no attention to the brilliant blue sky nor the gardens filled with all manner of flowers. She didn't notice the gardeners tending to every plant and flower with great care. Nor did she even wonder at what her mother and sister were giggling about.

Nay, she had more important things on her mind. Having been so close to death a fortnight ago, her perspective on life had changed. Not drastically, mind you. Just enough to make her truly and sincerely take a closer inspection on her life. More specifically, her future.

One of her very first thoughts after waking up from those many days near death shocked her to her very core: *I want children.*

Now, just where in the bloody hell that notion came from, she couldn't begin to fathom. Never, not once, in all her nearly seventeen years, had she ever longed for anything other than a life of freedom. A life where she wasn't bound to anyone or anything else but to her own heart and mind.

That distinct thought shook her. Shook her so much that she found it difficult to push it aside those first few days.

*Ye are far too young to be worryin' about such things,* she cursed her traitorous mind that bright afternoon. *Ye can think about such things when ye are older. Much, much older.*

Having a child didn't necessarily mean she would have to marry. Plenty of women had children out of wedlock. Oh, it might bother her parents for a time, but eventually, they would get over it.

*Nay, ye silly fool. Ye need neither a child nor a man to make ye happy. 'Tis naught more than a fever-induced thought that refuses to leave ye.*

The door to her chamber opened, and several beautifully dressed women walked in. Behind them was their Queen, Euphemia.

Orabillis started to stand but Euphemia waved her hand. "Nay, please sit."

Orabillis thought it an awfully disrespectful way to greet her queen, but her muscles were glad for her kindness.

One of the women grabbed a chair and sat it opposite Orabillis. The queen sat as the women stepped back, lining the wall like sentries.

"'Tis good to see ye recoverin' so well," Euphemia said with a smile.

"I am, thanks to the good care of yer healers," Orabillis said with a smile. "I dinnae ken how I will ever repay ye for yer kindness, yer majesty."

"Dinnae worry about that now, lass. Mayhap someday ye will be given the chance to help me or someone else."

Orabillis did feel indebted to her queen and her husband. "I will be forever in yer debt, my lady."

The queen smiled then turned her focus to the window. "I think we are all indebted to ye and yer sister. Were it nae for the two of ye, we might still be lookin' for that man."

*That man.* Homer MacGill. Silently, Orabillis hoped the man was burning in hell. "I am nae ashamed to say that I am glad he is dead. My only regret is that I was nae the one who sent him to meet his maker."

Euphemia turned her attention back to Orabillis. She leaned in, lowered her voice and said, "I wish I had been the one as well." She winked then and sat back in her chair. "Were it up to me, ye and yer sister would both be knighted."

She couldn't hold back her laughter at that notion. "A woman? Knighted?" She shook her head. "That would certainly send my da to an early grave."

"All good parents worry for their children. Ye will have yer own some day and will understand what I mean."

She felt a slight blush creep into her cheeks. *Children.* That was the very topic she had been trying so hard not to think about when the queen entered her room.

"Please ken that ye and yer family will always be welcomed here," Euphemia said with a warm smile. "And ye will always have our gratitude. If ever I can return the favor to ye, please dinnae hesitate to reach out."

*Me? Owed a favor by the queen?* Before coming to Edinburgh, she never thought such a thing possible. "We stopped the madman from harming anyone else. And, thanks be to ye and my king, I am alive to tell the tale. I think that makes us even, my lady."

With a graceful nod, Euphemia changed the subject. "I should like to think that ye and I can speak freely with one another."

"Of course we can, my lady. Ye are my queen. We can discuss whatever ye wish."

Grinning cheekily, the queen said, "I was much impressed by the way in which ye handled Gavin MacKendrick that night."

A deep blush crept up from her neck, her face heating with embarrassment. *Gavin MacKendrick.* Never a more arrogant man had ever graced God's green earth. "My da was tremendously upset by my actions that night. He was certain the king would have me hanged."

Euphemia giggled rather loudly. Orabillis noticed that the women standing against the wall exchanged confused glances with one another. Mayhap they weren't used to their queen's laughter.

"Och! Nay, never. My husband was more than a bit amused by it. He spoke of little else for nearly a week."

Orabillis wasn't sure how she should respond, so she simply smiled.

"I wish that I had yer courage, Orabillis."

Taken aback, she said, "My courage?"

"Aye, lass. Yer courage," she replied with a smile. "Ye were nae afraid to take on a knight, to put him in his place."

Orabillis cleared her throat nervously. "I am afraid my father dinnae see it that way."

"I think that, deep down, mayhap, your father was proud of ye."

She gave her a slight shrug. "Mayhap, my lady."

"How on earth did ye learn to fight like ye did?"

Orabillis giggled slightly. "Believe it or nae, my father. He wanted naught more than for his children to be able to defend themselves. I, however, wanted more than that. I have actually been training with his men since I was but six."

Euphemia's eyes grew wide with surprise. "Nay," she exclaimed.

"Aye, my lady. I have. Much to my mother's vexation, of course."

"I like yer mother," Euphemia said. "She is a woman of good character, I think."

Orabillis couldn't disagree. Her mother was a fine woman, indeed.

"As for Sir Gavin," she said, bringing the conversation back to the man whose mere presence set Orabillis's teeth on edge. "I do believe ye knocked some of the arrogance out of him. And he needed it."

"Most men do," Orabillis quipped.

Euphemia studied her closely for a long while. "Are ye aware that 'twas Gavin who pulled ye from that room and brought ye here?"

Another blush brightened her cheeks. "Aye, my lady. My father and sister told me."

Euphemia nodded. "Did ye ken that he refused to leave yer side?"

Orabillis's brow knitted. "What?"

"'Tis true, lass. 'Twas nae until ye finally woke that day that he finally left yer side."

She grunted derisively. "He was probably prayin' for my death."

Euphemia quirked a pretty brow. "Nay, I dinnae think a man would behave the way he did if he had no good feelings for a person."

"I fear I dinnae understand," she remarked.

Euphemia explained what had happened between Gavin and the healer, when the fevers had thrown Orabillis into the convulsions. "From what I have heard, he was ready to kill the healer, for he thought the man was being far too rough with ye."

Genuinely, she believed 'twas nothing more than an exaggeration. Whomever had told the queen about that night must surely have embellished the facts. She dismissed the idea that Gavin didn't hate her in its entirety.

"I think Gavin has the potential to be a good man, more like Sir Rory."

Orabillis hid her snort behind a cough and a laugh. "I think Rory has feelings for my sister."

"Oh, there is no doubt about that," Euphemia replied. "Anyone can see it."

"I doubt my sister does," Orabillis replied.

"I would nae be too certain about that."

For another quarter of an hour, they sat and talked as if they were old friends. The more Orabillis got to know her queen, the more she liked her.

"I fear I have taken up enough of yer time," Euphemia said as she gracefully got to her feet. "We shall talk again, aye?"

"I would like that, my lady," she said, once again trying to stand in her majesty's presence.

"Nay, remain seated, lass," she said with a smile. "Ye rest, and before ye ken it, ye will be back to your old self again."

Almost as quietly as they had arrived, the group left.

*I am nae sure anymore that I want to be back to my old self again,* she mused as she watched them leave.

*I am nae sure of anything anymore.*

# EPILOGUE

It hadn't taken long for Muriale to admit she did, in fact, have true feelings for the knight, Sir Rory MacLeod—a week, to be exact.

It came upon her all at once. She was standing at the window in Orabillis's chamber, staring out at the land below, her mind and heart having a battle of near-biblical proportions over what she might or might not feel for Rory.

It was a brilliantly sunny, warm day, with just a hint of fall in the air. The scent of heather wafted in through the open window, clinging to the afternoon breeze. Her sister had improved considerably this past week. Soon, they would be packing up and heading back to their keep.

Not long ago, she would have jumped with joy at the thought. She would have been packed by now and chomping at the bit to leave.

But, now, the thought of leaving this city—a place she hadn't wanted to visit to begin with—didn't quite hold the same appeal as it once had. For a long while, she stared out the window, trying to convince herself that she had grown to love Edinburgh, with all its hustle and bustle and its potential for excitement.

She'd also tried to convince herself that, since she had grown accustomed to the pungent aromas, she could grow accustomed to the crime and poverty. Court life might not be as bad as she had previously thought. And her Aunt Forvelith could certainly use the company. The poor woman had been alone for far too long. Why, the woman would be downright happy to have someone living with her, to keep her company and stave off the loneliness she must surely feel.

As she continued to lie to herself, staring out at the expanse of land, something kept niggling at the back of her mind. 'Twas the truth, but she continued to pretend it wasn't there, instead sweeping it away as if it was nothing more important than cobwebs hanging from a ceiling.

Then he came into her view.

*Rory.*

The pounding of her heart startled her to her marrow.

Aye, he was a tall, handsome fellow, who possessed more good qualities than anyone had a right to. Strong, determined, kind, honorable... And he made her laugh nearly every time they were together.

He was standing in the gardens below, his back turned to her now as he stared off into the distance. His black leather trews clung to his well-muscled thighs, his light-blue shirt stretching out over his strong back, broad shoulders, and muscular arms.

Before she realized what was happening, she was racing out of the bedchamber and down the stairs.

It took a while to make her way out of doors and to the gardens. By the time she reached the edge of the beautiful green space, her heart was pounding mercilessly against her breast. A bead of sweat had formed on her brow and upper lip, and she was short of breath. She paused, just at the edge, and stared across the grass and flowers at Rory. He hadn't noticed her yet.

*I am done thinkin'*, she mused. *I am ready to* feel *again.*

Without thought, she raced towards him, her brown locks coming loose from her braid along with any previous inhibitions she might have once possessed. Rory must have heard her coming, for he spun around, one hand on his dirk, ready to do battle.

He wasn't going to have to battle this day.

Grabbing a fistful of skirts, she ran towards him, all the while her heart felt close to bursting. Not from the exertion from running but from the sheer excitement coursing through her veins.

She flung herself into his arms, wrapped her arms around his neck, and kissed him. Stunned at first, he wasn't quite certain what he should do. But, in a manner of heartbeats, he was not only returning her kiss, he had taken over the plundering.

'Twas the most passionate of kisses, filled with thrilling anticipation, adoration, and excitement. She didn't want it to end, but knew that it must. For, if she didn't end it now, she might be tempted to pull him into the bushes and have her way with him.

Muriale pulled away, breathless, her fingers trembling, her legs weak. "I love ye, Rory MacLeod. I will marry ye."

The words had tumbled out so quickly, he wasn't sure he'd heard her correctly. "What?"

With more fervency, she repeated the words. "I love ye, Rory MacLeod, and I will marry ye!"

The warmth and joy in his smile made her legs feel all the more weak. "'Tis about time ye came to yer senses, lass," he quipped mischievously.

She didn't take it as an insult. Instead, she hugged him tighter and said, "How soon can we marry?"

From his surprised expression, he hadn't been expecting such enthusiasm. "Well, I will need to speak to Robert. Then I am sure ye will want to marry at yer keep with yer family around us."

She shook her head. "Nay, I dinnae want to wait, Rory. I want to marry ye now."

"Today?" he asked with more than just a bit of incredulity and surprise.

"Aye," she nodded with a smile. "As soon as we can."

He studied her closely for a moment, his brow drawn into a fine line. "Why so quickly?" he asked. "Are ye afraid ye will change yer mind?"

She smiled, a daring, mischevious smile, before pulling his head down so that she might whisper in his ear.

"Nay. I will never change my mind. I am tired of waitin' to see what life throws at me, Rory. Instead of waitin' for somethin' wonderful to happen, I want to *make* it happen."

In truth, she couldn't quite understand what had made her change her mind. All that she knew now was that she did love him, more than she could have imagined possible. And she wanted to begin her life with him as soon as possible.

"Verra well," he said, drawing her in again for a warm embrace. "Let us go and make it happen."

Before dusk descended, they were standing in the chapel, surrounded by her family and their king and queen, as well as Gavin and a handful of other knights. They exchanged their vows and promises.

As for what life might have in store for them, they didn't give it much thought that day or that night, nor the following three days. Instead, they hid away in a small private chamber, concerned only with the moment they were currently in. Tomorrow could wait.

# PROLOGUE TO ORABILLIS

### Prologue to Orabillis

1378

Orabillis McCullum could count on one hand—and have four fingers left—the number of marriage proposals she had received over the years. The first and only proposal took place when she was all of nine years old. She had been so insulted by young Robbie MacPherson's proposal that she kicked him in the shin and proceeded to pummel him into the ground. He went home crying and sporting one black eye and a bloody lip.

According to her family, had her father not intervened that day, Orabillis would most likely still be beating up the poor lad. From that day forward, her family referred to it as 'that incident.'

It was widely believed amongst her parents and siblings that the reason she had yet to receive another, some eleven years later, was the fact that the men in her clan were too terrified to even broach the subject with her. "Yer reputation precedes ye, Orabillis. The menfolk are terrified of ye."

Orabillis, however, knew that not to be the case. While she thoroughly believed most men were naught but addlepated eejits, those men she did know on a more personal basis were good, honorable, decent men.

In truth, she only referred to men as addlepated eejits when the subject of romance was brought up. She had no use for it, most likely because she didn't understand it. And she was far too busy to even make the attempt to.

So, it was widely understood amongst her family and clan that Orabillis McCullum would never marry. She was perfectly happy training with the menfolk on a daily basis. Truth be told, most of her clansmen were mightily proud of her skill with fighting and weaponry. Her father certainly was.

Or, at least, he had been when she was younger. Now, he would often remark he regretted spoiling her and teaching her to use any kind of weaponry. "I should have locked her away long ago," he would sometimes grouse.

Even though he refused to admit to it these past few years, he *was* quite proud of her. As was her family and the rest of the clan.

They loved and adored the young woman.

Outsiders might consider her manner of dress rather odd, for she much preferred to wear tunics and trews over dresses, but her clans people didn't mind at all. After all, they'd had more than a decade to get used to it. No one even noticed anymore.

Thus, Orabillis neither blended in nor stood out amongst her people. She was simply Alysander and Moirra's fourth daughter, a lass who wore tunics and trews and trained with the men. A comely lass who had a soft spot in her heart for the elderly and children, as well as animals of all kinds.

And she would remain happily single all the rest of her days.

Thus, when her father called her into her uncle Archibald's office that sunny afternoon, she could not have been more surprised had a horde of Nordic invaders busted down the gates of their walls and hied off with the McCullum fortune.

"What did ye say?" Her brow was furrowed into a hard knot, her eyes naught but slits. Certainly she must have misunderstood her father and uncle.

"The king sent a missive," Alysander said. He was holding the scroll in his hand as he stood behind his brother's desk. Archibald—a man she loved and adored almost as much as her father—was standing next to him.

"Robert has ordered that ye marry," Archibald added. His voice cracked like a lad on the cusp of manhood.

For a long moment, she stared at the two men. Oh, they looked serious, but were they truly?

"'Tis funny," she began in an even tone. "I thought I heard ye say that our king has ordered that I marry."

The brothers glanced at one another but otherwise remained mute. Undoubtedly, they were waiting for this proclamation to sink in.

Suddenly, she remembered that she would be turning twenty in a few days. *That's it,* she mused, rather relieved. *This is naught but a jest.*

So ridiculously funny she found this particular jest, that she didn't even bother to whip out her dirk and threaten to slash their throats if they ever uttered such disgusting words in her presence again.

Instead, she threw her head back and laughed. A good, full, deep belly laugh that brought tears to her eyes.

After several long moments of trying to catch her breath and to wipe away her tears, she slapped her hand on her lap and got to her feet.

"Truly, Father and Uncle, I think ye could come up with a better jest than *that.*" She shook her head and headed towards the door.

"Orabillis, this is nae a jest," her father called out to her.

She paused at the door, a wide smile on her lips and disbelief in her eyes. Nay, not for a moment did she believe either of them.

She'd met Robert a few years ago. He knew her stance on

marriage and romance, for they had had a very long conversation about it when she was recovering from being stabbed.

Another shake of dubious disbelief as she put her hand on the door latch. "Really, Father." She rolled her eyes and smiled. "Robert kens how I feel about marriage. And, since I have done absolutely nothing to anger the man, he wouldn't punish me in such a manner. He kens that I would rather be gutted and my entrails fed to the scavengers than ever to marry."

Archibald took the missive from his brother's hands and placed it in Orabillis's. "Ye need to read this."

# ALSO BY SUZAN TISDALE

### The Clan MacDougall Series

*Laiden's Daughter*

*Findley's Lass*

*Wee William's Woman*

*McKenna's Honor*

*The Clan MacDougall Boxed Set*

### The Clan Graham Series

*Rowan's Lady*

*Frederick's Queen*

### The Mackintoshes and McLarens Series

*Ian's Rose*

*The Bowie Bride*

*Rodrick the Bold*

*Brogan's Promise*

### The MacCulloughs

**Black Richard's Heart**

**Lachlan's Heart**

### The Clan McDunnah Series

*A Murmur of Providence*

*A Whisper of Fate*

*A Breath of Promise*

# ABOUT THE AUTHOR

*USA Today Bestselling Author*, storyteller and cheeky wench, SUZAN TISDALE lives in the Midwest with her verra handsome carpenter husband. All but one of her children have left the nest. Her pets consist of dust bunnies and a dozen poodle-sized, backyard-dwelling groundhogs – all of which run as free and unrestrained as the voices in her head. And she doesn't own a single pair of yoga pants, much to the shock and horror of her fellow authors. She prefers to write in her pajamas.

Suzan writes Scottish historical romance/fiction, with honorable and perfectly imperfect heroes and strong, feisty heroines. And bad guys she kills off in delightfully wicked ways.

She published her first novel, Laiden's Daughter, in December, 2011, as a gift for her mother. That one book started a journey which has led to fifteen published titles, with two more being released in the spring of 2017. To date, she has sold more than 650,000 copies of her books around the world. They have been translated into four foreign languages (Italian, French, German, and Spanish.)

You will find her books in digital, paperback, and audiobook formats.